CAPTIVE

CAL ROGAN MYSTERIES BOOK 6

ROBERT P. FRENCH

FOREWORD

Thank you for purchasing *Captive* the sixth Cal Rogan Mystery. At the end of the book there is information about the other books and contact information.

At the beginning of March, I was about a quarter of the way into writing this book, when we went into lockdown. As the book is set in the current time, I thought about giving COVID-19 a place in the book. But that thought was just too depressing. So Cal and Nick and the gang are operating like it never happened. I hope *Captive* give you a mental break from the realities of our current world.

Enjoy and stay safe.

Robert. Vancouver, August 2020.

ACKNOWLEDGMENTS

So many people go into the writing of a book and I would like to thank those who helped me with *Captive*.

A special thank you to Alan Woodruff, author of the Lucius White legal thrillers for his helpful analysis of *Captive*. Thanks also to Cynthia Gould for her proofreading skills from half a world away.

A million thanks to the wonderful members of my Launch Team whose encouragement and support have helped me through the whole process of writing this novel. You pointed out issues with the book and even found a few errors which slipped through. Alphabetically by first name, special thanks to Andrew Stewart, Andrew Tucker, Becky Chatelain, Cathie Austen, Cindy Warrick, Connie Charron, Deborah Bragg, Diane Griffin, Ed Campbell, Fiona Bradford, Ginny Sharma, Helen Heald, Holly Stolarski, Jamie DeAvilla, Janet Cline, JB, Jeffery Benham, Jim Bolger, John Mylett, Jyl Romain, Karan C, Karen Campbell, Kathi Defranc, Kenny Ray Fraley, Larry Branson, Linda DiMezza, Linda Harbour, Linda Longo, Lorraine Garant, Mary Clare Scully, Mel Calaby, Mel Mathews, Natoshia Avery, Neil Watson, Noreen Bloss, Pat Muddle, Patricia Ann Morgan, Patti Flanagan, Patty Laroche, Paul Morgan, Peter Lighthall, Rhiannon, Richard Pollack, Roger, Shae Curry, Terry

Cochran, Valerie Hykawy, Vicky Samson, and Wayne W. Bilow. If I missed anyone, I sincerely apologize.

As always, I would also like to thank the Vancouver Public Library for providing the perfect working location for any writer. Up until March, every word of *Captive* was written there... then the monster arrived.

Dedication

To my wonderful wife Penny who believed in me when I had stopped believing in myself.

ALSO BY ROBERT P. FRENCH

Junkie (Cal Rogan Mysteries Book 1)

Oboe (Cal Rogan Mysteries Book 2)

Lockstep (Cal Rogan Mysteries Book 3)

Three (Cal Rogan Mysteries Book 4)

Cabal (Cal Rogan Mysteries Book 5)

Jailed (Cal Rogan Mysteries Book 7)

All are available in paperback from Amazon.

1. ZELENA

Monday

So cold. The only light is from the moon as it crosses the tiny window, high up on the concrete wall. The sky is still dark. I put my head back under the threadbare blanket, hoping my breath will bring just a little warmth to my shivering body. I have to pray for what I dread: the morning. When it comes, *he*'ll come. *He*'ll take me and I'll be warm again—a brief moment of bliss. But then... My shivering redoubles at the thought of what comes next.

I can't think about that. I must focus on my plan. In a weird way it calms me. If I can just distract him for five, maybe ten seconds, then I'll be free. Free forever.

I think of my parents and the tears come, warm to my icy cheeks.

2. CAL

He looks at Adriana, then at me, then back again at her. We've seen this before, a client knowing he's at the point of no return, knowing that if he tells us why he's here at Stammo Rogan Investigations, he'll set a ball rolling which he will no longer be able to control. He looks down at the table, purses his lips, takes a deep breath in and speaks.

"I'm being blackmailed," he sighs. He looks up at me and I nod encouragement. He gives a grim little grin. "You did say this is completely confidential, right?"

"Completely," I say with a confidence I don't feel. It's a grey area; there is no legal confidentiality like there is between lawyers and their clients. A court can compel us to break our promise of silence but it's never likely to come to that... I hope.

He takes another deep breath. "OK," he says. He rubs the scar on his right cheekbone and turns his attention to Adry. This happens a lot. In the five months since Adry was promoted from Office Manager to Investigator, we have noticed that clients often feel more comfortable unburdening themselves to her, especially the male clients. Nick and I have made sure she's always in on the first meeting with any new client.

"I run a software company with eighty-five employees. We're good at what we do and we're very successful. Now anyway." He gives the same grin, then bites his top lip.

I wonder why he's so nervous. CEO's I've known are usually more self-possessed.

"So who's blackmailing you, Mr. McCoy?" Adry asks.

"Please, call me Connor," he glances at me then back at Adry. "About twelve years ago, we went through a bad patch. A client owed us over two hundred grand and I didn't have the money to make the month-end payroll. I was at my credit limit with the bank and I was desperate. I knew that if I didn't pay my employees on time, some of them might quit and if that happened, we wouldn't be able to complete the client's project, the client wouldn't pay us and we'd go down the tubes."

He looks down at the table and bites his lip again.

"What did you do to get the money, Connor?" I ask gently.

He doesn't look up. "I had this friend from high school," he says and, in a flash, I have an idea of what he's going to say. Maybe this is why he's so nervous. "He always had a lot of money," he continues, "he drove a Lamborghini, bought all his clothes at Harry Rosen and Zegna, expensive holidays two or three times a year. I thought I'd see if he'd loan me fifty grand to help me meet payroll."

In the pause I say, "Let me guess. He said sure... *if* you'd do something for him in return."

He looks up at me. "How did you know?"

I ignore his question. "What did you do?" I ask.

"He told me to meet him at some abandoned warehouse

in Burnaby. When I got there it looked really creepy. I almost turned the car around and left. Then he came out and told me to drive my car inside the place. When I got inside, I immediately regretted it. There were a couple of rough-looking guys waiting. I was scared as hell. He told me to get out of the car and I really didn't want to.

"While we stood and watched, he had his guys take the tires off the car. They packed them with tightly-bound plastic bags of white powder. When I started to object he showed me a big bag full of money. 'That's your fifty grand,' he said. 'If you want it you'll do this for me. If not...' he nodded towards his guys."

I can see the fear in his eyes now, even years after.

Adry pats his arm. "Go on," she says.

"They put the tires back on the car and sprayed them with some liquid they said would throw off the sniffer dogs. Mike told me I had to drive it to an address in Bellingham. I can tell you I was scared as hell driving across the US border, you know what those border guards are like when they give you that cold stare and ask you if you are taking any goods across. But it worked. I had to do it once a week for three weeks—every time from a different location and to a different address—and at the end of the month, he handed me the bag with fifty grand in it. I felt really embarrassed paying my people their salaries in cash, but none of them quit and we finished the project and got paid by the client. But as part of the deal, I had to do three more runs for them over the following two months.

"After that we shook hands and he said if ever I had a cash-flow problem, I could come to him. Fortunately, the business really took off after that and I never needed to."

"You were lucky," Adry says. "My uncle Reuben was a US

border guard. He told me those dogs are amazing at finding drugs."

"And your buddy ripped you off," I add. "You got fifty grand for six trips. That's only about eight grand each trip for smuggling drugs with a street value of maybe five million bucks."

"I never thought of it that way," he says. He mulls it over. "Son of a—" he cuts himself off and looks at Adry. "Sorry," he mutters.

She pats him on the arm again. "No prob," she says. He smiles gratefully and I am impressed with the way she is building rapport with him. "Tell us about the blackmail part."

"Not long after I did the, uh, deliveries for him, I saw on the news that he'd been convicted for possession and sentenced to ten years. I'd pretty much forgotten about the whole thing until last week. Out of the blue I got an email. There was a video attached. It was the warehouse with the tough guys filling my tires and putting them on the car. My face and the licence plate were really clear. Then it cut to another scene where he was handing over the money to me. His face was blurred out but mine was as clear as day."

"Can you email us a copy of the video?" I ask.

"No, I can't," he says. "I'd opened the email on my computer at work and I was so paranoid that someone might see it, I deleted it."

"I don't know a lot about computers," I say, "but when you delete something, doesn't it stay on the hard drive somewhere?"

"Usually yes, but I ran a program that removed all copies from my computer and from our email server." He looks a little rueful. "Sorry, I guess I never thought it through. If they send it again, I'll keep a copy for you."

"How much money are they demanding, Connor?" Adry asks.

"That's the thing," he says. "The email just said, 'We'll be in touch.' I got it last Thursday and I haven't heard anything since."

"It's only four days. They're playing you. Giving you time to worry yourself sick, so that when they contact you, you'll be desperate to do anything they ask." I open my notepad. "Doesn't mean to say we can't get started. What's the name of this slime ball who got you to run drugs for him?"

"Mike Anderson."

"Any idea where he lives?"

"No. I didn't even know back then, all I had was his cell phone number."

"No worries. If he's been to jail, we can probably track him down."

"Maybe I can find him on social media," Adry says. "Can you give me some personal details?"

"Sure," he looks up and thinks for a second. "He's the same age as me, thirty-seven, born in Calgary but moved here as a kid. Went to Prince of Wales high school but as far as I know he didn't go to university. That's about all I can think of."

Adry finishes typing the details into her laptop and asks, "Did you ever go to his house as a kid? Maybe his parents still live there, he might be staying with them if he's just out of jail."

He shakes his head. "No."

"You must have had some contact with him after you left high school," I say.

"Not really."

"How did you know he was rich?" I ask. "You said he

drove a Lambo and had expensive clothes. I'm guessing he didn't have those in high school."

"Oh, no. I see what you mean." He gives a nervous laugh. "I didn't know that at the time. When I was having my financial troubles, I was having a beer with a good buddy of mine from school and I mentioned I was having some cash-flow problems. He told me Mike was loaded, said he'd probably be good for a loan. He'd kept in touch with Mike and gave me his phone number."

"What's your friend's name?" I ask.

"Why?"

"Maybe he's still in touch with Mike. Maybe we can track down Mike through him."

He nods. "I see. Do you think it's wise to contact Mike?" He looks concerned.

"We're not going to contact him but I'd like to know where he is, so if we need to we can."

"Oh, OK. Well... Unfortunately, my buddy who put me in touch with Mike passed away a couple of years ago. A car accident, so..." He just leaves the sentence hanging.

"I'm sorry," I say. I look at my sparse notes. "Anything else you can think of?"

He shakes his head.

"One last question," I say. "Did you think of going to the police? They would probably overlook your indiscretion from over ten years ago and they are well equipped to handle blackmailers."

"Oh, no. Definitely not. If those videos ever came to light, it could ruin my business. We have some very prestigious, high-end clients who would drop us if there were any hint of scandal."

"Fair enough. Anyway, Connor, other than checking into Mike Anderson's background, there's not too much we can do until you actually get a demand for money. Get in touch with us straight away if they contact you and if it's by email, don't delete it."

"Definitely," he says. He reaches into his pocket and hands me an envelope. "That's the retainer we discussed on the phone."

We all stand, shake hands and head out of our tiny conference room. Lucy gets up from the reception desk and gets his rain jacket from the coat closet. As she hands it to him with a bright smile, I'm glad Adry asked Nick's daughter to be our new office manager and even more glad she accepted. Not only is she great at the job, but having her around is wonderful for Nick who still hasn't fully mourned the loss of his son.

As he's putting it on, I ask him, "I didn't ask you when you phoned, but who referred you to us?"

"My accountant at Beloff and Plasker. He said you'd solved the murder of one of their senior managers."

I remember them well and I'm a little surprised that one of their people would have known who I was. "Who specifically was that? I'd like to thank them for the referral."

"It's another Mike I went to school with. I'll email you his contact details."

He shakes my hand again and walks out through the main door of the office just as Nick wheels out of the elevator, back from his check up at St. Paul's. They nod at each other as they pass in the hallway and I hold the door open so Nick can wheel right in. He can be a bit touchy about being helped; he likes to be as independent as possible.

"Thanks Rogan," he says cheerily. "Now I'm here, it's time for morning prayers."

'Morning prayers' is his expression for our regular

morning meeting where we bring each other up to date on our cases.

Within minutes we are all sitting around his desk in the main office with mugs of coffee and a plate of his favourite chocolate-digestive cookies.

"Was that the new client?" he asks.

"Yes," Adry chimes in. "He's being blackmailed."

Nick's eyebrows raise. "Interesting. That's a bit different from our usual missing person or wayward spouse cases. Tell me about it."

"Sure," she says, her enthusiasm brimming over. "He's a businessm—" She stops mid-sentence. I follow her gaze.

It's a middle-aged man in a raincoat. His hair is awry and there is a crazed look on his face. It's a look I've seen on the faces of crack addicts living on the streets. But this man is no crack addict. He is short and well-dressed and definitely better fed than any crack addict I've ever met. He's just standing there breathing heavily and holding a large brown envelope.

Before any of us can say anything, he speaks.

"Please, you have to help me. Both my children are missing."

From the way he says it, I know that this too is not going to be one of our usual missing person or wayward spouse cases.

3. ZELENA

The kitchen is hot. The tea is hot. But I still feel cold. Why do they keep me in that room at night? And why is it so cold in there? It's May, or is it June now? I don't know. I've lost track of the days. Either way, the weather is warm here.

He's sitting opposite me at the table and the old woman is cooking. None of the others are here. At least they feed me and the food is good. It's the only good thing here. In half an hour, I'll be taken to the star room for the first session. The thought sends a shudder through me. I look at the counter where the woman is preparing breakfast and I see it: the instrument of my freedom. If I can use it today, I won't have to go to that room, I won't have to stand there while they shout, won't have to...

The door opens and a man walks in. He has a cardboard box full of groceries. The woman says something to him in Cantonese but he just stands there, his mouth hanging open. He looks like he doesn't understand what she's saying. She walks over to him, grumbling, and the man sitting opposite me turns around to watch what is happening.

It's my chance.

I leap up. But I'm too fast. My chair topples over backwards and crashes to the floor. I dash across the room to the counter and hear the shout behind me. I stumble but regain my footing and slam into the countertop. I grab the knife. It's long and sharp with a point like a needle.

I put the point under my chin.

One deep breath.

Can I?

I think of the star room.

Yes. I can.

With all my strength I push the knife upwards.

4. NICK

Lucy is the first to react. She jumps to her feet. "Come in and sit down, sir," she says. "Let me take your coat." Almost in a daze, he takes off his coat and hands it to her. She takes his elbow and leads him to the chair she has just left. "Would you like a coffee or a tea?" He just shakes his head. She takes his coat and vanishes into the reception area. For the hundredth time I'm grateful Rogan agreed to hire her.

Adry slides her chair closer to him. "Hi, I'm Adriana Locke. These are my colleagues, Cal Rogan and Nick Stammo. How can we help you, sir?"

Her quiet voice seems to shake him out of his dazed state. "I'm sorry, I'm forgetting my manners," he says in an accented voice. "My name is Janusz Gutkowski, I am pleased to meet you." He puts the brown envelope on my desk, gets up and shakes hands with each of us.

I ask, "You said your children are missing. Have you reported it to the police?"

"Yes, but they can do nothing. My children both went missing in Hong Kong."

Rogan and me exchange glances. I'll bet we're both thinking of the last time we had to track down a missing child and where that all led. As Lucy walks back into the room I'm glad I've still got her and that I get to see her every day. This poor bastard's got two kids missing. She hands him a glass of the fancy fizzy water we keep for clients and he takes a sip.

"How old are they?" I ask.

"My daughter Zelena is nineteen and my son Aleksander is twenty-three."

At least they're not little kids. Not that *that's* any consolation for him.

"I have photographs," he says. He pushes the brown envelope across the desk. I take it and slide out the eight by ten photos. The one on top is the son. He's a good-looking kid with a bright grin and dark, wavy hair. His father's hair probably looked like this twenty years ago. The photo was taken on a beach with palm trees in the background. I slide the picture across the desk so the others can see. I look at the picture of the girl. It's a graduation photo. The brother was handsome, for sure, but this girl looks like she should be on the cover of Vogue. She has long dark hair and large brown eyes. Unlike the picture of her brother, she is not smiling. The picture looks posed and I get the sense that the real Zelena is not the demure girl in front of me. I slide her picture across the desk, next to her brother's.

I watch them looking at her picture. Three different reactions. Adry is the first to speak. "Can you tell us what happened?" she asks.

"Yes. My daughter went missing first. She went on holiday with a friend, to Hong Kong." The way he says 'friend' makes me think he doesn't approve.

Rogan interrupts him. "Male or female friend?"

"Female. Zelena's not that kind of girl. She doesn't even have a boyfriend yet." Hmmm. I spot a man who might have a bit of a delusion going on here. A nineteen-year-old girl, looking like that, has at least one boyfriend. Unless, like me, she bats for the other team.

"You sound like you don't approve of her friend," Adry says. Good girl, she spotted it too.

"Stephanie is Zelena's best friend. They have known each other since high school. She's a nice enough girl, from a good family too, but just not serious."

Definitely old world.

"What made them choose Hong Kong?"

He stops and takes three breaths.

"I have no idea. They just said it would be a cool place to go." He makes quote signs with his fingers when he says the word cool. "I told them it was not a good idea because of all the protests and the crack-down by the Chinese government and the viruses you can pick up in places like that. But she insisted."

"Did you pay for the trip?" I ask.

"No. Never." He takes three more breaths. "She entered a contest and won a two-week trip for two, anywhere in the world. She could have gone anywhere, Europe, somewhere nice in the Caribbean, anywhere..." he shrugs. "But she chose Hong Kong. They left on April twenty-fifth, right after their final exams at UBC. I told her she had to text me every day and she did. She texted me every evening at six, until three days before the end of the trip, she didn't text. I texted Stephanie and at first she said Zelena was in the shower and would get back to me but I didn't hear anything, so at midnight I called Stephanie on her phone and she told me Zelena had gone out the previous night and hadn't returned."

His voice breaks and he takes another sip of his water. "I knew something was seriously wrong. I made Stephanie contact the local police but they said they couldn't do anything until she had been missing for forty-eight hours. When the forty-eight hours were up, Stephanie went back to the police and they didn't seem to take the matter very seriously. I spoke to the officer in charge, an Inspector Ho Lei Min. He took all the details but, in my opinion, he definitely did not treat the matter properly."

He pauses and he's breathing heavily like he's just run a race.

"Are you all right Mr. Gutkowski?" Lucy asks. "Can I get you anything?"

"I'm sorry," he says, looking back to Adry, "but I have a heart condition. My doctor tells me I must be careful. He has refused to let me travel. I wanted to go to Hong Kong but because of my heart, Aleksander offered to go there and talk to the police."

He stops again to breathe more deeply. He takes a bottle out of his pocket and pops a white pill in his mouth. Poor guy, it must be hell knowing your kids are in trouble thousands of miles away and you can't do anything. We have got to find this girl.

He picks up his water, takes a sip and continues. "Aleksander flew to Hong Kong and went to the police. He agreed with me that they were not being serious enough, so we decided to hire a private detective. Aleksander found one and the man started to work on the case. For three days Aleksander contacted me every day with progress reports. The detective was able to find a nightclub that Zelena had gone to and learned she had talked to a man there. The man was known to the staff of the nightclub, he was a regular there. The detective paid a couple of the staff members to contact him if the man showed up. But that was the last I heard. Aleksander didn't call me on Saturday evening with his progress report. I tried repeatedly to contact him all day yesterday but nothing. I was all set to take the risk and fly out to Hong Kong today, but my wife remembered that a year or so ago, you tracked down the daughter of one of our friends, Rebecca Bradbury, and that she recommended you highly. So Francesca insisted I see you. Can you help me?"

"Definitely." Rogan and I say it at the same time.

"Do you know the name of the private detective your son hired in Hong Kong?" I ask.

"I believe it was a Mr. Wang."

"Do you know his first names?" Rogan asks.

"No, I'm sorry, I don't."

"There are over ninety million people with the last name Wang," Rogan says. How does he know all these odd facts? "Do you remember anything more about him?"

He pauses, lost in thought. "I do remember one thing. Aleksander said his office was on, or maybe just near, the main shopping street in Hong Kong."

"Nathan Road," says Lucy. That's my girl!

"Yes, that's it," he almost shouts. "How did you know?" Yes, how *did* she know?

"Well done Luce. That narrows it down a lot," I say.

"How did Aleksander pay this detective?" Rogan asks.

"He used our family credit card."

"Then the name will be on the credit card statement."

Well duh! Why didn't I think of that? I must be losing my touch.

"Of course," Gutkowski says. "I can look it up online."

Adry pitches in, "Where are Zelena's things?" Good question.

"What things?"

"The clothes and personal effects she had on the trip. There might be something among her things that could help us, a diary or notebook or something."

The old man gives me a grim look. "I asked Stephanie to bring them back with her but the silly girl shipped them as freight. She said she had too much luggage to take Zelena's too. We would have paid for the excess baggage. As I said, not a serious girl."

"Will you let us know as soon as you receive them. There might be something useful."

"Did your son stay at the same hotel your daughter stayed at?" I ask.

"No, Mr. Stammo, Aleksander stayed at the Hilton."

"What happened to his things?" I ask.

"I don't know. I suppose they are still at the hotel."

"OK," I say. "We're going to need to get a whole bunch of details from you, starting with the name and contact information for her friend Stephanie."

Adry opens her laptop and we get down to it.

I'm going to make sure we get this man's kids back if it kills me.

5. CAL

I ring the doorbell of the ivy covered house situated in Kerrisdale, Vancouver's second most expensive neighbourhood.

After Janusz Gutkowski left the office today, we made two decisions: one, with two new cases today, and given our existing workload, we need to hire another investigator; two, because of the travelling that's going to be needed, it's better if I take the Hong Kong case and Nick takes the blackmailing case. Which didn't actually delight either of us. So I'm on Adera Street to interview Stephanie White, Zelena Gutkowska's best friend and travel companion.

The door is opened by an elegantly dressed woman in a conservative blue dress and a string of pearls that I'll bet cost more than I made last month. "Mr. Rogan?" she asks. I admit to my identity and she invites me in. "Stephanie's in the living room, come through."

The room is a reflection of the owner. Elegant, conservative, expensive and, predominantly, blue. Her daughter gets off the couch and shakes my hand. "Hi, I'm Steph," she says. She has slightly frizzy blond hair, blue eyes and a very genuine smile on a round face that exudes warmth. I don't feel any of the reservation Janusz Gutkowski expressed.

"Would you like coffee or tea?" her mother asks.

"No, I'm fine thanks," I say. She sits down next to her daughter and indicates a chair for me.

Something tells me to ease into the questioning about the trip to Hong Kong. I open with, "How did you and Zelena meet?"

"At school. We met in grade 8."

"Magee?" I ask. Obvious choice, it's just down the road. It's where I went, although I definitely did not live in this more ritzy part of Magee's catchment area.

"No. Crofton House."

"My wife went there," I say. Mrs. White smiles and nods in what I suspect is acceptance of my presenting an upper-class credential. Better not mention she's my ex-wife now.

"Stephanie was valedictorian. She's at UBC now."

"What are you studying?" I ask.

"Biology, for now," Stephanie says.

"She's going to be a doctor," her mother interjects and the hint of a frown passes across Stephanie's happy face.

"You must have been excited when Zelena won the trip and asked you to come along."

"Yes, it was great," she says but her answer lacks the enthusiasm I expected. It's probably because of what happened on the trip.

"What made you guys choose Hong Kong?"

She glances at her mother for a second. "It was Zel's idea. She said she'd always wanted to go there. I thought it would be pretty cool too, so we decided." Something in her demeanour tells me that what she said isn't completely true. But why would she lie?

"When I talked to her father, I forgot to ask how she won the trip," I lie.

Her smile seems less genuine this time. "It was on a YouTube fashion channel we both watch." Again she glances at her mother. "They said if you left a comment, they would choose someone at random to go on a trip anywhere in the world." This agrees with what the father told us. It still sounds odd. Do kids talking about clothes on YouTube make enough money to give away expensive trips and why would they?

"Did you both leave comments?" I ask with a smile. "Double your chances of winning?"

She looks up for a second. "Yes. But it was Zel who won." It's a lie.

I turn my most charming smile on Mrs. White. "Can I change my mind? If the offer's still open, I'd love a cup of coffee."

She frowns. She wants to say no but years of polite behaviour win out. "Certainly," she says, getting up and leaving the room without closing the door.

"Stephanie," I say, dropping my voice, "your best friend is missing. I need to find her. I can only do that if you are completely honest with me."

She glances towards the door, her face flushing. "I'm sorry," she says quietly. "I shouldn't have lied. It's just that my mother is so... I don't know... she just has to know every detail of my life *and* the lives of all my friends."

I hear the murmur of voices and drop my volume one more notch. "Tell me about the contest on YouTube, what channel was it?"

"There was no contest," she says, her volume matching mine. "We just made that up. My mother would have freaked if she knew the truth and Zel's dad... you've met him, can you imagine what he'd do?"

"So what did happen?"

She glances up. "Well," she says at her normal volume, "the hotel was very nice. It was the Kerry Hotel right on the waterfront and we had a room facing the harbour."

"Your coffee will be here in a moment, Mr. Rogan," her mother says, retaking her place on the couch next to her daughter. I was hoping for more time but clearly Mrs. White doesn't need to take time making coffee when someone else can do it for her.

I continue asking innocuous questions about the trip and get back equally innocuous answers which, incidentally, match perfectly with the answers we got from Janusz Gutkowski earlier. They match a little too perfectly in fact. I keep it up for about fifteen minutes—through the arrival of the housekeeper with my coffee—noticing that when Stephanie answers my questions, sometimes, if her mother's not looking directly at her, she will let me know the true answer by nodding when saying 'no' or shaking her head while saying 'yes'. I keep up the charade until I have drunk enough of the coffee to be polite.

"Thank you very much, Stephanie," I say as I stand up. "I won't take up any more of your time." I take out my wallet and withdraw a business card. I hand it to her. "Please text me immediately if you think of anything at all that might be important." She looks directly into my eyes and nods. As an afterthought, I hand a second card to her mother, just to take away any excuse she might come up with for taking possession of the one I gave to her daughter.

My darling Ellie is only ten and a half. I hope Sam and I never get so controlling of her that she feels she has to keep things from us. Or will everything change when she gets to be a teenager? I hope not, but maybe I'm being unrealistic.

As I drive away, I hope Stephanie doesn't wait too long before contacting me.

————

"WE'RE ON!" NICK WHOOPS AS I WALK INTO THE OFFICE. He sees my blank expression. "The new client. Me and Adry talked to him half an hour ago. He's received a blackmail demand for twenty-five grand. He's on his way in to plan how we're going to handle it." He wheels over to the cabinet where he keeps all the gizmos we bought when we set up the business and have hardly ever used. After fishing around for a few minutes he pulls out a box. "Tracking device," he says with a big grin. He wheels back and puts it on his desk. "How'd it go with the best friend?"

"Looks like the story she and Zelena told their parents isn't true. She couldn't tell me the details because her mother was there most of the time. She's going to text me I hope. If not, I'll go to her house again first thing tomorrow and ask to speak to her alone. I'm not too sure how the mother will react to that."

"I checked Zelena's social media accounts. They were easy to find. There aren't many Zelena Gutkowskas," Adry says. "She has a Facebook account and her posts all look very vanilla: her at school with friends, skiing at Whistler, pictures in restaurants. But no selfies with guys. Looking like she does, she has to have a boyfriend or, at the very least, a string of wannabe boyfriends. From what you just said, I suspect she uses Facebook for the benefit of her parents and their friends. However, she also has an Instagram account but it's private so I can't see any of the posts. I'm guessing it tells a different story. Maybe you could have her friend show it to you."

"Did you check the brother, Aleksander?" I ask.

"No, I didn't think to for some reason. I'll get right on it." She turns back to her screen.

I hear Lucy's voice greeting our other new client. Nick grabs the box on his desk, nods at me and we go out to the reception area and lead Connor McCoy to our conference room.

"Is your colleague not joining us?" he asks as he puts down his briefcase and takes a seat.

"Not just yet," I say. He looks disappointed and I think I know why. Maybe I should tell him that Adry already has a boyfriend.

Nick gets straight down to business. "Tell us about the phone call."

McCoy nods. "It was odd," he says. He pulls out his mobile and shows us the recent calls list. "It's the call from area code eight-oh-two, I looked it up, it's in Vermont."

"It doesn't mean anything," Stammo grunts. "It's easy to spoof area codes and numbers; telemarketers do it all the time. Did you recognize the voice?"

"It could have been Mike but I'm not sure. It's over ten years since I spoke to him."

"Did you hear any background noises?" I ask.

He frowns. "I don't think so."

"What did he say?"

"He asked if I wanted to buy a video for twenty-five thousand dollars. I told him yes and he said to have the money in cash, in a Safeway bag, and be at Victory Square at six this evening. He said to sit on a bench right by the memorial, the bench with the words 'To the Valour of our Sailors', and wait for his call. Then he just hung up."

I bring up a mental picture of Victory Square and start to formulate a plan.

"In cash, eh," Stammo says. "That's a bit old-school."

"What do you mean?" he asks.

"Serious blackmailers ask for bitcoin. It can't be traced and you don't have all the problems that go with a handoff of cash. This guy's an amateur. That's good, we're going to catch him."

"Catch him?" McCoy says. "Isn't that a bit dangerous?"

"The alternative's worse," Stammo says. "He must know you run a successful company. There's no way that twenty-five grand is going to buy his silence. If he gets away with this, he's going to ask for a second, bigger payment, probably *much* bigger. You could be paying him for ever. No, we have to take him down."

McCoy bites his lip. "I hadn't thought of that. Yes, you're right."

"There's another thing," Nick says. "I tried to track down Mike Anderson. I wasn't able to find anyone of that name from BC who'd spent time in jail during the time you mentioned."

"Hmm. That's odd." He thinks for a bit. "You know what? His parents were originally from Russia. They changed the family name to Anderson when Mike was a kid. Maybe try the Russian spelling of Michael."

"Do you know the original family name?" I ask.

"If I ever knew it, I don't remember it now."

"OK, we'll keep trying," Stammo says. "Anyway, I dealt with a couple of blackmail cases when I was with the VPD. If you're willing to risk it, it's better to use real money. There's always a chance that the person who picks up the cash takes time to check it. If the cash is phoney, he'll know something's up and he's going to throw it away and get out fast. If he sees it's real, he'll think he's succeeded and might just be lulled into a false sense of security." He checks his watch. "If you're OK with it, you might want to go to your bank and withdraw the money. You'd better call them first, banks aren't used to handing over large sums of cash."

"No need," McCoy says. He opens his briefcase and takes out a Safeway bag. He empties the contents onto the table: twenty-five bundles of twenty-dollar bills.

Nick whistles quietly.

"I have to get back to work. I have a client call at three-thirty." He starts to put the money back in the Safeway bag.

"Leave the money with us," Nick says opening his box. He takes out a device that looks like a white credit card with a red wire protruding from it. "I'm going to put this tracking device in one of the bundles."

"You can track the money?"

"Absolutely," Nick grins. "If we're going to use real money, we're going to do everything to make sure you get your money back."

While they've been talking, I've been developing the beginning of a plan. "There's a Bean Around the World coffee shop on the corner of Cambie and Hastings, kitty-corner from Victory Square. Meet us there not a minute later than five-fifteen," I tell him.

We get up and see him out. As soon as he's gone, Stammo gets to work with his tracking gizmo. I take out my phone and text Tina that I'll be home late tonight. Then I scroll through my contacts list and smile when I see the name. I make the call and I'm pleased the number is still active. It was only a fifty-fifty chance. "Hey, Rocky," he says, using my old street name. I give him detailed instructions of where and when I want to meet him, and tell him what the payment will be. I can hear the grin in his voice as he says, "Fuckin' A."

Now to go to Victory Square and think through all the options. And maybe I can get a handle on the nagging feeling something's going to go wrong, no matter how well we plan and execute this take down.

———

CONNOR MCCOY COMES OUT OF THE COFFEE SHOP'S bathroom and he is one nervous puppy. I speak as calmly as I can. "OK, this is it, just relax. Remember, we've got it all covered. It's three minutes to six: time to go and sit on the bench. And remember to check the other benches, like you don't know which one says 'To the Valour of our Sailors'."

He nods distractedly as he fumbles to put his earbuds in. "Can you hear me OK?" he says.

His voice comes through my own earbuds. "Perfectly. Remember, when he calls you, press the conference call button so I can hear what he says too."

He nods, takes a deep breath, and heads out the door.

I scan Victory Square. It is a one-block park, sloping up from Hastings to Pender, honouring the Canadian service men and women who died in the twentieth century's two world wars. The main feature is a concrete monument with the Canadian flag and the flags of the Army, Navy and Airforce. Due to the nice May weather, there are quite a few people around and because the square is on the cusp of downtown and the east side, they are a mix of social classes. Among them, I can see Ghost and his buddy Tommy. They are two homeless guys I know from when I too was homeless and living on the streets of the downtown east side. They fit right in with half of the denizens of the park.

I tap the mute button on my phone and pick up the other phone on the table in front of me. It is also set to a conference call. "Check in," I say.

"Here," says Stammo.

"Right," says Ghost.

"Yeah," says Tommy.

I can see all three of them. Ghost is closest to me, sitting on the steps of the monument. Tommy is on a bench at the south-east corner and Stammo is in his truck just up Hastings, illegally parked opposite the Amsterdam, Vancouver's original marijuana café.

Connor checks a couple of the benches then makes his way to the one facing the back of the monument. He sits and clutches his Safeway bag to his chest. He is the epitome of nervousness, which works in our favour, as the blackmailer is not going to expect him to be calm and collected.

"You're doing well, Connor," I say, then realize I have my own phone muted. I tap it and repeat my encouragement.

"Thanks," he says.

I examine the other people in the square. Half of them look like they are as homeless as Ghost and Tommy, or close to it. If the blackmailer is as big an amateur as we think, he is not likely to be using any of them. Of the others, no one seems to be focussed on Connor. There are a couple of lovers on a bench to the left, eating ice cream cones and deep in conversation. There's an elderly couple, probably tourists, standing, reading the words engraved on the monument. Up on the south side of the square is a well-dressed man sitting alone on a bench. He is looking down at the monument. From his vantage point he may also be observing Connor, but I can't be sure.

"It's ringing!" Connor says.

"Remember to press the button to conference call," I say

then hit the mute button fast. "We're on," I say into the other phone.

A new voice comes in through my earbuds. *"Look hard right,"* he says. Connor turns to his right. *"Do you see that garbage bin?"* Connor nods.

The well-dressed man stands up. He's looking down, maybe at Connor or maybe at the monument.

"Tommy," I say into the other phone, "do you see the well-dressed guy?"

"Yeah, Rocky," he says excitedly.

"Good. I may need you to follow him."

The blackmailer's voice says, *"I said, do you see the garbage bin?"*

Interesting. He hasn't got eyes on Connor or he would have seen his nod.

"Yes," Connor says.

I look up towards the well-dressed man but he's walking out of the square. He almost collides with a jogger running into the square.

"Forget him Tommy," I say.

The blackmailer says, *"Walk to the bin and place the bag on top of it."*

Connor stands up. Simultaneously the young lovers also stand and make their way, hand in hand, towards the bin.

"Ghost," I say. "Walk towards that garbage bin, straight ahead."

"OK, Rocky," he says and gets to his feet.

"If that couple grabs the Safeway bag, try and stop them," I tell him. I stand up and head out of the café. The lights are against me and the traffic on Hastings is heavy. I look back at the scene. Connor is nearly at the garbage bin. The young lovers have stopped and are standing beside the bin, kissing. "Move in, Nick," I say to Stammo.

Then I see it.

The jogger is running down the path, which cuts diagonally through the square. He will arrive at the bin at the same time as Connor and he's looking directly at him.

"It's the jogger!" I shout into the phone.

My view is cut off by a double-length trolley bus lumbering along Hastings. Damn! It takes forever to pass me. When it finally clears my line of sight, Connor is lying on the ground. Ghost has his hands over his face and there is blood on them. The young couple are moving toward him, and the jogger, clutching the Safeway bag, is running between cars as he crosses Cambie Street.

Nick turns his truck onto Cambie just as the lights change. I dash across Hastings and see the jogger run into the alley that divides the block. Got him. He may be able to outrun me, he won't be able to outrun Nick's truck.

I sprint as fast as I can to the alley's entrance. As I arrive, I hear an insistent car horn. A glance to my right and I see that Stammo can't turn into the alley. There is a Honda with out-of-town plates parked across the entrance. The people inside are studying a map. Nick is hitting the horn and shouting out his window at them, like a New York cab driver.

I head into the alley. My quarry is a good hundred meters ahead of me and he is getting into a nondescript grey car. I redouble my pace but before I have halved the distance, the car accelerates away and within seconds is exiting the far end of the alley.

I stand panting and turn around. The Honda is moving away, no doubt unimpressed with Vancouver driving manners, and within seconds Stammo roars towards me. I pull open the passenger door and hop in. It slams behind me as he accelerates.

He takes the tracker off his lap and hands it to me.

It's a high-end model and for a second I wonder how much it cost us. It shows a map on which we are a blue dot and the tracking device is flashing red and is moving east on Hastings. Stammo hangs a left on Abbott, to the screeching of brakes, followed by horns. He accelerates down the block but the lights are red and he is blocked from turning right by a car straddling the lanes. He swears in technicolour and hits the horn futilely.

The flashing red dot crosses Carrall and by the time the lights change and we turn onto Hastings, the dot has turned left off Hastings and onto Columbia. Stammo accelerates down Hastings and just makes the lights across Carrall.

I look down at the tracker. The red dot is stationary. "He's stopped by the lights on Cordova," I yell.

"Got him," Stammo says and his truck roars as he pushes the accelerator lever. I have to admit, he really has learned how to use his specially-equipped truck.

As we pull onto Columbia, the street is empty. "Where is he now?" Nick barks.

The red dot is steady. The grey car should be right in front of us.

He slows and our blue dot passes the tracker's red dot.

"Stop the truck," I shout. It jolts to a halt.

I jump out and scan the pavement behind us.

And I see it.

A white device, like a credit card with a red wire sticking out of it.

We were outsmarted.

We have just cost our client twenty-five thousand dollars.

Maybe this blackmailer is not such an amateur after all.

"WAS YOUR CLIENT OK?" TINA ASKS, CONCERN WRITTEN ON her face. It's a face I've loved since I first saw her at a Narcotics Anonymous meeting six months ago.

"He had a couple of bruises but he was OK. The jogger knocked him off his feet and snatched the bag of money but Connor fell on grass. Poor old Ghost got a bloodied nose but if anything, he was proud of it. It gave him a story to tell over a beer or ten. What was amazing was that Connor was OK about the money." I take a bite of the pakora. It's delicious. I love it when it's Tina's week to cook.

"So what's next?" she asks.

"Connor was more optimistic than he has the right to be. He thinks maybe the blackmailer will be satisfied with twenty-five grand and that it's all over. I doubt it. He said his software company has eighty-five employees so I'm guessing he's probably a millionaire. The blackmailer has to know what he's worth and it seems unlikely he'll stop now."

"What's the name of his company?" she asks.

"Why?" I ask. Tina is a reporter and I really don't want any of my clients to appear in the Daily News Hound dot com.

"You are sooooo suspicious," she grins. "I won't write a story about any of your clients, I promise. I was asking so that I could find out how rich he is. Just because he has eighty-five people working for him, doesn't mean it's a successful company."

"I'm not sure I remember. It was on his business card." I try to conjure up an image of it. "It was dark blue with white letters... 'Energy' something, I think."

"Oh, yes of course, 'Energy something', I know it well." She grins even more widely and I am torn between eating more of the wonderful meal and reaching across the table to kiss her. But then again, I can do both. So I do.

As we eat contentedly, I remember something else. "I got an email today," I say.

"Only one?" she laughs.

"It was from a friend of mine who I was at UBC with. We did our Masters together. He decided to stay in academe and he's now a professor at SFU in charge of the English Lit. department."

"Does he want you to spy on his unfaithful wife?" she says biting into a poppadom.

"No, he wants me to go and work with him and teach Shakespeare to undergrads, maybe do a Ph.D. at the same time."

"Would you want to do that?"

"Well, you know what..."

But my phone cuts me off by ringing insistently.

The caller ID starts 604-263. Although phone numbers are portable now, 263 used to be a Kerrisdale exchange and lots of the older residences still have that number. I give Tina a lopsided look. "I'm sorry, I have to take this."

She smiles and nods. We both have professions where it is important to take some calls any time of the night or day.

I accept the call. "Cal Rogan."

"Hello Mr. Rogan, it's Steph White, Zelena's friend."

I was right. "Hi Steph."

She is silent for a moment. Then, *"I really need to talk to you about what happened in Hong Kong. I couldn't say anything in front of my mother. She just went out to play bridge with her friends. Could you meet up with me?"*

"I would really like that Steph. If I'm going to find Zelena, I need to know the truth."

"Could you meet me this evening? I'm going downtown to meet some friends. We could meet before."

"Sure. When and where?"

She thinks for a moment. *"The Starbucks on Robson and Thurlow? 8:30?"*

"I'll see you there."

"Thank you so much," she says and hangs up.

I look across the table. "I'm sorry," I say.

"Some people will do anything to get out of doing the dishes." She laughs, gets up, comes around the table and gives me a wonderful kiss. "I'll be here when you get back," she promises.

I can't help but wonder if she will always be this forgiving of the pressures of my job.

————

"I'm soooo sorry I couldn't tell you the truth before. My mom is like so strict about stuff, she'd have killed me." Steph White leans towards me over the table, her hands clasped around her skinny latte. Although it's a Monday, she's dressed like she's ready for a party. She's not as stunning as Zelena looks in her picture, but Steph is very pretty. If her mother is as strict as she says, I'm betting she put on that short, glittery dress after her mother left for her bridge club and will not go back home until her mother is home and fast asleep in bed. Yet she's nineteen, old enough to vote and drink. Odd.

I smile encouragingly. "So what really happened in Hong Kong?" I ask, taking out my note pad.

She pauses. It's a typical reaction as a witness approaches the moment of truth. She smiles at me and runs the tip of her tongue over her top lip, removing a smudge of latte foam. She looks down at my notepad. "You have to promise me you won't tell my mother or Zel's parents. They would freak. Especially her dad, he's like a hundred times more strict than my mom."

I struggle not to show my irritation at these protestations of parental strictness. "Listen Steph," I say. "Your best friend and her brother are both missing. I don't see any reason I have to tell *your* mother but I can't keep anything from Zelena's parents if it will help me find her and Aleksander."

She looks me in the eye for a long moment but I can't read her expression. "OK," she says.

I try and ease her into talking. "When your mom was out of the room, you told me the story about winning the trip on YouTube wasn't exactly true."

"No, it wasn't," she says.

"When you mentioned it, I thought it was a bit far-fetched for someone on YouTube to give away a prize like that."

"Oh, no," she says. "There *was* a competition—there are lots of them on YouTube—and we both entered but we didn't win. We just told our parents that Zel had won." She bites her lower lip.

"Go on," I say.

She takes a deep breath and it all spills out in a rush. "Zel and I both had boyfriends but we never told our parents. They *so* wouldn't approve of them. Anyway, after we'd entered the competition, we were all at a party together and we were talking about where we would go if we won. Harvey, that's Zel's boyfriend, is from Hong Kong and he said it would be a great place to go. He said if we didn't win he'd pay for the trip anyway. Harvey is like super-rich. He said he would come with us for part of the trip and he even offered to pay for my boyfriend to go too. He said it would be his gift to us to celebrate the end of our first year at UBC. We thought he was joking but when we didn't win, he just gave us our tickets. He told us he also had tickets for him and Chad and that they would come over and stay with us for a few days."

"Chad's your boyfriend, I assume."

She gives a little pout. "Was," she says.

"So you told your parents you had won the contest and you went on the trip."

"Yes," she brightens up. "We flew first class on Cathay Pacific and Harvey had even arranged for a limo to take us from the airport to our hotel. The limo driver was in the arrivals hall holding up a sign with our names on it. It was like being a celebrity. He took us to the Kerry hotel and we had two rooms overlooking the harbour; it was amazing."

"What did you do there?" I ask.

"Oh, it was great. We went to visit all the street markets and shopped our faces off during the day and in the evenings, we went to nightclubs."

"Did you always go to the same club?"

"Not at first, but when Harvey and Chad arrived, he took us to a place called the Golden Dragon. It was amazing. We just kind of made it our place."

"How long did your boyfriends stay?"

"Just for a week. Zel was so happy. Before Hong Kong she and Harvey hadn't, you know, really hooked up before." She lowers her voice and leans closer. "She told me he was *fantastic* in bed and was more kind and gentle than anyone she'd ever been with. She just glowed all the time. She was lucky."

I remember what Zelena's father said about her not having a boyfriend. "Was Harvey her first?"

"OMG no! Zel's so beautiful that she had a constant

string of boyfriends. Don't get me wrong, she didn't sleep with all of them, she wasn't a slut. But she definitely wasn't a virgin either."

"Did Chad enjoy it too?"

"Yes, but it didn't really work out with us." I look into her face and the sadness I see is muted by an expression I can't quite read.

"So what happened after the boys left?"

"Zel was so over-the-moon in love that she wanted to fly back with them. But Harvey said he had to go to L.A. on business first, so she stayed."

"So Harvey's older than her?"

"Totally. He's thirty-one."

"Tell me about Zel going missing."

"Sure. It was the day after Harvey left. The weather was really nice so we spent the day just hanging out beside the hotel pool. That evening we had dinner at an open-air restaurant just by the Temple Street night market and walked to the Golden Dragon. We had a couple of drinks but it just wasn't the same without Harvey there, so we went back to the hotel. The next morning, we were planning to take the cable car and see the giant statue of Buddha, but when I went to her room, she wasn't there and her bed hadn't been slept in. When she wasn't back by the evening, I called the police. They were useless by the way."

"Did you talk to anyone who stands out in your mind?" I ask.

"Not really. There were a couple of guys at the pool who tried to pick us up but Zel shooed them away. Apart from that I can't think of anyone."

"No one at the restaurant or the nightclub."

"No. No one. Well, apart from Leo." She sees the question on my face. "Leo's the manager, or one of the owners, of the Golden Dragon, I'm not sure which. He was there every night and Zel was always flirting with him. But she flirted with everyone."

"Zel's brother Aleksander, does he know the truth?" I ask

"*Zander*? No way. I can't imagine that Zel would tell him. He's as bad as her dad. If he'd known, he'd probably have told his parents."

"What about Harvey? He must be really upset."

"Oh, poor Harvey, he's devastated."

"You've seen him since you got back?"

"No but I've texted him a *lot*. He never liked it that Zel flirted so much and he thinks she's met someone else and gone off with them."

"Does he suspect anyone? Maybe the manager of that club, the Golden Dragon," I check my notes, "Leo."

For a second she looks a bit flustered but covers it with, "No, not Leo. He and Harvey have been friends since they were little kids. Leo would *never* do that to Harvey."

I get the impression that maybe she had a bit of a crush on Leo. "How did you feel about Zel flirting with Leo?" I ask.

"Zel flirted with everyone," she says.

"So you said, but I asked how you felt about it."

"I didn't really care except that I felt sorry for Harvey." She says it a bit too casually. I wonder if she's covering up something. I just look at her but she doesn't add anything.

"On the subject of Harvey, I'll need to talk to both him and Chad. Can you give me their full names and phone numbers?"

"Sure." She taps at her phone and turns it towards me. It's the contact info for Chad Tucker. I scribble his number and address into my notebook. More tapping and she tells me Harvey's cell number.

"Do you have his full name?" I ask.

"No," she says. "I know it sounds crazy but I never knew his last name. I'm sure Zel must have known but I don't remember her ever telling me."

Odd, but no big deal. I'll find out when I talk to him.

"One last thing, we've been checking out Zelena's social media. The stuff she posts on Facebook looks like it's done for her parents' benefit. We couldn't see her Instagram posts because her account is private."

She laughs. "Yes, Zel wouldn't want her parents seeing that or her Snapchat. I can give you her username and password and you can log on as her and see everything." With an odd little smile, she takes my notebook, writes down the details and hands it back to me.

"Can you give me her username and password for Snapchat and any other sites?" I ask.

"It's the same. Zel used the same silly password for everything, that's how I know it."

I look at what she has written. Zelena's password is 'zelrocksit.'

"You've really been helpful, Steph. I can't thank you enough. I won't keep you from your friends any longer."

She gives a light-up-the-room smile. "No prob. If there's anything else you need to ask me about the trip, you can call me."

I stand and extend my hand. Without getting up, she takes it and gives a firm shake. And doesn't let go. It feels a bit disconcerting. I search for something to say and come up with, "I'm sorry it didn't work out between you and Chad."

She looks up unwaveringly into my eyes. "Don't be," she says. "Chad was way too immature for me. I think Zel had the right idea." Again she runs the tip of her tongue over her top lip and, this time, pauses it there for a moment. Holding my gaze, she lets go of my hand and says, "I think I would *really* enjoy a relationship with an older man."

A maelstrom of thoughts swirl through my mind but one comes to the fore: I need to keep this girl cooperative because I might want to interview her again. I smile innocently. "Sounds like a great idea, Steph. Can you give me your cell number because I'm sure I'll need to get in touch with you again."

"I was hoping you'd say that." She takes a piece of paper from her purse and hands it to me. Written on it is a phone number with a heart drawn underneath it.

Without another word, she stands, turns and walks out.

6. ZELENA

Tuesday

Today a guard stood beside me while I ate. Yesterday, *he* just managed to get to me before I could push the knife up into my brain. But at least I cut myself. The old woman had to bandage it and it kept me out of the star room for the day, so it was worth it.

But today's another day.

He came today.

He told me if I ever tried it again he would pull out my toenails, one each day for ten days, starting today. I had to beg him not to and he only agreed after I did what he wanted. I hated doing it. It means no one will ever find me. But I had to.

And now I'm following him down the corridor with the guard by my side.

As we get to the end, I hear the voices. Shouting the words I don't understand... but I know their meaning.

He opens the doors and I see the stars.

They make me want to cry.
But I must not.

7. CAL

It's a nice house, not opulent, but the house of a family who have achieved a certain level of financial success in life. The furnishings in the living room are elegant yet simple, in stark contrast to the conversation I need to have with the occupants.

I sip my coffee and look across the table at Janusz and Francesca Gutkowski. They both sit on the edge of their chairs, their faces hoping for, yet doubting, the possibility of good news.

"I've learned Zelena wasn't completely honest with you." I look at them. There is puzzlement in his eyes but something different in hers. "She didn't win the trip to Hong Kong—"

"Then how did she pay for it?" he interrupts.

I ignore the question and look directly at his wife. "Mrs. Gutkowska," I say, hoping that the correct form of address will build some level of trust with her, "did you know Zelena had a boyfriend?" Her face says it all but before she can speak, her husband interrupts.

"I told you before that she didn't have—" His wife grips his arm and he stops in mid-sentence.

"Janusz, please." Her voice is not loud but it is firm. "Zelena wasn't ready to talk to you about it. Yes Mr. Rogan, I did know." Her accent, unlike his, is not Polish but upper-class English.

"Why didn't—" but she squeezes his arm again and he goes silent. He puts his hand in his pocket, takes out his heart medication and pops a pill under his tongue.

"She told me she had a boyfriend a few weeks ago," she says to me, then turns to her husband. "She was worried about telling you. She said she would wait until the time is right."

He just looks confused and shakes his head, more in disbelief than in denial.

"Did she tell you his name?" I ask.

"Yes, it's Harvey."

"I need to talk to him, do you know his last name or anything that might help me track him down?"

"No, I'm afraid not. She showed me a photo of him." She glances at her husband. "He's Chinese."

The expression passing over his face tells me why his daughter didn't want to confide in him. My respect for my client just dropped a couple of notches.

With some trepidation about the effect it may have on his heart, I give them a précis of the details I gleaned from Stephanie White last night. When I finish, they sit in silence for a while, which he breaks with, "And to think, I sent Aleksander to find her. If I'd known..."

"Now, Janusz," his wife says in admonition. She turns to me. "Do you have any news of Aleks?"

"No, I'm afraid not. I will have to go to Hong Kong and retrace his steps."

"Spare no expense," Janusz says. "Go as soon as you can. I am happy to pay an advance on your expenses." I feel a wave of relief that I don't have to ask for the money—it's something I'm never comfortable doing—and also that Nick will be delighted because he's *always* comfortable asking a client for funds. Thinking of Nick, I remember what Adry asked me when I left the office after 'morning prayers.'

"Did Zelena have a computer?" I ask.

"Yes, but it won't be of any use to you. She had a password that she refused to share with us."

"I don't think that will be a problem," I assure them. They seem impressed.

"One other question, did you look up the name of the detective agency Aleksander hired?"

"Yes, I checked my credit card statement online. It was Jiang and Lee Investigations Company Limited."

"I thought you said the detective's name was Wang," I say.

"It was, I'm sure. He must work for the company."

Five minutes later, with Zelena's laptop under my arm, I am saying my goodbyes to her parents when my phone rings. I pull it out of my pocket. It's Zelena's friend, Steph White. "Excuse me, I have to take this."

I listen and try to keep the surprise from my face. It's a result I hadn't expected. I hang up.

"I have some good news. Your daughter is alive."

For a moment, their faces light up, but when I tell them how I know, Janusz looks me in the eye. "Mr. Rogan, please go to Hong Kong and find Aleksander for me. If you happen to run into Zelena you can tell her she is no longer a daughter of mine."

This time, his wife doesn't admonish him.

I'M ONLY HERE BECAUSE I MADE AN APPOINTMENT TO SEE HIM.
Now that we know Zelena's alive and well and that her
father only wants to pay for us to find his son, this interview
may be moot. However, maybe it can shed some light on
where Aleksander has got to. And I really want to know how
to get hold of the mysterious boyfriend, Harvey. I have
texted Harvey on the number Steph gave me but none of the
texts have been answered. When I phoned, there was no
reply and no voicemail. I'm guessing it's a burner phone,
which in my book makes Harvey a suspicious character.

I can see why her mother would not have approved of
Steph's choice of boyfriend. Every visible area of his scrawny
body, not covered by leather, bears an array of tattoos and
his hair is styled in a green mohawk. It would disqualify him
from just about any job, anywhere. Except for here. I have
waited patiently while he finished tattooing a lotus flower
on a girl's thigh and, although tattoos are not my thing, I
have to admit he did an excellent job.

We are now standing in the sun outside his place of
work on Granville Street. I maneuver myself upwind of him
to avoid the pot smoke from his joint. Pot's something else
that's not my thing and, since I've been with Tina and regu-
larly attending meetings, heroin seems not to be my thing
any more either. Or am I tempting the fates with that
thought?

"So Chad, how did you and Steph first meet? Was she a
customer?" I ask him.

"Steph? You've met her. Can you see her getting a tat? A
few months back, she came in with her friend Zel. Now *she*
was a wild one. I gave her a big red tongue on her stomach,

way below her waistband. You know, like the design on the Rolling Stones' album."

"I would have thought *Zel* was more your kind of girl," I say.

"Believe me, I would *love* to do Zel. She would be... like I said: wiii-iild." He takes in a lungful of smoke, holds it then breathes out the next words. "But she's Harvey's and he was paying for the tat. Steph was a Zel wannabe so I thought she might be interesting. Turns out not so much."

"Tell me about Hong Kong." I give him a smile he doesn't deserve.

"Fuckin' fantastic. Harvey picked up the tab for everything. He wanted me to come along and take care of Steph, so he could have uninterrupted time with Zel." He makes a lewd gesture.

"Did you go places together?"

"Sure, we went out together for meals and clubs but apart from that it was pretty much all at the hotel." He repeats the gesture and I can feel disgust starting to crawl into my gut.

"So while you and Steph were in her room, Harvey and Zel could have gone off somewhere together?"

"I s'pose."

"Did you ever meet Aleksander, Zel's brother?"

"Nah. I never knew she even had a brother."

"I need to talk to Harvey. Do you have any contact info for him?"

He shrugs as he holds in another lungful of smoke.

"No one seems to know his last name, I don't suppose you do?"

He lets out the breath with a contented sigh. "Funny you should say that. We always try and get the details of people who come in for tats. I tried to get his name but he wouldn't give it. Paid in cash too, so I didn't get to see his name on a card."

Why would this Harvey character hide his last name from everyone? One thought pops into my mind: drug dealers love anonymity. I mentally kick myself for not asking Steph if Zelena was into drugs. "Any chance he was a dealer?" I ask.

"Harvey? Nah. Didn't even use pot."

"When was the last time you saw him?"

"In the Hong Kong airport on the last day of the trip. He was flying to LA and his flight was a couple of hours after mine and on a different airline. We were in separate lineups. Mine was faster so I went through security a few minutes ahead of him. That was the last time I saw him."

His words trigger a thought.

"On the way to Hong Kong, did you and he fly out together?"

"Yeah, we took Cathay Pacific, first class."

"So you checked in together?"

"Yeah."

"So you must have heard *someone* use his last name."

"Yeah. Of course."

"I thought you said you didn't know it."

"No." He pauses and looks at me like I'm an idiot. "I said I didn't know it when he first came in to get Zel's tat done." He drops the tiny remains of his cigarette on the ground and grinds it out with his Fluevog shoe.

The worm of disgust turns to a mounting anger, which I try to keep out of my voice. "So what *is* his last name?"

He takes a long, supercilious look at me. "If he wants to keep his name private, why the hell should I tell *you*?"

I look up and down Granville Street carefully. No sign of any impediments to my just-devised plan of action.

My hand snakes out and grabs the front of his leather vest. I lift him bodily off his feet, turn and slam him into the window of the tattoo parlour. I push my face close to his and can smell the stale smoke.

"Listen to me you piece of shit, Zelena and her brother are missing and they could be in all sorts of trouble. Harvey may know something that could help me find them. I need to speak to him. So if you want to keep your teeth you'll tell me his last name now."

The fear in his eyes brings a smile to my face. "Lim," he says. "His name's Harvey Lim."

I lean in hard, crushing his puny chest into the glass. "How can I get hold of him?"

"I don't know." I straighten the arm holding him and make a fist with the other hand. I pull it back, ready to smash into his face. "I don't know," he squeaks. "Honest. I don't. All I know is he sometimes goes to the Roxy. He told me it was where he first hooked up with Zel. Honest, that's all I know!"

It's my turn to give *him* the long, supercilious look. Then I slide him down the glass until his feet reach the sidewalk. I let go of his vest and with a smile, straighten out the wrinkles I put in it. "If I find out you lied to me, I will be back and you'll be saying a painful goodbye to your teeth."

I turn and walk off, half hoping he has lied and that I'll have the satisfaction of coming back and making good on my word.

———

"I'm sorry to hear he reacted like that," Adry says. "Disowning his own daughter is harsh."

"You gotta see it from his point of view," Nick says. "For

years he has this idea that his daughter's like a good girl from the old country who's never had a boyfriend. Then he hears from Rogan that she's been shacking up with a guy in Hong Kong. Then, on top of that, she posts on Instagram saying 'My new guy' with a picture of her in a slinky dress fawning over some sleazeball. That's gotta be a shock to poor old Janusz's system."

"Yeah but disowning his own daughter and telling Cal to just concentrate on finding the son." Adry shakes her head.

"I've been thinking about it," I say. "My best way to track down Aleksander may be to find Zelena first. Maybe I can talk some sense into her and get her to go home. I'm pretty sure her mother could talk the old man into taking her back into the family."

"We could contact her through her Instagram account," Adry says. "I can log on as her and then post a message as her saying to contact us. She'd be sure to see it."

"Don't do that," Nick says. "If you do she'll know we have her password and she'll change it right away and we won't have any way to see her posts."

Adry mulls that over. "You're right. But what I can do is create a phony Instagram account with a name similar to one of her friends. Then I can log in as her, make her friends with the new account. We can follow her through the new account."

"Good idea," Nick nods enthusiastically.

I hand Zelena's laptop to Adry and tell her the password I got from Steph. "See what you can find, especially contact information for the boyfriend, his last name is Lim by the way."

Stammo cuts in. "Why don't we have Lucy do that. This isn't our only case you know. We need Adry on another case. She discovered one of our missing persons had a girlfriend on the side. She needs to go interview her."

He's right of course. I nod. "What about the Connor McCoy case. Any further communication from the blackmailer?"

"Nada," he grunts. "I'm gonna feel bad about billing him come the end of the month after we helped him lose twenty-five grand."

"You'll get over it Dad," Lucy grins. She opens Zelena's laptop and enters the password. It works. "I'll see if I can find something on Harvey Lim."

"Show me her Instagram and Snapchat feeds," I say.

After a few clicks she says, "Ta dah!" I sit down with her and look at the latest Instagram post, from eight hours ago. Zelena is in a very short designer dress with her arm draped round a well-dressed man. His face is partly hidden by a large-brimmed fedora. All I can see is about the bottom one-third of his face. It's night time and they are standing in what is obviously a street market. Behind them is a stall with what looks like thousands of watches. Her face looks serious. The post says, 'My new guy. Isn't he dishy?'

The previous post shows her and Steph, grinning like goofy kids in a candy store, as they toast the phone with brightly-coloured cocktails. I scroll down. There are lots of pictures of the holiday, showing Zelena in all sorts of happy poses with Steph and a few of them with Chad, his green mohawk looking very out of place. There are only three with Harvey. He is tall, good-looking and wearing clothes that I would bet cost more than the holiday. Something's bothering me; something's out of place but I can't quite see what. I scroll down further going back in time until I come to a picture that is obviously the Vancouver Airport. She and Steph are posing in front of the Bill Reid sculpture. I continue scrolling. There are a few pictures with Harvey. I stop at one. He is posing, standing at attention, in front of a dark grey Lamborghini Huracán. Unfortunately, his legs completely obscure the registration. We could have called in a favour at VPD—if we still have any favours to call in—and got an address.

Lucy grunts, "Huh," then gets up and goes to her own desk in reception. After a second, I hear her talking on the phone. I was hoping she would do as Nick suggested and scour through Zelena's computer for any lead to Harvey.

I scroll through lots more pictures but can't find anything that would get me closer to finding him. The last post I look at is a picture of Zelena just looking straight into the camera. It's a selfie. She's grinning broadly. And that's it! I scroll right back up to the latest post. She's just smiling. In all of her other posts she is grinning or laughing but here she's just smiling. This is not how Zel would announce a new boyfriend to the world.

I'm not sure what it means but I'm going to find out.

It's time to go to Hong Kong, though it bugs the hell out of me that I won't get to talk to—

"Here's Harvey's address!" Lucy is sporting a big grin and waving a piece of paper.

"That's my girl!" Stammo says proudly.

She hands me the slip of paper. It's an address complete with postcode.

"How the heck did you get that?" I ask.

"I put on my sexy voice and phoned the Lamborghini dealership. I told them my car had broken down last night and that a *really* nice man named Harvey Lim, driving a grey Lamborghini, had helped me out and I wanted to send him a huge bunch of flowers as a thank you and could they please, *please* give me his address."

"I told you we should hire her, didn't I Rogan," Nick crows.

Adry gets up and gives her a big hug.

"You just earned *yourself* a huge bunch of flowers," I say.

She puts on a phony pout. "I was *hoping* for a Lamborghini," she says.

Amid the laughter, I think what a great place this is to work.

"Will you settle for lunch?" Nick says. "We've all been working pretty hard, let's go out and have a nice lunch on the Company."

I really want to get nose to nose with Harvey Lim but a break for lunch won't make any difference will it?

———

THE HOUSE IS A 'VANCOUVER SPECIAL,' BUILT TO OCCUPY THE maximum footprint that the city bylaws allow. I'm guessing it's at least five thousand square feet, maybe even six. The doorbell gives a muted chime and is opened almost immediately by a fresh-faced teenager who is definitely not Harvey Lim. "Hi, can I help you?" he says with a big smile.

"Hi, yes, I think so. Is this the Lim residence?"

"Yes, it is, but I'm afraid my parents are out at the moment."

"Actually, I was hoping to speak to Harvey Lim. Is he in?"

"You just missed him. He left about twenty minutes ago."

Damn. I knew I shouldn't have taken the time for lunch.

"Do you know how I can get hold of him?" I ask.

His face takes on a suspicious aspect. "Why?" he asks.

If I tell him the truth, he's going to be less than helpful because he's going to call his brother and say there's a detective looking for him. It might spook him. I say the first thing that comes into my mind. "I work for his lawyer and I have some papers he needs to sign urgently." I wonder where that lie popped up from?

"He's flying out to Hong Kong this evening but he went home to pack. If you go over there you can probably catch him before he leaves for the airport."

"That's great, he said he wanted to sign them before he left," The lies trip off my tongue. "I got this address from our office files, I thought he still lived here. Can you give me his proper address, please?"

"Sure, come in for a second." He opens the door wide and I walk into a very grand entranceway with curved stairs leading up to the next floor. He walks over to an antique-looking table bearing a white orchid. He slides open a drawer and takes out a pad of paper and a pen. As he writes the address, I look around. Everything is expensive. The Lim family is worth a few bucks for sure.

The kid hands me the address. "I'll text him and tell him you're on your way," he says.

Not a good idea. "Don't bother, I'll call him from the car and find out if he wants me to go to his home or meet him at the airport."

He nods. "OK." He seems like a nice young man. I just hope he doesn't try to be helpful by calling his brother and blowing my cover story out of the water. He holds the door open for me and I head for my car.

After thirty minutes of maneuvering the Healey in and out of the early afternoon rush-hour traffic, I arrive at Harvey Lim's house in Richmond. Although somewhat smaller, it's every bit as impressive as his parents' house. Best of all, there is a grey Huracán in the driveway so he's almost certainly at home; if he'd already left for the airport, he would have parked it in the three-car garage... unless it's already full of even more expensive cars.

When he opens the door, I recognize him from the pictures on Zelena's Instagram, but simultaneously, I can see a strong family resemblance to the young man who so kindly gave me this address. He has a pleasant, open face and a nice smile but there is the hint of 'bad boy' in his features. I can see why Zelena would have been attracted to him.

"Can I help you?" he asks.

"I hope so. I'm Cal Rogan. I'm a private investigator and I've been hired by the Gutkowskis to find their daughter, Zelena. Could I come in and talk to you?"

A look of what I can only describe as relief washes over his face. "Yes, yes, come in." He holds the door open. There is a suitcase in the entranceway. "I'm getting the late flight out tonight. I'm going to try and find Zel and get her back." Still talking, he leads me into the living room. "I didn't know what had happened to her and I was starting to fear the worst but when I saw her Instagram post, I knew I had to go over to Hong Kong and get her back." There is the desperation of a jilted lover in his voice.

He indicates for me to sit.

"I'm going to go over to Hong Kong soon too," I say.

"Great. Maybe we could work together on finding her," he almost pleads. "You have the detective skills and I speak the language."

"That might work," I say, feigning enthusiasm. "But I need to know some things first." I take out my notebook. "Would you mind answering a few questions?"

"Ask me anything."

I start with an easy question. "How did you and Zelena meet?"

"At the Roxy on Granville." He smiles at the memory.

"I know you didn't meet her parents but did she meet yours?"

"No." He smiles sadly. "My parents are old-fashioned. They wouldn't approve of me dating a girl who wasn't Chinese."

I can't help thinking of Romeo and Juliet. Harvey and Zelena were *a pair of star-cross'd lovers* but they had a less drastic ending. So far anyway.

"Is that why you decided to go to Hong Kong? To get away from your respective parents."

"Mainly to get away from Zel's parents. Even though she was nineteen they still had a curfew for her. They said while she was in their house she had to follow their rules. I offered for her to move in here but she said she just wasn't ready for that, which I totally get. So we thought a trip to Hong Kong would work out well. I have business interests there. I had to pay for Steph to go too, just so Zel's parents wouldn't freak."

"What about Chad?"

He makes a grimace. "Yes, Chad," he says. "Zel's idea. She thought he would keep Steph occupied while she and I were together." As he says the last word he almost blushes.

"Steph told me about the Golden Dragon. She said Zel had been flirting with your friend Leo. Could he have been involved in her disappearing for a while?"

"Leo? No way. He's a good friend of mine. He wouldn't do that to me."

"How about the guy in her last Instagram post. Did you recognize him?"

"It's funny," he says. "We had lunch at the restaurant beside the Kerry hotel and there was a guy at the next table who couldn't take his eyes off her. After lunch, we walked down to the ferry over to Hong Kong Island and he was on the ferry too. We joked that he was following us. Now I think about it, he might have been the guy in the post."

"Did you see him again during your trip?"

"I don't think so... Maybe... I don't know."

"Anyone else make you feel suspicious?"

"Not really. I mean I was used to people looking at Zel, she's so beautiful, but no one suspicious."

"Did you ever meet Aleksander, Zelena's brother?"

"No, never."

"One thing I don't understand," I say, "is that she didn't make a post on Instagram from the time she disappeared until about ten hours ago. That wasn't like her. She would normally post at least five times a day."

"You're right," he says. "I never thought of that."

"Also, in that post she didn't look as happy as she normally did in her posts."

"I noticed that. It's one of the reasons I'm going over there to find her. I'm sure she's not happy with this new guy and I really love her." I can't help feeling sorry for him and I know it's no use telling him that, even if we find her, Zelena is likely to walk all over him.

I stand up. "I'm planning to fly out soon too. Steph gave me your phone number but when I've tried to text and call you, you didn't reply. What's a good number to contact you on?"

"Oh," he says. "That was you. I get so many spam texts and phone calls I ignore them if they don't come from someone in my contacts list."

I hand him my card. "I'll put you in for sure," he says.

Walking away from the house, I review our conversation. The only helpful thing was that the man in the Instagram post may have been stalking them. It triggers another thought. I pull out my phone.

"Hi Cal," she says. There is an undertone of seduction in her voice, which I find disconcerting.

"Hi Steph. Thanks for telling me about Zelena's post."

"Yes. I was so relieved she wasn't, you know... I tried to text her but it didn't go through."

I mentally kick myself. Why didn't I think of texting her?

"Did you recognize the guy in the photo with her?"

She pauses for a moment, perhaps searching her memory.

"No. I'm pretty sure I never saw him before."

I rush through a goodbye and hang up.

I have virtually no clue as to how to track down Zelena except that there is one man in a population of seven million, who appears on her Instagram post, and might have been stalking her.

I get the feeling I'm missing something obvious.

Maybe I'll have better luck finding her brother.

———

"Come and look at this, guys." Adry's voice pulls me away from the report I've just put the finishing touches to. Lucy managed to get me on a flight to Hong Kong tomorrow morning and I'm rushing to clear up some of the other cases we have on the books before I go.

I get up and walk over to her desk and Nick joins us. She is logged into Zelena's Instagram account. There is a new post. It's a selfie. She is smiling broadly and there is a guy sitting beside her but it's not the same one as in her previous post. It's daytime and in the background I can see what looks like a poster, with pictures of food on it with prices beside each dish. They are maybe at a street vendor or on a restaurant patio.

"It's a different man," Nick grunts. "She moved on pretty fast."

"Maybe she's just flirting with this one," I say. "Her friend Steph says that's her style." The thought of Steph brings back the feeling I'm missing something.

"Anyway," he says, "the old man said to forget her and concentrate on finding his son. That's what we should be doing. She looks like she's back to normal."

"You're right," I say.

"You guys. You are such... *men*," Adry sighs.

"What?" Nick says.

"Look at the two posts," she says like something should be obvious to us.

"They're just pictures of her with a couple of different guys, one at night and one in the daytime." There is frustration in Nick's voice.

She looks at us like we're idiots.

"What?!" we say in unison.

She scrolls down to the posts prior to Zelena's going missing.

"Look," she says. "Every day she's in a different outfit, sometimes she appears in two or even three different outfits in the same day. Now look at the new posts." She scrolls back up. "She's in the same dress. I'll bet you a hundred bucks something's wrong. There is no *way* she would wear the same dress two days running."

In the silence, Lucy's voice wafts in from the reception area. "Watch out, male brains at work," she says.

And then it comes to me. It's what's been bothering me. "You know, you're right. If everything was OK with her, she would have been texting with her best friend, but Steph didn't have any communication from her, even though she tried to text her." I think it over for a second. "More to the point, Steph didn't seem to be that worried about not hearing from Zelena."

I grab my phone and dial Steph's number; it goes to voicemail. "It's Cal Rogan. Please call me as soon as you get this."

I check my watch. "I'd better go. I haven't even told Tina I'm flying out tomorrow. Adry, can you see if you can get hold of Steph White? Maybe meet with her and see if you can get a read on her." I give her Steph's number. "I'll see you guys when I get back."

"Yeah, good luck Cal," Nick says. Softie! He never calls me Cal.

"Bon voyage." Adry gets up and gives me a kiss on the cheek.

I go to the reception area and give Lucy some last minute instructions to check the client reports I've written before sending them out.

As I turn to go, I almost walk into the front door, which has just been opened by Connor McCoy, our client who's being blackmailed.

"Hi," he says. "You guys were right. I just got another blackmail demand. A hundred grand this time. I have to get the money together and be ready to hand it over tomorrow afternoon."

"That's not good. Again, I'm really sorry we couldn't catch the guy yesterday."

"We have to try again. If I can't stop this I don't know what I'll do."

"Have you thought again about going to the police?" I ask.

"No. I just can't risk it coming out that I did all that drug smuggling for them. You guys are my only option."

"Unfortunately, I have to go out of town tomorrow

morning but Nick will work it all out for you." He looks disappointed but that can't be helped.

I say my goodbyes and leave.

———

MY PHONE BURBLES THE FACETIME RINGTONE. THAT CAN ONLY be one person. Ellie. I reach over and press the green button on my phone, which is sitting on the passenger seat, in blatant violation of BC's driving bylaws.

"Hi sweetie!"

"Hi Daddy, you'll never guess wha— Where are you?"

"I'm in the car. You're looking at the underside of the soft-top."

"Oh, OK. Anyway, guess what!"

"What?"

"We're moving back to Vancouver."

I feel a wave of elation roll over me. "You are? When?"

"On July first. I marked it on the calendar, it's only forty-two sleeps."

I can't believe it. "That is so great. What made Mommy decide?"

"That's not the best part," she says, laughing.

"What could possibly be better than that?" I chuckle.

"Not this Friday, but next Friday we're coming out for a visit to find an apartment and get me registered back in St. Cecilia's and stuff like that. I am sooooooo excited."

"Wow! That's fantastic. I'll meet you at the airport." It hits me that I may not be back from Hong Kong by next Friday. I decide not to bring that up right now.

She prattles on about all the things we'll be able to do when she moves back and I just sit in the glow of knowing my life has really turned around. Four and a half years ago I was a drug-addicted ex-cop living on the streets. For the last year or so, Ellie was the one thing missing from my life. Now I have a real chance of a wonderful life.

It seems too good to be true.

———

SHE SEES THE FLOWERS IN MY HAND. "OK, CALIFORNIA Rogan," she says putting on a strong Indian accent, which makes her sound like her mom, "what have you done wrong."

"Nothing, but I have good news and bad news. Which do you—"

"The good news. I'm an optimist."

"Ellie is moving back to Vancouver."

She runs and hugs me. "That is wonderful." The hug lasts a long time. Then, "What's the bad news?"

"I have to fly to Hong Kong tomorrow."

She keeps hugging but looks up at me. "Why?"

"That missing girl and her brother. I need to try and track them down."

"Huh," she says, giving me a quizzical look. "Hong Kong?"

"Yes."

She thinks for a moment... then smiles... then gives me a sweet, lingering kiss.

"What flight are you on? I think I'll come with you."

My second shot of elation for the day hits me. "What about the Hound?" I ask. The 'Hound' is the Daily News Hound dot com, the online news website she works for.

"I was talking to my editor yesterday. Now that Beijing is taking a hard line there, the protesters are going underground; he was asking me if I knew any reliable reporters there. I don't, but I think I should go over there myself and do a story on where the protesters are hiding out and what they're planning."

"That's fantastic. Let's celebrate. I think I should open that bottle of champagne we have left over from New Year's Eve."

She smiles and does a Groucho Marx with her eyebrows. "I can think of another way to celebrate too," she says.

That bottle of champagne may never get opened.

———

SHE RUBS HER LIGHT-CARAMEL FINGERS THROUGH THE HAIR ON my chest. "Now *that's* how to celebrate," she purrs. She gets no argument from me. I pull her closer to me and run my hand gently down her side. She laughs. "Oh, no, no, Mr. Sexy. I have to get up, text my editor and book my flight. You can go into the kitchen and start getting us something to eat."

She slips out of bed and into a robe and heads for her second bedroom, which doubles as an office. I get dressed and go into the kitchen. As I open the fridge, my phone rings. I pull it from my pocket. "Hi Sam." I wonder why my ex is calling so late. It's eleven in Toronto.

"Hi Cal. I hope I'm not interrupting anything."

"No, not at all." It's a good job she didn't call fifteen minutes earlier. "What's up."

"I didn't want to tell Ellie this, I don't want to worry her, but the reason we are moving back to Vancouver is that my MS has taken a turn for the worse and my parents suggested it would be better if I were closer to them, in case things start going downhill."

"I am so sorry to hear that Sam. Is there anything I can do to help?"

"If you could just be there for Ellie, that would be great."

"Of course, no prob. I have to go to Hong Kong on business but I should be back by a week from Friday. I'll pick you guys up from the airport."

"That would be nice, but if you're not back, my parents can pick us up."

"It will be so nice to see Ellie on a regular basis."

"Yes it will."

She is silent for a moment.

"I was wondering..."

A longer silence.

"...if maybe we could think about... well... getting back together."

It is something I have yearned after for so many years, except now I have Tina.

I stumble over the words, "Oh... I... I guess I'd need to think about it Sam."

"Of course. I don't want to rush you. Maybe we can talk when we're in town. Maybe have dinner together."

"Yes, sure."

More silence.

"I'll let you go now," she says breezily. *"See you at the end of next week."*

"Sure. OK. 'Bye," I say and hang up.

I stand stunned and silent.

"I got the same flight as—" Tina's voice goes from excited to concerned. "What's the matter? Are you OK?"

"Yes, I guess. That was Sam. The reason she and Ellie are coming back to Vancouver is that her MS has got much worse."

She envelopes me in a big hug. "Oh Cal, I am so sorry to hear that."

Normally Shakespeare would come to my aid but instead I think of Jonathan Larson.

> How do you leave the past behind when it
> keeps finding ways to get to your heart?
> It reaches way down deep and tears you up
> till you're torn apart.

I feel a building turmoil.

8. ZELENA

Wednesday

Last night was terrible. The last winner was horrible and he smelled bad. He was very rough with me. He didn't break the rules but he still hurt me. He was quick but that seemed to make him angrier. It was very difficult to pretend I was enjoying it but I managed it because I had to.

The more I pretend to like it, the happier the customers are. The happier the customers are the better room I get to sleep in. I didn't have to sleep in the cold room last night.

Maybe tonight it will be better. Maybe I'll get some gentler winners.

He takes me into the star room and ties my wrist to the restraining strap. Why they bother with that I don't know. We couldn't run away even if we tried. The blond girls are here again but the redhead is still missing. She hasn't been back since she was won by the huge fat man with the scar.

He moves to the front of the stage and says the opening words, whatever they mean. The lights come on over my head and I smile and pose as they taught me. It makes me feel cheap but I have to do it. It's the only way to keep Aleksander alive.

The men start to shout what I assume are numbers.

The bidding has begun.

9. NICK

Rogan will be getting onto the plane about now. Already the office doesn't seem the same without him. I'm mainly worried about how we're going to handle the handover of the money to the blackmailers. I really tried to get Connor to bring the VPD into it but he insisted we didn't do that. We have to catch the blackmailer this time and that's gonna be a bit more difficult without Rogan being on the scene. Adry has been in touch with Rogan's homeless squad but I don't hold out much hope they can make a difference.

"This guy looks like a good candidate," Adry says. She drops a file on my desk. In addition to her caseload, she's trying to find a new investigator for the firm. I flip open the folder and scan the paperwork.

"What kind of name is Zeke Stone?" I say.

"What kind of name is Nick Stammo?" she throws back at me.

Point taken. I look at the information in the file more carefully. A former member of the Victoria Police Department, he made detective Sergeant and then got injured in the line of duty and retired early on a disability pension. Sounds like me—except for the detective Sergeant bit. There is a picture Adry got off his Facebook page. He looks too young to have been a Sergeant but then again everyone puts their best picture as their profile photo. "Looks good," I say. "Before you bring him in for an interview, let me check him out with a guy I know in the VicPD."

I hear Lucy's voice. She's greeting someone. Maybe a new client; we get quite a few walk-ins—go figure. But it's not. It's Connor McCoy. Lucy brings him into the main area. I can see his worry from across the room. He comes over, puts a briefcase on my desk and sits down.

"I got the call. They asked if I had the money. I said yes and they said be ready to hand it over this afternoon at four-thirty. They said they would phone at four and tell me where and how, *and* they said not to put a tracking device in this time. They said if we did, they'd come back for more money."

"I take it the money's in the briefcase," I say.

He nods. "I just got it from my bank. They're the Royal Bank right next door so I thought I'd bring it straight here for safekeeping."

"Listen, it's not too late to call in the VPD," I say. "I really don't think they're going to care about what you did all those years ago. They could make sure we caught this guy and put him behind bars."

He thinks it over for a bit. "Not this time. I can't take the risk that it would all come out and affect my business. But listen, if they come back for more money, we can get the police involved, OK?"

I shrug. "It's your money."

He stands. "Anyway, I have to get back to the office. I'll be back here before four and wait for the call."

When he's left, Adry looks over at me. "There's a hundred grand in that briefcase?"

I nod.

She gives a half smile. "I don't even know what a hundred grand looks like."

"You'll have to use your imagination," I say. "That's client property. We can't go fiddling about with it. It stays right there until he gets back."

She looks disappointed.

I go through my contacts and find my guy in the VicPD. Let's see if this Zeke Stone guy is as good as he looks on paper.

———

FEAR. I CAN HEAR IT IN HER VOICE. "DAD, YOU'VE GOTTA COME here."

Adry hears it too and moves fast towards the reception area. I wheel there just in time to see him coming through the glass doors, assault rifle at port.

"Get down! On the floor! Now!" He demands.

Adry is down first followed by Lucy.

But I'm just as angry as hell.

"What the fuck!" I yell at him. "I can't get on the floor, I'm in a fuckin' wheelchair. I'm a former VPD—"

"Hands on your head!" He points the rifle straight at me and I do as he says.

"What's going o—"

"QUIET!"

Three other officers have followed him in. One pushes past me. The second comes at me and quickly frisks me and checks my chair for weapons, and the third, a woman, pats down Lucy and Adry. "Clear," they say simultaneously. "Clear," comes from the first guy behind me.

Everything slows back down.

Two plain-clothes officers walk in. One looks vaguely familiar. The more senior one looks at me. "Name?"

"Nick Stammo. What's going on here? I'm a former VPD member."

He ignores me and walks past me into the office while his partner comes over and cuffs my hands behind the back of my chair. I hear the snap of cuffs as the female officer cuffs Lucy and Adry. Now I'm really angry, no one does that to my girls.

I look over my shoulder at the senior officer. "I said, what's going on here," I growl.

He and the one with the assault rifle are standing by my desk. "Is this your briefcase?" he asks.

"No, it belongs to a client."

He puts on a pair of nitrile gloves and opens the briefcase. He reaches in and takes something out. But it's not money. It's a large ziplock bag. It's full of smaller bags of what look like a white powder. Oh Jeez. He opens the big bag, removes a smaller bag and opens it. He sniffs the contents.

He nods to his colleague and returns the bag to the briefcase.

"Where's your partner, Cal Rogan?"

"Out of town on business."

"Where out of town?"

"None of your goddamn business. Listen to me. We've been scammed here. That briefcase belongs to a client. A guy called Connor McCoy. He's a big wheel in some high-tech company."

"You can explain it all later." He walks over to me. "For

now, Nicholas Theodore Stammo, I am arresting you on suspicion of dealing in a controlled substance. You have the right..."

As he says the words, which I've probably said more often than him, I grind my teeth and wonder why would the CEO of a software company want to frame me and Rogan.

Then a horrible thought hits.

10. CAL

Thursday

It feels weird. We got on the plane at midday on Wednesday and here we are fourteen hours later and it's Thursday evening in Hong Kong. It was nice travelling with Tina. Fourteen hours with nothing to do but chat, eat and drink. It's economy on Air Canada, not the Cathay Pacific first class, which Harvey Lim probably took, but I guarantee he didn't have a better time than we did. Tina's been here before and knows a lot about the city. With a bit of luck we'll get some time to enjoy it together. Starting this evening.

I pull out my phone. "I'd better check in with the office." I go to take it off airplane mode when she reaches across and stops me.

"It's three in the morning back home. Let's just enjoy the evening, have dinner and get back into the real world tomorrow."

How can I resist. I put the phone away and lean back in the seat of the cab and enjoy my first sights of Hong Kong.

11. ADRY

The alarm snaps me awake. It's still dark. What the — Then it all comes flooding in: the arrest, the paddy wagon ride to the police station, the body search by the callous female cop, the interrogation by the police, letting Lucy and me go but saying that Nick was being held in custody. I feel myself flush at the embarrassment of it all.

I grab my phone. Five AM, Cal should be there now. But there's no text message from him. I'll go old-school and phone him. I get the 'phone not connected' message. Maybe his plane was delayed. It's early but I'd better check with Nick, maybe, just maybe, his lawyer Jim Garry got him released from custody last night. I press the number but it goes to voicemail.

My third call gets through. "Luce," I say. "Sorry to call so early, have you heard anything?"

"No prob, I was awake. I phoned the Cambie station lots of times during the night but they wouldn't say anything about Dad. They wouldn't even tell me if he was there or not. I'm going to wait until seven o'clock and call his lawyer."

"That's great. Why don't you go in and open up the office at the normal time. I'm going to go see Connor McCoy at his office and find out what the hell he thinks he's doing planting a suitcase full of drugs on us."

We agree and hang up.

I try Cal again but he's still not online.

I'm going to have to do this alone.

———

THE YOUNG GUY AT THE RECEPTION DESK AT DARK ENERGY Systems Inc. is tall and thin and wears Harry Potter glasses. He gives me a snotty look. "Do you have an appointment with Mr. McCoy?" he asks. I haven't had a lot of experience dealing with corporations. My last job was office manager at that sleazy film company. I guess I'll have to wing it.

"No I don't but it's very urgent that I see him."

"As you might imagine," he says, "Mr. McCoy is extremely busy. Now if you would like to phone in and make an appointment, I'm sure he could fit you in at some point."

He is patronizing in the extreme. I need to take another approach.

"Have you heard of the Me Too movement?" I say and from his eyes I can tell he has and I'm betting that *now* he wants to hear what I have to say. "You can tell Mr. McCoy my firm has been asked to look into certain, shall we say, inappropriate behaviour at this company and if he wants to get ahead of it, he had better speak to me right now."

He leans forward. "What sort of inappropriate behaviour?"

I also lean forward and drop my voice. "I'll tell you if you promise to keep it a secret." He nods expectantly. "But I have to speak to Mr. McCoy first."

He nods and picks up his phone. "Hi Pat, it's Mark at reception. Would you tell Connor there's a lady here who I think he should talk to." He pauses while McCoy's secretary speaks. "I think it would be better if Connor speaks to her directly about that." Another pause, then he looks at my card. "It's a Ms. Adriana Locke. She's a private investigator." After a third pause he hangs up. "Sooooo," he says, "what's this all about? Have Connor and Pat been...?" He leaves the question hanging.

"I think I'd better talk to him first," I say turning away.

In less than sixty seconds a man walks into reception but, to my annoyance, it's not Connor McCoy. He's dressed in jeans, a tee shirt and expensive shoes, but dress doesn't say anything about his status in a software company. He shakes my hand. "How can I help you Ms. Locke?" he says. He seems like a really nice guy and cute too.

Trying to push down my irritation at being fobbed off like this, I say, "It's a bit of a delicate issue. I would really rather speak to Mr. McCoy personally."

"I'm Connor McCoy," he says.

But he's not the Connor McCoy who came into our office three days ago.

Oh crap! We have *really* been conned.

———

LUCY LOOKS AGITATED TO PUT IT MILDLY. "HI LUCE," I SAY IN my calmest voice. "Have they released your dad yet?"

"No. I spoke to Mr. Garry, his lawyer, and he's trying to get him released on bail this morning. He says the chances are good, with Dad being in a wheelchair and all. But we have a bigger problem now." We've been conned by an expert, one partner's in jail and the other's ten thousand kilometres away. What could be a bigger problem than that? "Look at this." She hands me a paper copy of the Vancouver Sun. The page one headline reads, HIGH PROFILE PIS BUSTED FOR DRUGS. There is even a picture of Nick being pushed out of our office with his hands cuffed behind his wheelchair.

"Ho-ly crap." She's right, we do have a bigger problem.

"It gets worse," she says. "Look."

She swivels her computer screen towards me. It's the CBC website. In addition to the article about the arrest, there's video, taken from outside our building, of us all being lead, handcuffed, into the waiting paddy wagon. My parents are news junkies and they love the CBC. I have to call them before they see this. Jason too. I don't want him to think his girlfriend's a jailbird.

I am not going to take this lying down. "Whoever it was calling himself Connor McCoy, I'm going to hunt him down and make him very, very sorry he messed with us."

"But how?" she asks.

Good question.

Cal will know.

Except when I try to get him, his phone's still off.

———

IT'S GONE FROM WORSE TO MORE WORSE. I'VE SPENT A GOOD part of the day trying to placate clients who have phoned in, worried about their cases. Despite assuring them that we are the victims of a con job, four have cancelled their contracts with us and two have asked for repayment of their retainers. Nick is going to freak when he finds out. And on top of that—

My phone rings.

Thank God. "Cal, why didn't you call before?"

"Sorry. When we got into Hong Kong it was in the middle of the night in Vancouver. It's six AM here now. I just remembered to turn off airplane mode and saw your texts. What's up?"

I give him the details of how we were conned and the client cancellations.

"Nick's in jail?" he says. *"This is bad. I'll get the next flight back."*

"Are you sure, Cal? By the time you get back, I'm sure he'll be—"

"Dad's back!" Lucy shouts.

"Hang on Cal. Nick's back." I put him on speaker phone and go to the reception area. Lucy's holding the door open so Stewart, Nick's guy, can push his wheelchair through the doorway.

Lucy gives Nick a big hug. "Are you OK?" she asks.

"Of course I'm OK. Twenty-four hours in jail isn't gonna faze a Stammo. Jim Garry got me out on bail and Stewart came and picked me up."

"That was the hardest part," Stewart says. "trying to drive Nick's truck to the courthouse. I don't know how he manages to use those hand controls." He pats Nick on the shoulder. "Anyway, I've got to get off to the hospital. See you later." He squeezes Nick's shoulder. I sense he would like to give him a kiss but knowing Nick, I doubt he's ready for such a public show of affection just yet. He's only been out for a short time.

When Stewart has left, we all go into the main office and stand around my phone.

"Are you OK, Nick?" Cal asks.

"Why does everyone keep asking that?" Nick says.

"I should come back."

"No way, Rogan. Adry and I can handle this."

I tell them about my meeting with the real Connor McCoy.

"*So we don't even know the identity of the person who scammed us.*"

"The not-real McCoy was just a front," Nick says. "I'm guessing it's all being managed by someone with a big grudge against one or both of us."

"*That could be a long list. Each of us put a bunch of bad guys in jail when we were with the VPD. It could be any one of them.*"

"We've gotta start with finding Connor or whatever his name is. The question is: how?"

"*Have we got anything with his prints on it?*"

"No, the drug squad took the briefcase. Besides, no one in VPD is going to run the prints for us. It would weaken their case against us."

"*Did you talk to Steve, I'm sure he'd help us out.*"

"On the way back from the jail, I tried to call him and tell him we were conned. I couldn't get through to him. I've got a feeling he's not going to call me back." That bites. When a former colleague and friend decides to cut you off, it hurts. If we don't sort this mess out, nobody in the VPD will have anything to do with us.

I think back to our first meeting with the phony Connor. "Wait a minute," I say. I get up and go back to the reception area. "Luce, you remember on Monday I gave you an envelope with the retainer cheque from Connor McCoy?"

"Yes," she says. "I deposited the cheque on Tuesday morning."

"Do you still have the envelope? His fingerprints will still be on it."

"No, I remember dropping it in the recycle bin. But I could call the bank and try and get the details of the bank account it was drawn on."

I nod and give her the thumbs up. "Did you hear that Cal," I say as I walk back into the office.

"Yes. I was just thinking that someone has gone to a lot of trouble and expense to screw us. The retainer was twelve grand and, from what you said, there must have been over a hundred grand's worth of heroin or cocaine or whatever it was."

"Maybe it was a drug gang. That would be small change for them," Nick says. "Oh," he adds. "What if it was your ex-wife's ex-boyfriend. He may be locked up in Millhaven, but he's still got contacts on the streets."

"No point in speculating. We've got to find a way to track down the Connor character."

"It won't be through the cheque he gave us," Lucy calls from the reception desk. "I just phoned our bank. They were going to call us. The cheque he gave us bounced."

"Crap," says Nick, summing up the general view. "We're never going to find him."

We all sit in silence.

Then I think over the words Cal just said and it gives me an idea. It's a long shot but I'll give it a try.

12. CAL

My words have garnered their full attention. All three are wearing nicely tailored grey suits but their smiles have been replaced by worried expressions. I lay out the pictures on the Kerry hotel's concierge desk; Adry printed them off from the photos in Zelena's Instagram feed before I left. "Do you recognize any of them?"

"Yes, him." The younger woman says. She is pointing at a picture of Chad with his green mohawk and tats. Yes, he'd be very noticeable in the lobby of any five-star hotel. She looks at her more senior colleague beside her, who gives a slight nod. "He was not as polite as our usual guests," she says in only slightly-accented English. "He asked me to go on a date with him."

I point to a picture of Zelena. "Do you remember her?" I ask. The lone male concierge nods. "Yes. She and her friend," he points to a picture of her with Steph. "They came often to the concierge desk. They would ask for advice about their plans. They were very friendly and polite."

"And we know Mr. Lim of course." The older woman points to Harvey's picture. "He's a regular guest here."

A fourth young man joins us. Just how many concierges does this hotel have? His male colleague introduces me. "This is Mr. Rogan, he is a detective from Canada. He is looking for this lady who is missing," he says, pointing at Zelena's picture.

"Yes, I know," the new arrival says. "Last week, Thursday I think, a young man was here. He said she was missing and that he was looking for her." I pull Aleksander's picture from beneath the others. "Yes, that's him. He was here with another man. Chinese man." That would be the private detective Aleksander hired, Mr. Wang.

"Were you able to give them any useful information?"

"Not really," he says. "I wasn't on duty the day the lady went missing."

I check my notes from my meeting with Steph. "That was Friday, two weeks ago today."

"I was on duty," the younger woman says. She looks up for a moment, thinking. "I think that was the day before the young ladies were going to see the statue of the Buddha. They were planning their trip and asking about where to get the cable car."

"Yes, that's right. She went missing the night before."

"I went off duty at six o'clock," she says. "Sorry."

The older woman says, "Just a minute let me check something." She taps away at her keyboard. "That was Friday, May eighth... Yes. Mr. Zhao was on concierge duty in the evening. He will be on duty again this evening after six."

I ask them if they remember anything else unusual—especially if they saw either Zelena or Steph with anyone different or suspicious—but they don't, which is pretty much what I was expecting. It was a long shot. I thank them profusely and hope my next appointment will be half as friendly and cooperative.

However, I don't hold out much hope of that.

———

THE MONGKOK POLICE STATION IS JUST OFF NATHAN ROAD and it is just like any police station in Vancouver or anywhere else for that matter. Inspector Ho holds open the door of the interview room for me and we sit at the metal table bolted to the floor.

"How can I help you Mr. Rogan?" he asks. His English is excellent and he has a British accent. He's short and is carrying a few extra pounds around his middle. And he's older than I expected.

"First, thank you for seeing me, Inspector."

"My pleasure," he says. "I used to live in Toronto, so I love to meet Canadians."

I haven't done business in Hong Kong before, so I don't know the protocols. Maybe 'getting to know you' is first on the agenda. "My ex-wife lives in Toronto, it's a great city."

"It is," he says, nodding but not showing any level of warmth.

There is a moment of silence, which I fill with, "You have a British accent, did you live there too?"

"I did, I studied English Literature at Cambridge."

"No way. I have a Masters in English Lit. but it's not from Cambridge. Just UBC, I'm afraid." It reminds me of the job-offer email from SFU.

He gives a sigh. "And here we both are, humble detectives." He sits more upright. "But you didn't come here to discuss literature, I expect."

The rapport-building phase is over. "As I told you on the phone, I've been hired by her parents to find Zelena Gutkowska."

"Yes, as you said. Unfortunately, we have been unable to find her and, to be frank, our inquiries indicated that she was, how can I put this politely, a... party girl."

I feel a little jab of annoyance. Just because she liked to flirt with men shouldn't mean she doesn't have the protection of the law. "Maybe she was, but she's still missing."

"So no one has had any communication from her?" he asks.

"She has posted a couple of pictures on Instagram but we have reason to believe they may have been coerced."

"Why do you say that?"

I tell him about Adry's observation of Zelena wearing the same dress on consecutive days, but saying it out loud makes me doubt its importance. Ho clearly feels the same way. "Hardly conclusive," is all he says.

"I was wondering if you could give me copies of your files, so that I don't have to go over ground you've already covered."

He sighs. I don't think he relishes the work needed to do the copying. "You read Chinese then?" he asks.

"No, I don't, but I'm working with someone who does."

He gives me a long look. "Who would that be?" he asks.

"Mr. Gutkowski has also hired a local detective with whom I'll be working." Not entirely true. I haven't yet contacted Mr. Wang of Jiang and Lee Investigations Company Limited. For some reason, a little voice in my head tells me to just drop in on him. His office is five minutes from here.

"Who's that?" he asks again.

The same little voice tells me to withhold the information but I resist lying to the police; it's never a good policy. "Mr. Wang," I say.

"Never heard of him." His British accent is starting to grate on me. "You should be careful who you deal with. There are some shady unlicensed operatives who you don't want to get mixed up with."

I force a friendly smile. "So, could I have copies of your files?"

"I'm afraid that's against our policy," he says. "I shouldn't really be talking to you about an ongoing investigation anyway."

"Can you at least tell me what lines of inquiry you have opened up?"

"I'm afraid not," he says.

I know what's going on here. He wants to cover up how little he's done to try and find Zelena.

"So," I say innocently, "your investigation is still ongoing."

"It's ongoing until I decide to close the file," he says.

I was right. He is orders of magnitude less cooperative than the people at the Kerry.

"Her brother came to see you," I say.

"Yes. A nice young man."

"Did you know that *he's* now missing?"

There is a flicker of surprise in his eyes. "No," he says. "For how long?"

"Almost a week."

He thinks it over for a couple of seconds.

"Do you want to file a formal report of a missing person?"

A big part of me wants to say no but I can't leave any

option untried. He may be a washed-up, lazy cop but just maybe he'll unearth something.

"Yes, I do."

He sighs again. "OK, I'll get the paperwork." He waddles out of the interview room.

Something tells me this is going to be a long use of my time for little or no result.

———

I GET OUT OF ONE OF THE RED TAXIS WHICH ARE EVERYWHERE in the Kowloon district of Hong Kong; there seem to be more of them than there are private cars. The road is one-way, narrow and teeming with people. Except for a few people who are obviously tourists, everyone seems in a hurry.

My destination is an arched doorway between a restaurant, packed with lunchtime customers, and an empty jewellery store, the name of which would make Ellie giggle. Restaurants and jewellery stores are also ubiquitous here. I pull open the glass door and walk down a narrow hallway. Beside the elevator is a directory in both Chinese and English. One of the legacies of a century and a half of British rule is bilingual signage. The Jiang and Lee Investigations Company Limited is on the third floor. After a long wait, the ancient elevator arrives and takes me slowly upward.

I step out into a dim corridor, lined with wooden doors, each door with a frosted-glass panel bearing the name of a company. It makes me feel I've gone fifty years back in time. The last doorway on my left is covered with the names of seven companies, the last of which is Jiang and Lee. I turn the handle. It's locked. This does not bode well. I tap my knuckles on the glass panel.

Out of a movie, long-forgotten, an image springs into my consciousness of an octogenarian, wearing a green velvet jacket and a fez, opening a squeaky door and peering out. But the man who actually opens the door is the polar opposite. He is about my age, dressed in business casual and he looks energetic. He reminds me of the former US Democratic hopeful, Andrew Yang. He gives me a broad smile. "How can I help you?" he asks in slightly-accented English.

"Hi. I'm looking for Mr. Wang."

"I'm sorry there's no one of that name here," he says. The second thing not to bode well.

"He's a private investigator with Jiang and Lee."

"I think you've been misinformed. I'm Philip Jiang and I can assure you we don't have a Mr. Wang here."

That's why Inspector Ho didn't recognize the name as a private investigator.

"My name's Cal Rogan, I'm a private investigator in Vancouver. I have a client named Janusz Gutkowski," I say. "His son Aleksander said he hired a Mr. Wang at your firm."

He throws me a puzzled look for a moment, then steps back and opens the door wide.

"You'd better come in," he says.

The office is the antithesis of the building. It is bright, clean and modern, with vivid, framed prints on the walls. There are two desks both with dual-screen Apple computers. There is a single two-drawer filing cabinet and there are two bookshelves, bursting to the point of overflow, with books of all types. In one corner of the office is an area with what look like Ikea leather chairs and a couch. It is to this area he gestures. "Please have a seat Mr. Rogan."

"Call me Cal," I say.

He smiles and extends his hand. "I'm Phil." His shake is firm and warm. "I think your client must have just got my name wrong, Jiang... Wang..." He smiles.

"I guess he must have."

"I haven't heard from Aleksander in over a week," he says. "Do you know how I can get hold of him?"

"No, he went missing a week ago."

"So they're both missing now?" he says.

"Kind of." I pull out my phone and show him Zelena's Instagram feed using the phony Instagram account which Adry created.

He looks at the posts. "So she's not missing but Aleksander is. It's odd."

"Maybe," I say. "One of my colleagues thinks maybe these posts were coerced." He looks puzzled. "Like someone forced her to do the pictures," I add.

"Why would he think that?"

"She," I correct him. "Zelena's wearing the same dress in both pictures. My colleague says Zelena would never wear the same dress two days running."

"Maybe the pictures were taken on the same day but posted to Instagram on consecutive days," he suggests.

It makes sense. This guy's good. "How about we work together on this?" I say.

He thinks for a second or two, then extends his hand. "Deal," he says. We shake.

"Are you hungry?" he asks.

I realize I am. All I had this morning was a coffee and it's already one o'clock.

A few taps on his phone and he says, "I've ordered from the restaurant downstairs. Why don't you tell me what you've learned so far about the case?"

I give him a full debriefing of what I learned in Vancouver. The food arrives just as I get to the end. While we eat, he speaks. "I haven't found out as much as you but the first thing I did, after Aleksander hired me, was go to the hotel. I know the security manager at the Kerry and he told me Zelena and her friend Steph had their boyfriends stay over and that it was one of the boyfriends, Harvey Lim, who paid for the rooms. He also let me look at the security videos from the time she and her friend got back to the hotel until the next morning when her friend found out Zelena was missing. Just before midnight, she appeared in the lobby and then took a cab."

"Was she alone?" I ask.

"Yes."

"Did anyone know where she went?"

"She told one of the doormen she wanted a taxi to take her to Hong Kong Island."

"Did he remember where specifically?" I ask.

"No. But I was able to see the taxi's licence plate on the video. I was able to track down the driver who drove the cab that night. I showed him Zelena's photo and he remembered her. He took her to a nightclub in Stanley."

"Was it the Golden Dragon?"

He frowns. "No. The Golden Dragon is near here and it's a very respectable, well-known place. The nightclub he took her to was called IF. It has a reputation. A lot of prostitutes operate from there. I have no idea why Zelena would go there."

"Did you go and check it out?" I ask.

"No. Aleksander hired me on a provisional basis to see what I could discover. When I tried to get hold of him to get his agreement to investigate further, he didn't call me back. I assumed that maybe he had hired someone else."

"Did you speak to his father in Vancouver?"

"No."

I grab my phone. "I'm going to email my partner and have him tell Mr. Gutkowski to contact you and give you a retainer. I'm sure he'll agree."

"Thanks, I appreciate it."

"How did Aleksander find you, by the way?"

He thinks for a moment. "You know, it's odd. I don't think he ever said. Normally I ask new clients who referred them but I don't remember asking Aleksander."

"How do you feel about going to this IF nightclub tonight and see what we can learn?"

"Sounds good. How about we meet for dinner first and we can drive over there together."

"That would be gre— Oh, wait a minute. My girlfriend's over here with me. She's a journalist and she's doing a piece on what the protesters are up to after the crack down by Beijing. I really ought to at least have dinner with her before I ditch her to go to a nightclub."

"Wise man. Why don't I pick you up from the Kerry at about nine-thirty?"

"Sure, but how did you know I was staying at the Kerry?"

He laughs. "A guess. It's where I would stay if I were new in town and the person I was trying to find was last seen there."

He's *good*.

This is going to be a great partnership.

———

THERE ARE NOT QUITE AS MANY STAFF AT THE HILTON'S concierge desk as there are at the Kerry, but they seem equally eager.

"I'm trying to find one of your guests," I say, "a Mr. Aleksander Gutkowski." I spell the last name for them.

"Certainly sir," one of them says as he taps away at the keyboard. A small frown crosses his brow. "Mr. Gutkowski checked in on May thirteenth for five days but he never checked out." He makes a couple more taps on the keyboard. "The front desk held the room for twenty-four hours but then released it."

It fits with what Janusz said; Aleksander stopped communicating after three days.

"Can you tell me what happened to his clothes and luggage?"

Another one of the concierges, a young woman, says, "It's our policy to store the items for the guest. Would you like me to check for you?"

"That would be great. Thanks."

She disappears through a door behind the desk and returns within seconds bearing a big smile. "Yes, we have them here."

"Do you think I could see them?" I ask.

She cuts a glance to her colleague who intervenes, "Are you a family member sir?"

"No," I say, "but I'm a representative of the family. They have asked me to find their son." I take out a business card and offer it to him with both hands and a slight bow. He takes it with a matching gesture and a deeper bow.

"One moment sir," he says. He picks up his phone and talks rapidly in Cantonese. There is a pause and he says a few more words before hanging up. He smiles. "Yes sir," he says, "my superior has authorized you looking at the items, but emphasizes that you may not remove anything."

"Thank you so much."

He says a few words to his female colleague who takes

me through to the back room. She leads me over to a shelving unit and points to two items of luggage, a suitcase and a soft, leather carry-on bag. I take them off the shelves, place them on the floor then squat. I open the suitcase first. It has been meticulously packed with each item carefully folded and wrapped in tissue paper—all part of the Hilton service I suspect. I check through it but it holds only clothes and toiletries. I unzip the carry-on, take out the most obvious item, a computer, flip it open and power it up. While it boots up, I remove one of those neck pillows for use on planes and sort through the remaining items, which are just things you might have on an aircraft: books, a couple of maps, breath mints and bottled water. Nothing of interest. The computer has come to its log in screen and, as expected, it's password protected. Just for dogs, I try Zelena's password 'zelrocksit' then 'aleksrocksit' then I enter Aleksander's name spelled backwards, with and without the capital A. None of them works but it was a very long shot. I power it off and return everything to the carry on. I look up at the concierge who is standing beside me, ostensibly to answer any questions but probably more likely to enforce the mandate that I don't remove anything.

"There's no passport," I say. "Do you keep passports and valuables separately?"

"No sir," she says. She squats beside me and takes the carry-on. She rotates it, unzips a side pocket, peers in and removes a passport, an envelope—which looks like it contains currency—and a notepad, similar to the one I always carry with me.

The envelope isn't sealed. It contains a thick wad of five-hundred Hong Kong dollar notes. I close it and put it back. The passport is Aleksander's. I put it back and open the notepad.

The first page is a to-do list with several items checked off, the last of which reads 'Find private detective.' I flip the page. There are notes about his conversation with the concierge staff at the Kerry. The last item says, 'Talk to night concierge, Mr. Zhao.' He obviously had the same conversation I did. I flip to the next page. It's headed, 'Private detectives.' There are three names with addresses, written in neat block capitals. The first is Phil Jiang. There are four stars outlined beside his name. The second is a Mr. Paul Yip. His name and address are neatly crossed out. The third is a Mr. Henry Wang. There are no stars beside his name but there is a double exclamation mark. It's the name Janusz Gutkowski mentioned. So there is a Mr. Wang. Janusz wasn't confusing it with Jiang. I think back to my conversation with Inspector Ho this morning. He said he had never heard of a PI named Wang. I remember his words. '*You should be careful who you deal with. There are some shady unlicensed operatives who you don't want to get mixed up with.*' I wonder if Aleksander's double exclamation marks indicate he had his doubts about Mr. Wang too. I put my finger beside the address. "Where is this?" I ask my watchdog.

"About a ten-minute walk from here," she says.

I flip the page, it's blank. I riffle through the remaining pages, also blank. Three clicks with my camera records the notebook's details. I return it to the side pocket and replace the carry-on and suitcase on the shelf.

It's four hours until dinner with Tina.

I've got time.

————

THE BUILDING IS OLDER AND SEEDIER THAN THE ONE HOUSING Phil Jiang's office but the corridor has the same fifty-year-old feel to it. The door numbered two-oh-seven has Chinese characters painted on the glass but there is no English translation. It is one of the few things I've seen without bilingual signage. I knock. I see no movement behind the frosted glass and no sounds come from within.

I knock again and, after a decent interval, try the door handle.

It opens.

Unlike Phil's office, it doesn't open into a large room. It's a small, old-fashioned, wood-panelled waiting room with two doors leading off it and three, wooden, waiting-room chairs. It looks like a doctor's office from a bygone era. There is a stillness to the air and a disquieting silence.

"Hello," I say. "Anyone here?"

Nothing.

I tap on the first door and open it.

It's a file room crammed with filing cabinets and shelves stacked with papers, files folders and boxes. It's lit by a bare bulb hanging from the ceiling. On top of one of the filing cabinets is a printer, its green 'on' light glowing.

There is no response to my knock on the second door.

I open it slowly.

I notice the buzzing first.

Then the smell.

Then the sight.

The body is held bolt-upright in its chair by the wire around its neck. Even from where I'm standing, I can see the flies and maggots feasting on the protruding eyes. The hands are flat on the desk, held in place by knives through their backs.

I close the door before the smell makes me gag.

I guess I'll be meeting with Inspector Ho for a second time today.

———

INSPECTOR HO'S INVESTIGATION WAS PERFUNCTORY TO SAY THE least. The dead man was, as I suspected, Henry Wang, the other private detective whom Aleksander Gutkowski engaged. Ho asked me a few questions and let me go. I couldn't get hold of Phil Jiang but I left him a voicemail telling him to watch his back.

My text with Tina said she wouldn't be back here at the hotel until seven so I have about forty-five minutes. I text Harvey Lim and get lucky. He's in the Red Sugar bar on the fourth floor. I take the escalators from the lobby and go into the bar. I have to walk along two corridors, flanked with private rooms and booths, before coming out to the main bar. At the far end it has a spectacular view of the harbour. Harvey is sitting at a table drinking a red cocktail of some sort.

He stands when I arrive at the table and shakes my hand. "Have you found out anything?" he asks.

The waiter arrives as we sit down. This must be the service that staying at a five-star hotel buys you. I order a local beer. "Yes, I have," I say to Harvey. I tell him about my meeting with Phil Jiang and his lead to the IF nightclub but omit any reference to the late Mr. Wang.

"Can I come with you?" he asks.

"I don't think that's a good idea; the place sounds a bit sleazy. Don't worry, I'll keep you informed." He looks a bit crestfallen. "Have you discovered anything?" I ask.

"I haven't had a lot of time. I had some important business meetings to attend but I did talk to my friend Leo. He's one of the owners of the Golden Dragon nightclub, he's there every night. I asked him if Zel had been there but she hasn't. He's a very well-connected guy and he's agreed to send her photo to a bunch of other nightclubs and bars, asking them to let him know if she shows up."

He takes a sip of his cocktail.

"I was looking at the map of Hong Kong. The IF nightclub is in Stanley, which is on Hong Kong Island. You said there was a man who you thought might have followed you and Zelena on the ferry to the island. Did you think any more about whether he might be the man in the Instagram post?"

"It might be but I can't be sure." There is a bleep. He takes out his phone taps on it and gives a big sigh. Without speaking, he turns the phone in my direction. There is a picture of Zelena in what looks like a market. She has a big grin on her face and her arm's around a handsome young man in jeans and an expensive leather jacket. It is a different guy from the ones in the previous two posts. And she's wearing a different dress. The message says, 'Look what I found in the Stanley Market. Helloooo extremely lovely person?'

I look at the pain on his face. "I'm sorry."

"Do you think I should comment?" he asks.

I think about it for a bit.

"Sure, see if she replies."

He does.

We wait.

She doesn't.

"Will you let me know, if you hear anything?" he asks.

I can't help feeling sorry for him. "Absolutely," I say.

He hands me his business card. "Here's my Hong Kong number, call me any time, night or day." I smile encouragingly at him and pretend not to see the tear in his eye, looking instead at his card. In Hong Kong fashion, it is printed on one side in Chinese and on the other in English. The name of his company is vaguely familiar.

I need to track down Zelena. She's the only lead I have to finding her brother but when I do I'm going to give her a piece of my mind.

Doesn't she care about the pain she's putting people through?

13. ZELENA

They took me out again today but this time it was to a different market. He made me pose with some random guy. He gave me my phone so I could post it on Instagram then took it away again. He makes me do the posts because his English isn't very good. I hope someone sees what I did in the post. Maybe it will make them contact the police. Maybe if he gets me to do more posts, I can put in more clues. Someone will get it. Please.

At one point, I could have run away. He was talking to the other guard and they weren't looking at me. I thought about it for a moment but then remembered what they said they would do to Zander if I didn't obey them.

It was nice to be out in the fresh air for an hour but it makes it so much worse to be back here tethered in the star room. The first winner of the day comes to take me off to one of the silk bedrooms. I hope he's gentle. But he won't be. They never are. That's why they come here.

14. CAL

I walk past the concierge desk on my way to the entrance door. At this time in the evening there's only one person on the desk. He must be the one who was on duty the night Zelena went missing. Mr. Zhao, the head concierge called him. I check my watch. Nine thirty-five. Better not stop and talk to him now, Phil Jiang is probably already here waiting patiently.

As I walk through the main door, a grey Lexus LC flashes its lights at me. Nice ride. Jiang must be pretty successful. With Nick running the business, we've been pretty successful too... anyway we were until this scam hit us. I wonder how many other clients have cancelled. It's still early in the morning in Vancouver, I'll call later and get an update.

An attentive doorman holds the passenger door open for me and I climb into Jiang's car. "Hi Phil," I say.

"Mr. Rogan?"

It's not Jiang behind the wheel. It's a short, squat man, with a chubby face showing no hint of a smile. He's as different from the urbane Phil Jiang as I am from Nick. I start to apologize for getting into the wrong car and then realize he knows my name.

"Yes," I say, "I'm Cal Rogan."

"I am Mr. Lee, Mr. Jiang's partner." He doesn't offer to shake hands. "He had appointment. I drive you to club. Meet you there." His voice is heavily accented.

"Thank you."

He drives down the ramp to the street, checks the traffic and accelerates so hard the tires squeal. "About how long is the drive to IF?" I ask.

"Sorry, no English."

I'm not sure if it's a statement of fact or an order, so I keep quiet, trying not to wince as he throws the car into turns and around roundabouts with seemingly no regard for any speed limit. It is all made more frightening by the fact that they drive on the left in Hong Kong and my heart keeps pounding every time I think he might be in the wrong lane.

To my shredding nerves, it seems to go on for ever, but I'm sure it's not been much more than twenty minutes before he pulls the car to a halt.

He points a fat finger at a doorway.

"This is IF?" I ask.

He just nods and jabs his finger again.

I get out of the car and close the door behind me. Mr. Lee peels another layer of rubber from the tires and screeches around the corner. I take a deep breath of air—grateful I still can—and survey the scene. It's not like Kowloon. There are far fewer people on the streets, the buildings look generally poorer and the brass door, which Lee pointed at, looks out of place. There is no signage indicating this is the place I'm looking for; nothing that even hints there's a nightclub here. I cross the sidewalk and grab the door handle. This close, I can see a Chinese character and the word IF pressed into the brass of the door. I pull the door open and step into a darkened lobby area. I am confronted by a man the size of a small house. He is about my height—he's the first person I've encountered here who is—but almost wider than he is tall. As my eyes get accustomed to the lower light level, I see that he's perched on a stool and when he stands... well, make that a large house.

He steps past me and opens a door. "Please step inside sir," he says in perfect, unaccented English. I think of Caliban: *I must obey: his art is of such power.* I have no option, so I step through the door.

The IF nightclub is bright and simultaneously part-garish and part-elegant. There are more men than women and many of the women are draping themselves over their male companions and sipping champagne. Everyone is very well dressed. To my left, there is a restaurant area where couples and groups of men are dining. Ahead of me is an almost-empty dance floor, beyond which is a bar.

From my right I hear a voice. "Cal, over here." I look and see Phil Jiang sitting alone on a couch with a martini in his hand. I walk over and join him.

He stands and shakes my hand. "Sorry to subject you to Lee's driving but I had some business near here on another case, so I thought it would be better to have him bring you. He lives a few blocks from here." We sit down and he waves over a waiter. I order a Hoegaarden. He lowers his voice. "This place is very well-known in Hong Kong. The girls are all independent and very expensive. The management lets them use rooms upstairs, provided they make the men buy a couple of bottles of the overpriced champagne and give a percentage of their fees to the house. It's not exactly legal but it is... what's the word...? tolerated.

"I've only been here for about twenty minutes but I've

been observing operations. You see the guy in the red shirt behind the bar?" I nod. "He's running the place. The girls get room keys from him and when the men come in, they go to him and he makes sure there's a girl to take care of them. He's the guy we should talk to. Nothing happens here that he doesn't know about. Whether or not he'll talk, I don't know. But what I do know is he won't talk for free. Are you prepared to give him a few bucks?"

"Sure. How much?"

"A thousand, maybe two." He sees my eyes make like saucers and grins. "That's Hong Kong dollars." My eyes settle back into my head as I do the math. Janusz Gutkowski will be OK with me spending about three hundred Canadian, I'm sure.

Except there's a problem. "I don't have that much cash on me."

"I can cover it," he says.

"OK. Let's do it." We down our drinks and head over to the bar. As we sit down, a pretty barmaid comes and says something in Chinese. Phil replies to her and she goes over to the man in the red shirt and says something to him. He takes a long look at us and then nods. The girl goes to serve another customer and red shirt comes over to us. He has a slight limp.

"How can I help you, gentlemen," he says in serviceable English. Jiang looks at me and nods.

I pull out my phone and show him a picture of Zelena. "Do you remember this girl being in here two weeks ago today?"

"Two weeks?" he says. "That's a long time." I'm the only Caucasian in here and I'm betting someone looking like Zelena would be remembered for months to come. But before I can say anything, Phil slides a brown note across the bar. It disappears into red shirt's pocket.

"Yes, she came in here at about eleven o'clock."

"Was she alone?"

"Huh," he grunts. "A girl looking like that doesn't come in here alone."

I flip to the latest Instagram post. "Was she with *him*?"

He looks at Jiang and a similar note appears. This time I see the number on it: five hundred. It disappears. He shakes his head. I scroll down. Again he shakes his head. I scroll to the post of her with the guy whose face is partly covered by the fedora. "How about him?"

"Probably. I can't really see his face so well but he had that hat."

"Did she seem happy, worried, frightened or what?"

"She was having fun. What do you say? Party girl?"

"Did they stay long?"

He shrugs.

"What did they do?"

"Drank."

"They just drank and left?"

He looks at Phil and another note appears on the bar. This time it doesn't disappear. He looks at it for a moment and then looks back at Phil. A second note joins it. They are accepted. "The guy paid me for the use of a room and they went upstairs."

How the hell do I tell *that* to Mr. Gutkowski?

"What time did they leave?"

We get the answer for free. "I don't know, customers who use the rooms leave by the back door."

"The guy she was with, has he been here before? Do you know him?"

He looks at Phil but no new note appears. Phil just says a couple of words in Cantonese.

Red shirt just shrugs. "He comes in sometimes," he says.

"How often?"

He says something to Phil and another five-hundred note passes hands.

"Maybe two times a week. He lives round here."

"Do you know his name or where he lives?"

Yet again he just shakes his head.

———

WE WALK THE THREE BLOCKS TO MR. LEE'S HOUSE IN SILENCE. Phil seems to sense I need to process what we've just heard. The Lexus is parked outside. We get in and Phil eases it away from the curb. "Was he telling the truth?" I ask.

"Almost certainly," he says. "Generally you get what you pay for in Hong Kong."

"It just doesn't make sense. Zelena spends a week with her boyfriend at the Kerry. She tells her best friend she's head-over-heels in love with him and then, the day after he leaves, she sneaks out of the hotel, meets some guy, goes to a sleazy bar with him, goes upstairs to have sex with him and never goes back to the hotel."

"The guy must have been—what was the word you used?—coercing her."

"But how?" I ask.

"That's the question. But what we *do* know is that if she's anywhere, it's around here. The guy in the hat is local and the last Instagram post was in the Stanley market. If we're going to find her this is where we have to start looking."

He's right.

We lapse into silence.

As we enter the tunnel under the Hong Kong harbour, he asks, "Was your girlfriend OK with you working this evening?"

"Yes. She wanted to get a start on the article she's writing and I promised I would take her out for dinner tomorrow night and take her to a nightclub. You said the Golden Dragon was a reputable place so I thought I'd take her there. It would also give me a chance to talk to Leo; he's one of the owners. Zelena and Harvey used to go there, maybe he can tell me something useful."

"Maybe." He doesn't sound hopeful. "Anyway, while you're having fun with your girlfriend tomorrow evening, I'll come back here and see if our mystery man comes in."

When we get to the hotel, a doorman opens the car door for me and I get out. I check my watch. Eleven-thirty. Hopefully Tina will still be awake. But I just need to make one phone call first. I pull out my phone and see there's another email from Simon Fraser University, repeating the offer.

I'll have to talk to Tina about it. But first that phone call.

15. ADRY

Nick is worried. We've had four clients bail on us and one of them was an airline which has given us ongoing business ever since he and Cal started the business. I wonder if he's worried about having to lay me off. I'm certainly worried about it. I can't afford to be laid off. I'll have to get a new job somewhere else and I'd hate that. I love working here. I can feel a prickling in my eyes. It's twenty-four hours since that piece in the Sun. Maybe it's all going to die down now.

"Cal's on line one," Lucy calls from reception.

He must be up late. It's around midnight in Hong Kong.

Nick puts the call on speaker.

"What's up, Rogan," he grunts.

"Hi Cal," I add in the cheeriest voice I can manage.

"I'm working with a local PI, the one Aleksander hired. We're pretty sure she's in the Stanley district of Hong Kong." He updates us on all he's been doing and sounds pretty positive. *"Adry, did you get a chance to speak to Zelena's friend Steph? I'd like to know if she's had any communication with Zelena other than via Instagram."*

"No, sorry," I say. "I'll talk to her today."

"Thanks. So... what's the status of the scam?"

"Not good," Nick says. "We've lost four clients and we spent a good part of yesterday trying to track down the guy who called himself Connor McCoy. We came up with a big fat goose egg. Hopefully it'll all die down and we won't lose any more." Nick shrugs. He really looks beaten down by this whole thing.

I put on my happy voice. "While we've got you on the phone Cal, why don't we do 'morning prayers?'"

This seems to perk Nick up, or is that just me being hopeful?

After we've reviewed all our cases, I pick up my office phone and dial Zelena's friend, Steph.

"Hello Mr. Rogan." Caller ID has let her down this time. There is a coyness in her voice. Either she's got a big old crush on Cal or she's trying to manipulate the hell out of him. Either way, she's *not* going to want to talk to me rather than him. But I can use that.

"Hi, Ms. White," I say brightly. "This is Adry Locke from Stammo Rogan Investigations. Mr. Rogan wanted me to make an appointment with you for later today."

"Oh, yes." The sexy tone has gone from her voice. *"I'll be free at lunchtime. I could meet him in the bar at the Hotel Van at twelve."*

"That's perfect. Thank you very much for being so cooperative."

We hang up just as Lucy comes into the main office. "Dad," she says to Nick, "there's someone on line one. She says she's a client and would really like to talk to you. She says it's urgent."

"Oh Jeez," Nick says. "Another cancellation." He takes in a big breath. "OK. I'll take it." The words come out as a sigh.

Grim-faced, he picks up the phone. "This is Nick Stammo," he says. He listens, nodding his head. Then a strange look comes into his eyes. "Really?" he says. As he listens more, the look changes. It's like a weight is being lifted from his shoulders. He has a big grin on his face. But it's more than just a grin, he looks like a wolf with a lamb in his sights. "Can you come into the office?" he asks. He nods his head as the caller talks. "Great," he says, "I'll see you at one this afternoon."

His grin widens.

"Gotcha!" he says.

"Who was that?" I ask.

The grin gets even wider. "You'll see."

I wouldn't want to be that lamb right now.

———

"Hello Ms. White, I'm Adry Locke." She looks up and frowns. "From Stammo Rogan Investigations," I add.

"Oh, yes, of course," she says. "I thought my appointment was with Cal." She doesn't seem disappointed that I'm not him, so the sexy voice on the phone wasn't because she has a crush on him. But does it mean she wants to manipulate him? We'll see.

"No," I say. "He's in Hong Kong trying to track down Zelena. He asked me to meet with you. I'm so sorry I wasn't clearer on the phone."

"No problem, how can I help? Call me Steph, by the way." If anything she seems relieved it's not Cal. Curiouser and curiouser.

"I assume you've seen the Instagram posts Zelena has been making?" I ask.

"Yes."

"You sound like you don't approve."

"Well, Zel's a friend, she's like my *best* friend, but I think she has been really unfair to poor Harvey. He paid for all of us to go on that trip and then she just ditches him for another guy. That is like so harsh."

"It is," I say. "Harvey must be devastated."

She softens. "He was. But at least he sees Zel for what she really is. She's a good friend but I have to say, she's a rotten girlfriend."

"Harvey sounds like a good guy," I say.

"Oh, he is. He's really great."

"You really like him don't you?"

She looks at me for a second or two. "Yes, I do."

"How do you feel about him going over to Hong Kong to help find her?"

"Oh, he's mainly going for business reasons but he said while he's there he would see if there's anything he can do to help find her or her brother. Even though she hurt him, he still wants to help."

"If I had to guess," I say gently. "I would say you're in love with him."

She smiles. "Yes but don't tell anyone. We want to keep it on the down-low for a while." She pauses. "When that first Instagram post came out, he was *so* upset. I went over to his place to like help him and we kind of hit it off. We want to keep it quiet because it's so soon after Zel dumped him and he didn't want to seem like he had just, you know, dated me to show her. He told me he already had feelings for me even when he was seeing Zel. He hated having Chad there. So did I."

"No one will hear anything from me," I assure her. I am *such* a liar. "Apart from the Instagram posts, have you heard from Zelena? Has she texted or anything?"

"Yes. She's sent me a couple of texts. They were odd."

"How do you mean odd?" I ask.

"Zel's always enthusiastic about everything. She just seems to be, I dunno, down."

"Would you mind showing me the texts?"

She pulls her phone out of a purse, which must have cost her the equivalent of two weeks of my salary, taps it and hands it to me.

I scroll up to see some previous messages, just to get an idea of Zelena's style. Then I scroll back down to the last two messages. I see what Steph means. The words are stilted. The first one is an apology for leaving; it reads, 'So sorry for leaving like that, don't blame my new man.' It certainly lacks her usual flair. Then one of them catches my eye. It says, 'I am so enjoying my new life here in honkers. Hope everything looks perfect.'

"That one looks odd," I say.

"You mean 'honkers,'" she smiles. "That was Zel's nickname for Hong Kong."

That's not what's odd. The first sentence is obviously Zelena's but the second sentence is like someone wrote it for her, someone who doesn't speak English very well. I read it again.

Holy crap.

Without asking permission, I switch to Instagram and go to her latest post. Holy crap squared. I was right.

My hands trembling with excitement, I switch back to messages. This time I ask for permission. "Would it be OK if I sent Zelena a text from your phone?"

"Sure," she says.

I think about it carefully. I need to word it just right. I start typing. 'I understand how everything looks perfect.

btw matt standing says hi and watch out for his posts.' I say a silent prayer and hit Send.

I hand her back the phone. She looks at the text and frowns. "I don't get it," she says.

A part of me wants to tell her we think Zelena is still being held captive, but I remember what Nick said. I just say, "Don't worry, Zelena will."

She looks even more puzzled. "You made a mistake. You got his name wrong. Our friend Matt's last name is Standish, not Standing."

"I know."

———

I HATE THE WOMAN I'M SHARING THE ELEVATOR WITH. NO ONE has the right to look so beautiful yet be so nice.

"It's so good to see you again Adry," she says.

Damn. She even remembered my name. "Nice to see you too Ms. Summers." I say awkwardly.

"Please, call me Marly," she says.

We do the Canadian thing—talk about the weather—as we head down the corridor to the office. She gets there half a step ahead of me and opens the door for me.

Nick hears me introduce our former client to Lucy and wheels into reception. He smiles and extends his hand. If I didn't know he was gay, I would think he had a crush on her.

I lead the way to the conference room and hold the door open for them both, then run back to get my laptop. I am bursting to tell Nick what I just learned from Steph White but it will just have to wait.

When I walk into the conference room they are, you guessed it, talking about the weather, but as soon as I sit down, she gets straight to business. "Someone is trying to ruin me financially," she says.

I think back to her case. It was the first case we had after I joined the firm as Office Manager. Her husband, Dale, who was from a super-rich family was murdered. Cal and Nick suspected her at first.

"After Dale's death, his brother, who administers their family trust, offered me a cash settlement of seven and a half million dollars. I probably could have got more but I didn't want the hassle of a law suit, so I agreed. I signed the documents and they wrote me a cheque. I invested the money conservatively and got on with my life. I now work for a non-profit helping indigent teenagers get off the streets and helping them turn their lives around."

Wow! Beautiful, nice, rich and a thoroughly good person. Now I really hate her.

"Two months ago," she continues, "I got a call from the Royal Bank in Toronto. They said I owe them five million dollars."

"Let me guess," Nick says. "They say they lent you the money and you haven't made any payments on the loan."

She frowns. "That's right. I told them it wasn't me who had taken out the loan but they said they had all my information including my signature on the documents. When I told them I haven't been in Toronto in the last ten years, they said they had video footage of me, taken in their offices. They also said their loan officers had seen recent pictures of me and swore I was the person who took out the loan. I told them it wasn't me but they won't listen and have put a lien on my investments, awaiting a court date. My boyfriend is a computer specialist and he did something on the dark web and found my financial details out there. I just don't know what to do. Do you think you can help?"

Nick gives his wolf-lamb smile. If I didn't know him, I'd find it scary as hell. "Yes, I think we can help," he says. "You see, I know who's scamming you."

She frowns. "How can you possibly know that?"

"Funny you should ask," Nick says. "Someone is trying to ruin us financially too."

"Who?" she asks.

"It's just too much of a coincidence. I'm guessing it's the same person who is trying to ruin you. The only person who hates you and hates us too."

She gasps. "Bob Pridmore?"

When she says his name an image of him pops into my mind: six foot six inches, built like a line backer, cruel face and the slimiest lawyer in town.

"He's the only one I can think of," Nick says.

"If it is Bob, what are we going to do?"

"You remember how we got him out of your life before?" he asks.

"Yes," she says awkwardly.

"We could remind him of the threat to send the video to the Law Society. He wouldn't want to risk disbarment."

"We could..." she leaves it hanging.

"OK," says Nick. "Why don't I give Big Bob a call?"

"Wait a minute Nick," I interrupt. I remember the video of Marly with Pridmore and I can sense her discomfort. "How do you feel about it Marly?" I ask.

"Not good," she says. "There was some pretty explicit stuff in the video. Sure, we could use it against him but if Bob got hold of it, he could also use it against me. The charity I work for now wouldn't be impressed if they got to see it. In fact, I would feel a whole lot better if you just deleted any copies you have of it."

"She's right Nick," I say. "Besides, we can't be a hundred percent sure it *is* Pridmore."

"I suppose," he says. "But maybe just the threat would make him back off."

"That doesn't help Marly," I say. "He's hardly going to go to the Royal Bank and say he fraudulently took out a loan in her name."

"You're right," he agrees. "And it doesn't help us either. He's not going to go to VPD and tell them he and his side-kick planted drugs on us." He mulls it over for a while. "I don't usually believe in coincidences, but in this case, maybe we should consider whether the scams being perpetrated on us are in fact connected."

We sit in silence for a moment until Marly says, "If it is someone who has got my financial details from the dark web, there's nothing I can do is there?"

"Oh yes there is," Nick says. "No one arranges a five million dollar loan over the internet or by phone. The bank told you they have your signature on the documents. This gives us two lines of investigation. One: you can get copies of the signed documents and have a hand-writing expert verify that the signature is not yours. And two: the bank has video of the person who came in to sign those documents. If we can get our hands on that video, we can prove it's not you."

Marly gives a big beam. "Thank you so much." She gets up from the table and leans over to give Nick a big hug, which makes me hate her a lot less. "But how are you going to deal with *your* problem?" she asks.

Nick looks at her.

"Damned if I know," he says.

"Me neither," I add.

We may be able to help Marly with her problem but Stammo Rogan Investigations may still be screwed.

———

As soon as Nick has given Marly's big, fat retainer cheque to Lucy, I drag him into the main office. "Nick you are never going to believe this." The words bubble out of me. "Zelena sent a message. We can communicate with her. We can find out where she is and get her back. Cal can get the police to rescue her. It's so simple but I would never have—"

"Whoa," he says, a wide grin spreading across his face. "Slow down. What have you found out? And for heaven's sake start at the beginning."

I take in a big breath and then another.

"OK look at this Instagram post of Zelena's." I open my phone, find the post and show it to him.

"So," he says.

"It says, 'Look what I found in the Stanley Market. Helloooo extremely lovely person?' The first sentence is something Zelena would say, but the second sentence is kind of odd. I thought it might have been written by someone whose first language isn't English. But it isn't. It's an acronym: Hello Extremely Lovely Person. H E L P. Zelena's sending a message."

"Hmm, could be, I suppose." He doesn't sound convinced.

"Now look at this," I grin at him and show him Zelena's text to Steph. "It says 'I am so enjoying my new life here in honkers. Hope everything looks perfect.' The first sentence was definitely her normal style—she called Hong Kong 'honkers'—but look at the second sentence, it's awkward English and it's another H E L P."

"Ho-ly! You're right." A big smile spreads across his face. "You are amazing." As I sit here glowing, he thinks it over for a bit and I smile, because I know what's coming next. "But how do we communicate with her?" he asks.

I remind him about how I logged into her Instagram and made her follow the fictional Matt Standing, which is the account we use to see her posts, and how the name is similar to her actual friend Matt Standish. "So I sent her a text on Steph's phone that said, 'I understand how everything looks perfect. btw matt standing says hi and watch out for his posts.' She will know someone understood her message and that everything posted by the fictional Matt Standing is a message back to her."

"What's the time in Hong Kong?" he asks.

I check my phone. "Six o'clock tomorrow morning."

"OK, let's wake Rogan up. He'll want to hear this." He gives a short laugh. "If we get that girl back, there is a big bonus in your future."

He thinks a bit longer and his face becomes grim. "Provided we've still got a future."

———

IT'S A BIT OF AN ANTICLIMAX NOW. CAL IS GOING TO THINK how he can best communicate with Zelena while Nick and I are working on the cases of our remaining clients. I'm just about to do a google search for a client's supposedly wayward husband when Nick says, "Coffee time." He wheels over to the kitchen area and after a few moments comes back with a tray on his lap with three mugs and a plate of the inevitable chocolate digestive cookies. "Coffee, Luce," he calls.

We gather round his desk and sip appreciatively. Somehow our coffee tastes better when Nick makes it.

"We've done good work today," he says. "Or I should say, you guys have."

He looks a bit down. Lucy spots it too. "What's up Dad?" she says.

"Nothing really." He picks up his second cookie and takes a bite. "It's just that I've been nosing around on the dark web to see if I could find Marly's financial details, you know, bank account numbers, Social Insurance Number and so on, but I couldn't find anything. It bugs me that her boyfriend could find it but I couldn't."

Lucy smiles. "Don't sweat it Dad. She did say her boyfriend's in the computer business; maybe he's a pro at that sort of stuff."

"Yeah, but it still bugs me. I really want to look at what might be out there," he says.

"If you think it's important Nick," I say, "go with your gut. Give her a call and get her boyfriend's details, then give him a call. Maybe he can point you in the right direction."

"Yeah, maybe I'll do that. Good idea." He takes a bite of his cookie.

Lucy gives him a long look. "I know you Dad," she says. "That's a delaying tactic. If you mean it, do it now."

"OK, OK," he says and grabs his phone. When Marly picks up he says, "You were saying your boyfriend found your financial details out there on the dark web?" There is a slight pause. "Yes," he says. "That's right." A look of shock appears on his face. "Could you repeat that please," he says. The look of shock slowly transforms into that grin: the wolf-with-the-lamb-in-his-sights grin. I can almost see the wheels turning in his head as he thinks through whatever it is he's just learned. "Yes, I'm still here," he says into the phone. He thinks some more. "Can you come back into the office?" He listens some more. "In that case, you'd better come back in right away... Cancel and don't say anything... Definitely, right now...OK... Good. We'll see you in half an hour."

He hangs up.

The grin is back. "You know what? Criminals *always* make a mistake," he says.

16. NICK

She sits down at the conference table. "What's this all about, Mr. Stammo?" She looks a bit ticked off at being asked to come to our offices for a second time, without any explanation.

"Do you have any pictures of your boyfriend?" I ask.

"Why?"

"When you told me his name over the phone, it rang a bell, shall we say."

She frowns. "Sure." She takes her phone out of her purse and after a few taps, hands it over to me. I show it to Adry and she nods. The smiling face staring out at us belongs to the guy who calls himself Connor McCoy.

"What?" Marly looks equal parts worried and annoyed.

"Connor's the CEO of Dark Energy Systems?" Adry asks.

"Yes, why?"

Adry turns her laptop around so Marly can see the screen. "This is their website. That's the real McCoy, as you might say."

Marly reaches over and scrolls up and down. "There must be a problem, maybe they got the pictures mixed up."

As Adry tells about her visit to Dark Energy Systems, Marly's face begins to crumble and when Adry tells her that her boyfriend is the one who scammed us, a tear runs down her cheek, holds for a moment on her chin and then drops onto the table.

We give her time.

After a moment, she says, "I sure know how to pick boyfriends, don't I? My husband was gay, Bob Pridmore was an abusive slime and Connor is a con-man." Another tear appears and I push across our ever-present box of tissues.

She takes two, dries her eyes, then takes a big breath in and straightens her back. "So, what's the plan?" she says.

I nod at Adry.

"It's pretty obvious that if someone is trying to ruin both you and us, then it's almost certain Bob Pridmore's behind it. He's the only connection between us who would want to harm us both. It's almost five o'clock, so we have to move fast."

As she tells Marly our plan, I can see she's not too happy with one aspect of it, but she knows she's got to go along with it. I feel bad we're having to ask her to do this but it's the only way we're all going to get out of the mess the phony Connor McCoy has got us into.

———

It's a flashback to just over a year ago. I'm sitting in my truck outside Marly's house, waiting for her boyfriend to leave. The only difference is that it's a different boyfriend, with a different car and Adry is here in the truck, sharing a pizza and keeping me company.

"Game on," she says.

I look up. She's staring out of the window.

Marly and 'Connor' are standing in the doorway. He gives her a peck on the cheek then goes to the blue Prius in the driveway.

"He bought the migraine story," Adry whispers.

"Also known as 'not tonight honey, I have a headache,'" I grunt as I hand her the paper plate holding my third slice. "He didn't give me time to finish my pizza. Now I really don't like him."

As he drives away, I follow. Before long, we are on Marine Drive and I can let a couple of cars get between us. We follow him over the Lions Gate and into Vancouver. We start-stop, start-stop in the rush-hour traffic all the way along Georgia Street until we get onto the viaduct. Two blocks along Prior, he hangs a left onto Princess but now there are three cars in front of me and the lights go red. Quietly fuming, I wait until they go green again but I can't turn left because of the oncoming traffic. Beside me, Adry is muttering swearwords under her breath.

Finally we make it onto Princess but the Prius is not in sight. "We've lost him." Adry spits out.

"Maybe," I say.

"How the hell are you going to find him?" she asks.

I give her my favourite answer. "Watch and learn," I say. I know that phrase drives Rogan nuts, Adry too if her grunt is anything to go by. "This is a residential area. You don't take Princess Street to go somewhere else. He's going home. I'll bet you a buck, his car is going to be parked within a four-by-four-block area."

"Huh," she says.

She sits in silence as I drive up and down, block by block, until we see the blue Prius. It's parked on a block with a wide variety of old buildings. Some are little houses, some are big; some are gentrified and some are run down; some have been converted to multi-family dwellings. He could be in any one of twenty buildings.

I drive on past the Prius, hoping 'Connor' isn't looking out of a window at his car and recognizing my truck as the one parked outside his girlfriend's house in West Van.

"OK, I owe you a buck," Adry says. "But we still don't know what his real name is and where he lives."

She's right. Rogan's the one who knows the ins and outs of the downtown east side. And so he should; he lived on the streets here for long enough. Then it hits me. I know how to find out where 'Connor' lives. Connor. Stupid millennial name! Why Connor? Oh! I feel the grin appear on my face.

"True," I say trying to keep the smugness out of my voice.

"So what are we going to do? Sit in your van all night watching the Prius and hoping he comes out to use it in the morning?"

"No need. By the morning, we're going to know where he lives and maybe, just maybe, what his real name is."

"How?" she asks.

It takes a lot of control not to say my favourite phrase.

17. CAL

For what feels like the hundredth time, I check Instagram. Nothing. As Matt Standing, I posted a comment on her post where she's with the guy in the Stanley Market. 'Looks cool. Where are you staying in Stanley?' but there's been no response. Not that I expect her to give me an address, but at least an acknowledgement that we've made contact would ease my fears.

My phone burbles. FaceTime.

When his face appears on the screen he has a big smile on it. He's in his truck. "Hey Nick."

"Hey Rogan, guess what." He tells me about what's happened with Marly Summers and the discovery of the phoney Connor McCoy. He outlines his idea and I give him the information he asks for.

"Sounds like a plan Nick. Well done," I say.

"So how's it going over there?"

"I've been hanging around in the Stanley area, walking around the streets. I don't have any great expectation of running into Zelena but if this is where she's living or being held captive, it's good to get a sense of the neighbourhood. Every time I've seen a shop or café I think she might like, I've gone in and shown her picture around but no one has shown any signs of recognizing her."

"Good old-fashioned police work," he says. *"Have you been to the Stanley Market, where she said the picture was taken?"*

"I'm standing outside it right now, just about to go in."

"Great. How's Tina doing?"

I feel the broad smile take over my face at the mention of her name. "Great. She's made good progress with the protester groups," I say. "Under promise of strict anonymity, she's managed to get interviews with some of the leaders of the movement and she's very excited about the article she's working on."

"Good for her," he grins at me. *"You should take her for a nice night out."* Clearly the break in the 'Connor' case has put him in a good mood.

"Already planned, dinner and a nightclub. Phil Jiang has promised to hang out at IF tonight and see if he can spot the man in Zelena's post, so I don't feel too guilty about taking the evening off."

"She's a keeper Rogan. You take good care of her."

"I will Nick, I will"

We say our goodbyes and hang up.

———

THE STANLEY MARKET IS NOT WHAT I EXPECTED. FOR SOME reason, I thought it would be a street market but it's in an old building that looks like a warehouse. I walk up the steps and am faced with a vast array of market stalls. Most of the customers look like locals and the stalls all sell items that locals would buy. There are stalls selling meat, herbal medicine, pots and pans and colourful clothing of all types. It has a nice, friendly vibe.

I take out my phone and find Zelena's post where she's posing with the guy in the market. As I walk around I check it against the various stalls but can't find anything that looks like where the picture was taken. Maybe it wasn't actually taken here. I look more closely at the post. Right at the edge of the frame there is the head of a chicken in what looks like a cage. I turn to a man at a stall selling meat and show him the photo. I point to the chicken. "Can you tell me where I can find this stall?" I ask. He says something in Cantonese and points upward. I remember there was an escalator at the entrance. "Mgòi, mgòi," I thank him, trying out one of the three words of Cantonese I learned on the plane. I backtrack and make my way up to the next level. Right there, twenty paces from the top of the escalator, is a stall with a cage containing three live chickens. I walk over and recognize a face. He is standing beside the stall with an older lady who looks like she might be his mother. It's the well-dressed young man posing with Zelena in the post.

I walk over. "Hi," I say, adding a silent prayer that he speaks English.

"Hi," he says. "You want to buy chicken?"

Saying a silent thank you, I show him the post. "Do you remember this girl?" I ask.

A big grin breaks out on his face. "Oh, yes. She was very pretty. Very nice lady."

"Was she alone," I ask?

"No, she was with two men."

I scroll to Zelena's first post after she went missing, the one that says 'My new guy.' "Was this one of the men?" I ask.

He takes a long look at the picture. "Maybe, without the

hat. Yes, maybe." He nods. "He was the one took the picture."

"Have you seen her since?"

"No, sorry."

"Did she say anything to you?"

With a sad look, he says, "No."

After last night at IF, I remembered the value of having cash in my pocket and paid a visit to an ATM this morning. I take a five-hundred Hong Kong dollar bill from my wallet and give it to him with my business card. "If you see her again, follow her and find out where she lives. If you can take me to where she lives, I'll give you five thousand." Janusz and Francesca Gutkowski can easily afford the thousand Canadian. For a second, I remember that Janusz told me to forget his daughter and look only for his son. But I have no other lead to his son than through his daughter.

I leave the young man talking excitedly with his mother and begin the long, slow job of going from stall to stall with Zelena's photo, asking if they've seen her.

———

IT'S NOT THE RESTAURANT YOU WOULD ASSOCIATE WITH A romantic dinner. The tables and chairs are green plastic and placed outside on the sidewalk. There are no cars allowed on this street in the evening. On one side of us is the restaurant and across the narrow street is the fish market where you can choose the fish or lobster you want them to cook for you. The maitre d' doesn't stand behind a lectern but patrols the street competing with the other restaurants for customers. And the food is fabulous. We have eaten ourselves to a standstill. Lobster, chow mein and ribs, washed down with a couple of Heinekens—people in Hong

Kong seem to love Dutch beers—and I'm a happy camper. Tina went for more exotic foods including chicken feet but I'm not that brave.

"That was great and I managed not to spill anything on my dress," she says.

"That's good." She is wearing a stunning white dress with a delicate pattern woven in gold thread. I'm no expert on women's clothes, but I'm betting it cost a lot.

"I'm stuffed," she sighs. "Why don't we take a walk through the market and burn off some of those calories before we go to the nightclub?"

"It's a deal. If I can get out of this chair."

The street we are on intersects Temple Street, the home of Mong Kok's famous night market. Hand-in-hand, we stroll the few paces towards the market. Temple Street is narrow with stalls cramped on either side. Behind the stalls are strips of sidewalk lined with shops, all open and ready for business. The market runs in both directions. I point north. "This is the general direction of the Golden Dragon," I say. To our right is a stall with brightly coloured women's dresses and robes, and on our left is one with kids' backpacks. We walk between them. Immediately the stall owners start their sales pitches and before long Tina has bargained the owner down by thirty percent and purchased a bright-red, high-collar dress. "I love this place," she grins.

Unlike the Stanley market, the customers here look to be mainly tourists. We manage to make it through a couple of blocks, with Tina buying only three items, but when she stops at a leather goods stall to bargain for a purse, I wander ahead past four stalls selling electronics parts, dolls, china and tee shirts respectively. The next stall on my left has what must be a thousand watches. "Very fine watches," the owner says. "Look at this one. Perfect for you." He holds a garish sports watch with an orange and grey strap.

"Not my style," I say. I look at the vast display and see some watches that may be more to my taste. I point. "What about tho—" My jaw drops. While the owner continues to extoll his wares, I pull out my phone and open Instagram. I scroll to the first post, the one with Zelena and the man in the hat. Behind them is a stall full of watches. I move to the approximate position from which the camera must have taken the shot. It's the same stall. On the right side of the picture, I can see suitcases. I look to the right. Sure enough there's a stall selling suitcases. This is where the picture was taken.

"How about these?" the stall owner asks.

"Sure," I say. "How much is that one?"

"Two hundred eighty."

I take three hundred out of my wallet and hand it over.

He takes it with a look of amazement and I realize I should have bargained him down. I hope I haven't committed some form of *faux pas* by not haggling over the price. As he gives me my change, I turn my camera around and show him the picture. "Do you remember this girl?" I ask.

He peers at the picture, starts to smile and then his face shuts down. He looks at me, eyes blank. "No. Never seen her." Why the hell is he lying?

I take out a five-hundred-dollar bill and hold it out. "Just look again, please." I hold out my phone in the other hand.

He ignores both and just shakes his head. This time, I see fear in his eyes.

"Listen," I say gently. "This girl is in a lot of trouble. I'm trying to find her so I can take her home to her parents. Can you please help me?"

"Sorry. Don't know her." He grabs a watch and moves towards another potential customer. "Very fine watches," he says. "Look at this one. Perfect for you." The man starts bargaining with him.

I feel Tina's arm slipping around mine. "What did you buy?" she asks. I show her the watch. "Nice. How much did you bargain him down?"

"I didn't."

While she gives me a tutorial on market haggling, I watch the owner of the stall out of the corner of my eye. He completes his sale and, with what is clearly a terrified glance in my direction, he disappears behind his stall. I have done enough interrogations to know he knows something and there's no way he's going to tell me what it is. Reluctantly, I put my arm around Tina and move away from his stall, wondering if there's any way to unlock what's in his mind.

———

THE GOLDEN DRAGON IS EVERYTHING THE IF ISN'T. IT'S COOL and sophisticated and if there is a bouncer, he is not obviously in evidence. The music is loud but not deafening and it is early enough that there are still seats available at the bar. A smiling cocktail waitress brings us huge menus with seemingly every drink known to mankind listed in Chinese and English. Even the cheapest drinks are eighty-eight Hong Kong dollars which, at about fifteen bucks Canadian, is a hell of a price to pay for a beer.

From what little I know of Zelena, I can see why she liked this place. It's fun, friendly, noisy, and the tiny dance floor is packed with smiling glitterati. It even makes me want to get up and dance and I'm betting that if I don't ask Tina to, she's going to ask me.

But this is the last place where Zelena was before she went back to the hotel with Steph and then disappeared. I'm hoping Leo, the owner who's friends with Harvey, will be able to tell me something, anything that might help me find her.

We order and when she brings our drinks, I say to the cocktail waitress, "I'd like to speak to Leo, the owner. I'm a friend of his friend Harvey."

A flicker of a frown crosses her face, which quickly reverts to a broad smile. "I'm sorry sir, Leo isn't here tonight."

Damn. "Will he be back tomorrow?" I ask.

"No sir, he's on vacation. I'm not sure when he'll be back," she says.

I think back to my conversation with Harvey in the Red Sugar bar at the hotel. He said Leo was here every night. Come to think of it, when I spoke with Steph at the Starbucks on Robson, she said the same thing. I look the waitress directly in the eye. "Are you sure?" I ask.

"Yes sir," she says... but she's lying. "He won't be back for a long while." For an instant, her eyes flicker across the room and I follow her gaze. Sitting on a couch, wearing an expensive suit and holding a glass of what looks like Coke, is a well-muscled guy with a serious expression, completely out of sync with the ethos of the club. He is the bouncer. His eyes lock mine and he gives the smallest shake of his head.

I've been warned off.

The waitress moves away to serve another customer.

"What was that all about?" Tina asks.

"I'm not sure. Zelena came here the night she disappeared and I wanted to ask the owner if he noticed anything out of the ordinary. But now it seems *he's* disappeared too."

"Well…" she says, a serious look on her face. "That only leaves one thing for you to do."

"What's that?"

She grins. "Dance with me."

———

AS WE LEAVE THE GOLDEN DRAGON, TINA HAS A FIT OF THE giggles. Her enthusiasm has made me forget about missing people and whoever is trying to scam Stammo Rogan Investigations and just enjoy the moment. My legs ache from dancing and my jaw hurts from grinning. She is clutching the bags containing all the purchases she made in the market and I have my arm tight around her, not just because I like it but also to help steer her on a steady path. She kisses my cheek and breathes, "I love you," in my ear sending a tingle the length of my spine.

"I love you too."

We are on a quiet side street—quiet by Hong Kong standards anyway—so I lead her towards Nathan Road, where we are sure to find one of the ubiquitous red taxis.

Sure enough, when we are half a block away, a cab turns off Nathan and comes towards us. I flag him down and hold open the back door for Tina to get in.

"Thank you kind sir," she says as she puts her many bags into the back seat.

Three things happen in quick succession.

Tina tries to step forward to get into the cab but sways unsteadily and lurches backward.

An "Oooof" sound explodes from her lips.

A man bounces off her and into me and pushes me into the side of the cab.

As I gain my equilibrium, I see the man running away towards Nathan Road. For a second, I think to follow him but he has too much of a start and I know that once he turns the corner, he'll disappear into the throng on Hong Kong's busiest street.

"Rude bastard," I say. "Are you OK?"

Tina doesn't answer. Instead she collapses at my feet, a stain of red spreading over her white dress.

18. ZELENA

The last one was really bad. He made me fight back hard. I hurt my hand punching him and he punched me back when he finally held me down and raped me. I'm hoping it leaves a bruise. The last time one of the customers from the star room bruised me they gave me the next night off. Then I had to wear heavy makeup for a couple of days while it healed.

But at least the day wasn't bad today. They took me out in the van. We went about half an hour away from here. I think it was near where the Stanley Market is. They brought along a whole bunch of outfits and made me change into a different one for each set of pictures. Just for a moment, I could enjoy being in the open air. At one point, I saw a policeman. I so wanted to run to him and ask for help but if I did, they would punish Zander, probably kill him. And I don't know where they're holding us. It's my fault he's here.

I hear footsteps. They're *his*. I have learned to recognize the different people's footsteps as they come up the stairs.

He unbolts the door and walks in.

He hands me the phone.

"Text friends. Say having good time. Post Instagram with first pictures in green dress."

He stands over me so he can see what I write.

I go to text Steph and feel my whole spine catch on fire. 'I understand how everything looks perfect.' OMG, she got it. I try to look calm and stop my hands from trembling. I text back. 'Thanks for understanding.' I look at her message again. She got Matt's name wrong. It's Stand*ish*, not Stand*ing*. I go to Matt's texts. There's nothing recent. Just to be safe, I text, "having a great time in honkers. miss you guys in vancouver. having enough luscious pizza?'

"What that about pizza?" he says over my shoulder.

I clear my throat to give me time to try and calm down. I say the first thing that comes into my head. "That's my friend Matt. Just about all he eats is pizza. Everyone jokes about it."

He just grunts.

I got away with it but I have to be careful.

I switch to Instagram and look at my last posts. There are lots of likes and comments. There's one from Matt. But it's Matt Stand*ing*. 'Looks cool. Where are you staying in Stanley?' I can feel my heart in my chest. Someone's trying to communicate with me. They want me to tell them where I am. But I don't know. Except once, we have always gone in a van with no windows in the back. To give me time to think, I do as I was asked and make posts with the first two pictures they took today. It breaks my heart to make light-hearted posts about having a good time. But it gives me an idea.

I go back to the Stanley market post. I reply to a few of the comments and then get to Matt's. I reply, 'That's for me to know and you to guess. Or the other way around.' I add a googly-eyes emoticon and press send.

"OK, that's enough," he says and snatches my phone away.

Without a word, he leaves the room.

I hear the refrigeration unit start in the next room.

The client must have complained.

Another cold night.

19. NICK

I haven't been here in a dog's age. I think the last time was years back when Rogan and me were still in the VPD, before he got hooked. It hasn't changed in the last ten years, probably not in the last fifty. We sit down across the table from Rogan's two buddies, Ghost and Tommy.

"Thanks for meeting us at the Ovaltine, Mr. Stammo," Ghost says.

"You didn't give us much choice."

He chuckles. "Yeah, well Rocky always treats us to breakfast when we do some work for him."

"Who?" Adry asks.

"Rogan's street name," I tell her. "From when he was a junkie, living on the streets."

I take Ghost's hint and call the waiter over. They order. I'm tempted to order too. I'm betting the breakfast here is as good as ever.

"So did you find out where the owner of the Prius lives?" I ask.

"Course we did," he says with pride and his buddy Tommy gives us a big toothless grin and nods.

I stare at him for a moment and he cocks his head to one side.

I get it.

"OK," I say and take out the two hundred bucks in twenties that I promised them on the phone yesterday. I hand it over. It gets split between them and disappears into their pockets. Ghost pulls out a piece of paper and hands it over.

"I wrote it down so's I wouldn't forget it," he says.

It's an address.

"You're sure about this?" I ask. They both nod. "Well done guys. You did good." I take out an extra four twenties and hand them over. "That's a bit of a bonus for staying up all night to keep your eyes on the Prius until he came out and used it this morning."

The bonus disappears into their pockets... then they look at each other and burst into laughter.

"What?" I ask. This only makes them laugh more. Adry joins in and I can't keep a straight face either.

Tommy is the first to get it together. "Thanks for the extra Mr. Stammo," he says, wiping his eyes with the back of a dirty hand, "but we didn't stay out all night. Right after your call, we walked to Strathcona and found the car. Ghost went and hid and I sat on the hood of that Prius and bounced up and down a couple of times until the alarm went off. In no time flat, the guy comes out of his apartment to chase me off and Ghost went and wrote down the address. Easy peasy. Then we went and had a beer."

They may be a couple of homeless alcoholics but they're definitely not stupid.

Now I see why Rogan likes to hire them.

"HELLO ROLAND," I SAY. "CAN WE COME IN?"

Before he can get over his amazement at seeing us, Adry pushes past him into his apartment and I wheel after her.

"What the fuck d'ya think you're doing?" he asks.

"Sit down, Roland," Adry says and takes a step towards him. It's a side of her I've never seen before.

He points a finger right at her face. "Fuck off bit—" His words are cut off with a yelp. She's grabbed his hand and twisted it somehow and pushed him backwards until he flops down in his chair.

She turns to me and sees the stunned look on my face. "Krav Maga," she says. I don't know what it means but I'll definitely ask her later.

I wheel closer to him. "Who put you up to this Roland?" I say.

He rubs his hand. "How do you know my name?" he asks sullenly.

"Because like most small-time criminals, you're stupid. You came to scam us using the name Connor McCoy because you knew there was a real Connor McCoy who did own a real computer company. But you were also scamming Marly Summers and you used the same name with her. I couldn't work out who would be so lazy as to use the same name for two marks who knew each other. And then it clicked. I figured you stuck with the name because you must have a connection with the real Connor McCoy. So Adry here emailed him the picture of you that Marly gave us. Connor told us you were his lame-assed brother Roland who was a bit actor trying to make it big in Hollywood North. It's funny you don't look alike. If you had we'd have spotted it a lot sooner."

Even more sullenly he grunts, "How did you find me? Connor doesn't even know where I live."

"That's for me to know and you to guess. The question is... who put you up to this?"

"No one. It was my idea."

"Come on Roland. You're too stupid to scam Marly Summers out of five million bucks."

His eyes go wide. "What did you say?"

I can't keep the grin off my face. "You didn't know, did you?"

"Know what?"

I take a guess. "He told you to look around Marly's house and find out things like her bank account details, Social Insurance Number, driver's licence number, email password and anything else you could get your dirty little hands on. What he didn't tell you is he used that information to steal five million bucks from her."

"Son of a—" Stupid bastard can't find the words.

I let it all sink in for about fifteen seconds. The only thing to break the silence is the ping of Adry's phone.

"He scammed you too, didn't he?"

He just nods.

"Who was it, Roland?"

When he says the name, it's my turn to be stunned.

Because it's not Bob Pridmore.

————

"I DIDN'T EXPECT TO SEE YOU IN THE OFFICE ON A SATURDAY Luce," I say as she puts coffee and cookies on my desk.

"I had some filing and stuff to do and I knew you guys would be in anyway. What did you find out?"

"We found out it's not Bob Prid—"

"YES!!" Adry's yell cuts me off. "Zelena replied to 'Matt Standing.'"

"What did she say?"

"Huh," she says. "That's funny. It was the same thing you said to Roland. Her reply to the question 'Where are you staying in Stanley?' is 'That's for me to know and you to guess. Or the other way around.'" She thinks it over. "It's the sort of thing Zelena would say to tease someone," she adds.

"Yes, but if you read it the other way round, it would say 'That's for *you* to know and *me* to guess.' She's telling us she doesn't know where she's being held but wants us to figure it out."

"Good one Dad," Lucy says.

"Good one Zelena, you mean. She's bright."

"Right," Adry says. "But it's easier said than done. She's got to give us some sort of a clue." She thinks some more. "How about I message her something like 'Stanley sounds great. What do you like best about it?' Maybe she can tell us what she sees out of a window or maybe a sound she hears, like a church bell or traffic or something."

"No," I say. "Too risky. She's obviously being watched while she uses Instagram. They would spot if she tried to give us some sort of clue." We slip into silence. We've got to come up with something. I start nibbling on a second cookie. If she's being kept somewhere and they are just taking her out to take photos she can post on Instagram, maybe she can tell us about something she sees in transit. "Maybe we could message her something like—"

My phone rings. Rogan.

"Perfect timing," I say. "What time is it there?"

"Just after one in the morning."

"You're up late. Did you see Zelena's Instagram post? We're trying to think out what to reply. I was thinking—"

"Listen Nick, I'm in the hospital."

Oh my God, what's he done now? "Holy shit, are you OK?"

"I'm fine but Tina's been stabbed."

A chill cuts through me. I remember what it's like to be stabbed. "Was it anything to do with those protesters she went to interview? I thought it was risky, I was saying to Adry—"

"No, it wasn't. I think it was me who was the target."

"Oh crap. Is she OK?" He's silent. Jeez. I think I know what he's going to say next.

"No."

I knew it.

"Oh, Cal..."

"She's lost a lot of blood, but she's hanging in there. The doctors are fairly close-lipped about the prognosis. I don't know, but that doesn't seem too good to me."

"Is there anything we can do?"

"No. I'll call you when I know more. I've got to call her parents too. I have no idea what to say to them. What time is it there?"

"Just after ten AM. Listen buddy, you hang in there," I try to sound positive but that's not really my long suit. "Keep us informed and if there's *anything* we can do, just let us know."

"Thanks Nick. I appreciate it." He pauses for a moment. *"I'll check her Instagram post when I get a moment."*

"Don't you worry about that. We'll handle the Instagram posts. Oh, and we got a break with the guys who planted the drugs on us."

"That's great Nick. What have you—" I hear voices in the background. *"Listen, I've got to go. One of the doctors just came in. I'll call you later."*

"Stay positive and keep us posted," I say, but he's hung up.

I put down the phone and look up. Four eyes are drilling into me.

"What's happened?" Adry asks.

When I've told them, they're both in tears. Lucy is taking it real bad.

I try not to think what would happen if something like that happened to Stewart and it was my fault. If I think about *that* I'll be bawling too, just when I need to be strong.

I let them cry it out for a bit, then say, "Remember Tina's young and she's strong. If an old bird like me can survive being shot and damn near choked to death like I did six months ago, she'll pull through just fine."

They dab their eyes and try to smile. I change the subject. "OK ladies, we need to work out what to say to Zelena and how we're gonna handle what we learned from Roland."

"OK ladies?!" Lucy says giving me a lop-sided grin. "What century are we in Dad?"

Adry tries to hold in a laugh. She fails.

"Alright, alright," I say, faking grumpiness. "Let's get to work." But all I can think about is Tina lying in that hospital. I force the image out of my mind. "Zelena first. Let's do some brainstorming. Adry, just before Rogan called, you were going to say something about sending a message to Zelena."

"Yes," she says, "We need to do two things. We need to tell her we're coming to help her and we need to get her to give us a clue, any clue, as to where she might be."

"The first one's easy, just mention Mighty Mouse." I just get blank looks. "You know, *here he comes to save the day, Mighty Mouse is on his way*...?" More blank looks. "OK, wrong generation," I grunt. Maybe I'm getting too old for this stuff. "It was a cartoon back in the day," I explain.

A look comes into Adry's eye. "Maybe a pop-culture reference would work," she says. "A song maybe."

An image of my father pops into my head. I usually try not to think about him. "Lucy, do you remember your grandfather? He used to kinda sing quietly to himself all the time." Lucy nods and smiles. Her memories of him are good ones. He'd mellowed by the time she was a kid. "He loved a group from back in his day called The Doors. He was always singing one that went something like, *And we're on our way, and we can't go back.*"

Adry smiles. "Wrong generation agai—"

"The Royal Concept!" Lucy whoops. She looks at us and laughs. "Your faces!" she says. "There's a Swedish rock band called The Royal Concept. Their best known song is called 'On Our Way."

"Yeah, but she might not know them."

"Doesn't matter," she says. "We could do an Instagram post as Matt Standing and say something like. 'Just downloaded a great song by The Royal Concept, On Our Way.'"

"Might be a bit obvious," I say.

"Maybe we can be a little less obvious," Adry says. "Wait a minute." She turns to her keyboard and taps away for a second. "Look at this." She turns her computer round so we can see the screen. There's a brightly-coloured image with the words ON OUR WAY. "It's the cover for the song. We can use it as the picture on the post."

"Alright! Now we're getting somewhere. Good work you guys."

I can tell Lucy is pleased. She says, "That will tell her we're trying to get to her but how do we ask her to give us a clue as to where she is? She doesn't even know where she is herself."

We lapse into silence.

This is a more difficult problem. "It's a puzzle," I say.

They both nod. "It sure is a puzz—" Adry sits bolt upright in her chair. She turns her computer around and starts tapping at the keyboard. A big smile spreads over her face. She turns it back so we can see it again.

"How did you—"

"My little brother. He loves games and puzzles. Whenever I visit my parents he always wants me to play this with him."

It's perfect. Now we're getting somewhere.

My phone rings.

When I see the caller ID the good feeling disappears. It's my former partner, former boss, at VPD.

"Hi, Steve," I say.

"Hey Nick," he says. The tone of his voice says more: he's got bad news. *"I'm going to need to speak with Rogan."*

"He's out of town, Steve," I tell him.

"Where?"

I think for a moment but I can't find a reason not to tell him. "Hong Kong."

"When's he due back?"

"I dunno. Depends on how he does on the case."

He goes silent.

But not quite. I can hear the sound of muffled words. He's talking to someone but he's got his hand over the phone. I strain to hear what he's saying. There's two voices but I can't quite catch what's being said.

He comes back on. *"Listen Nick, you know that briefcase full of drugs we found in your office—"*

"Jeez Steve, I don't remember..." I say in my innocent

voice. "Hmmm...Wait a minute... Oh yeah, *now* I remember. The one the fuckin' drug squad arrested me for," I say.

"*Yes. I'm sorry about that. They now know you weren't involved.*" He takes in a deep breath. "*We've got some new evidence.*" Now I'm all ears. Maybe they're onto the scam that was pulled on us. "*We think this is all down to Rogan. We've got a warrant for his arrest.*"

"You can't be serious. This is bullshit. What new evidence are you talking about?"

"*You know I can't discuss that with you, Nick.*"

"I told you, those drugs were planted on us. We even know the name of the person behind it."

"*I admire your loyalty to Cal but you have to face facts. He's screwed you on this.*"

"First, I can't face your so-called facts if you won't tell me what they are. And second..." I stop in mid-sentence. I don't have a second.

"*Alright,*" he says, "*I'll tell you. The drug squad has a picture of Rogan talking with a drug dealer about six months ago.*" He's talking about the time Rogan had his little relapse. "*We believe the drugs in that briefcase came from the same dealer. We estimate the street value of those drugs at around two hundred and fifty grand.*"

"The guys who planted the drugs on us scammed a client of ours for five million. They could afford it."

Silence with muffled talk again.

"*If what you say is right, why would they spend a quarter of a mil just to make you look bad?*"

Maybe he's got a point. The same question has always been in the back of my mind too. Why *would* they— Wait a minute. Maybe there's another explanation. "In the suitcase, there was a big Ziploc bag with a bunch of smaller bags inside, right?"

"Yeah." It's not much more than a grunt.

"What was in the small bags?"

"Heroin. Bad shit too. Cut with fentanyl and a whole bunch of stuff with long chemical names. This batch would have caused a lot of deaths if it had got onto the streets."

"How many bags, did you test?"

"I don't know. The lab probably randomly sampled two or three. They're pretty busy."

"Maybe not all the bags have drugs in them. Maybe just a few of the bags on the top."

"Come on Nick, you're just clutching at straws."

"Maybe I am, but if you arrest Rogan, his lawyer's going to ask you if you tested every bag." He goes silent. "Maybe you should have *all* the facts before you think about falsely arresting someone."

"Just tell Rogan to call me, OK."

He hangs up leaving me to worry.

As I think over the call, I realize I may have screwed up. What if all the baggies *do* actually contain drugs? If they test them now, it will remove a seed of doubt that our lawyer, Jim Garry, might have been able to use in court.

Maybe I should have kept my big mouth shut.

20. ADRY

I was never into pot. As I walk through the shop door, the smell gives me a flashback: as a kid, both my parents used to smoke it, and I remember just how much I hated that smell. But I've got to say the decor is amazing, all white and lime-green. It looks kind of healthy and hip at the same time. Now it's legal, I guess some of the money that was made when it was illegal has found its way into the legit economy. The guy behind the counter fits Roland's description, Caucasian, medium height and muscular, with one side of his head shaved and the hair on the other side kind of longish and greasy-looking. His name tag confirms his identity. If this is the guy who paid Roland to scam us, I'm guessing he's just a front. He doesn't look like he's got the brains to plan something like this. Roland said he just knows his first name, my job is to find out who he really is.

"Hi Lee," I say with my sexiest smile. "I'm Skye, I'm a friend of Roland's." Nick said it wouldn't be a good idea to tell him my real name. I just hope Roland does as we told him. Nick promised to keep his name out of our investigation if he cooperates.

"Oh, yeah, he said you'd be in," he says. He looks me up and down and his eyes settle on my boobs, encased in my sexiest bra; in this case, it's a good sign. After he's had his little stare, he smiles and says, "Roland and I go way back. How can I help you, Skye?"

"He told me you have some real good local bud."

"Sure do." He points at the display of pot under the glass counter. "That one on your right. It's excellent. World class."

"How much?" I ask.

He tells me and I can't keep the surprise out of my face; luckily I don't need to. It fits with the plan. I lean in towards him. "That's a bit out of my price range." I give him a smile. "As a friend of Roland's I don't suppose you could, I don't know..." I lean further in and bite my bottom lip for a second, "...find a reason to give me a discount."

He smiles and looks up and over my shoulder. I'm guessing he's checking a camera. He licks his lips nervously. "I can't give you an actual discount," he says. "But if you were to buy, like, half of what you need now, I could deliver the other half, free, this evening."

"It's a deal," I say. "Could you bring it to me at my apartment?"

"Absolutely," he says.

"You are so sweet," I say. I reach over and touch him on the arm. "We could maybe smoke a joint together." I get out my phone. "I live in the west end. Text me when you're ready to deliver and I'll text back the address." I give him the number of the burner phone that I picked up on my way here. "What's your number?" I ask. When he gives it I tap it into my phone and look up into his eyes. "...and what's your last name, Lee?"

He smiles. "Let's keep some mystery," he says in what he must think is a sexy voice. "First names only."

Damn! He's not as stupid as he looks. I knew it wasn't going to be that easy.

I give him a big smile. "I like that."

So it's all down to Plan B.

Roland better stick to the script we gave him if Lee calls him again.

———

I AM SO LUCKY TO HAVE JASON AS A BOYFRIEND. AS SOON AS I told him about the plan to check into Lee, he said we should use his apartment rather than mine. He doesn't want Lee to have my real address. Lee texted me twenty minutes ago and he should be here any minute now. We are standing in the underground garage waiting for him. Jason has an arm protectively around my shoulder. It feels nice. I tell him I love him and he gives me a kiss, which makes me all tingly. When this is over, I'm going to drag him back upstairs and—

My phone chirps. It's a text from Lee. *I'm here.*

I text Nick first and then text Lee back. *Drive down the ramp to the garage and I'll open the door for you.*

Jason and I move into the elevator lobby so we can't be seen through the garage door.

OK. I'm at the garage door, he texts.

On my way down, I reply.

I wait for Nick's text but it doesn't come. I look at Jason and he shrugs. "I don't know if I can do it without Nick," I say.

"Don't worry," he says. "We can do it."

God, I love this guy.

We wait.

My phone chirps again. There are two texts at the same time. Nick's is a thumbs-up emoji. Lee's is three question marks. I nod at Jason and he presses the fob to open the garage door. I walk out of the elevator lobby back onto the garage floor. As the door becomes fully open, Lee's Corvette purrs in. It's an older model and has a personalized plate, POT R US. I move into one of the visitor parking spots and wave him over. Nick's truck follows him in. Lee pulls into the parking spot and Nick brings his truck to a halt right behind him, blocking any chance of him making an exit. Lee doesn't notice and gets out of his car. He gives me a big smile. Out of the corner of my eye, I see Jason circle round so that he's about ten meters on the other side of the Corvette.

Lee swaggers over. He waves a brown paper bag. "Hey babe," he says. "Let's party."

I hear the purr of the electric motor on Nick's ramp. So does Lee. He turns. "What the f—"

"Here's the deal, Lee," I say. "You're going to give us some information and I'm going to let you leave unharmed and get on with your pathetic life."

He turns back to me as Nick rolls up beside me. He looks down at Nick and I can see the light dawn. "Roland gave me up, did he?" I don't know whether the sneer is for me, for Nick or for Roland. All three probably.

"Yes," Nick says, "and you're gonna give up the name of the person who gave you the order to screw us over."

"Not a chance." He says it quietly and there's a different tone in his voice. I'm not sure how to interpret it.

"It would be better for you if you co-operated, Lee," I say.

"I don't think so," he says. "You have no idea what you're dealing with bitch."

Jason has moved up behind him. "Don't talk to her like that," he says.

I have to hand it to Lee. He doesn't turn around. He may be more dangerous than I thought.

"We need a name," Nick says.

I see the subtle change in his posture as he balances on the balls of his feet. Before I can shout a warning, he spins and his foot comes up and jabs hard into Jason's chest, crashing him backwards into the side of the Corvette. It's a good kick but not black-belt level. I can handle this. As Lee's leg snaps down, his fist is heading for my face. Deflect, hold, twist, pull. Using his own momentum, I throw him to the concrete and follow him down. I'm rewarded with the thud of his head on the hard, grey surface and the ooof of breath as my shoulder slams into his chest. I put a lock on his hand, hard enough to be painful but with a lot in reserve. His eyes flicker open and I almost laugh at the surprise in them. I hear Nick's voice over my shoulder. "What did you say that was?" he says.

"Krav Maga," I say. "It's an Israeli martial art."

"Huh," he grunts. "Well done."

Lee starts to struggle and I increase the pressure. He yelps.

"Are you OK, sweetie?" I throw over my shoulder.

"I think I'll live," Jason replies.

Nick leans forward in his chair. "OK ass-wipe," he says. "Who's behind this?"

"Not a chance," he says again. And this time I recognize the tone. Fear.

I increase the pressure on his hand and he writhes underneath me. I increase it more.

"Arrrgh," he yells out in pain.

I look up at Nick, the obvious question on my face.

He nods and I bear down on Lee's hand.

"I can't tell you!" he screams.

"More," Nick says.

I increase the pressure.

"They'll kill me if I tell you," Lee shrieks.

"More."

I say, "I can't Nick. If I do, I'll start to break stuff."

Lee is whimpering and Nick is thinking. I hear his wheelchair move. "OK. Plan C," he says. "Come and give me a hand, Jason."

I relax the pressure just a little and Lee exhales.

For a few moments, I hear them rustling around and muttering behind me until Nick says, "Got it."

I look Lee in the eye. "OK," I say. "In a moment I am going to let you up. You are not going to try anything, because if you do, I will break at least one bone. You are going to go and sit in your car and after my partner has moved his truck, you are going to leave here and never come back. Understood?"

He nods.

Keeping the lock on his hand, I stand up and let him get to his feet.

"If I were you," Nick says, "I would forget this ever happened. If your bosses heard about it, it would reflect very badly on you."

I let go and he slinks over to his car, massaging his hand, and gets into the driver's seat.

Nick wheels over to the open passenger door. "I'm gonna move my truck so th—"

In a blur of motion, Lee leans over and snaps open the glove box. I feel my blood run cold. His hand darts inside and comes out holding... absolutely nothing.

I sigh, Nick chuckles and Jason laughs.

"Looking for this?" Nick says. He's holding up a wicked looking black handgun.

He hands it to Jason. "Keep an eye on him," he says.

Nick wheels over to his truck. I look over at Jason. He's holding the gun casually. He looks like he does this every day. I'm getting very turned on watching him. He glances at me and I see it in his face too. He smiles and his eyebrows flicker up. I can feel my body reacting.

Please God Nick won't want to come up to Jason's apartment to discuss Plan C.

Because I have a Plan A of my own, which I really want to put into action.

21. CAL

Sunday

I stand on the sidewalk in front of the Kwong Wah Hospital and watch the morning rain. It's the first time I've stepped outside. Inspector Ho came to interview me. He dismissed the idea that the assault on Tina is connected with my case. He blames the protestors she has been dealing with. "They are very bad people, Mr. Rogan. In the west, you think they are some kind of freedom fighters but they're not. They're criminals."

I'd like to believe him but I'm sure he's just toeing the Beijing party line.

Tina's life is hanging by a thread because of me. I think of all the people who have been put in danger because of me. It reminds me of Ellie. I haven't called her in a few days. Toronto is twelve hours time difference. She'll probably be getting ready for bed and I don't want to speak to Sam right now. I must remember to call Ellie tonight.

I should— My phone rings. "Hey Nick, I was just going to call you," I say.

I update him on Tina and he gives me the news on 'Connor McCoy.' His enthusiasm would normally be infectious but right now my enthusiasm antibodies are in full force.

After I hang up from Nick, I call Phil Jiang.

"Hi Cal. I spent last night at IF. The guy in the photo didn't show up. But I showed a couple of people the picture and they said he's usually there on a Sunday night so I'll go there again tonight and see if he shows." I tell him about last night and what happened to Tina. He says, *"That's bad Cal. But Inspector Ho's wrong. The protestors would never do that. Foreign reporters are their best friends. Those in the police who are pro-Beijing have a very biased view of them. Someone's trying to send you a message."*

"Maybe it's a message I should listen to. No case is worth the life of someone you love."

He's silent for a moment. Then says, *"I can't advise you about that. You must do what you have to."* There is another pause, *"If you do decide to drop the case and go back to Vancouver, I promise you I'll do my best to follow up on it from over here."*

I feel a rush of relief. It makes the decision for me. I need to stay with Tina and get her through this. I'm going to drop the case. I'll call Nick tomorrow morning Vancouver time and tell him to talk to Janusz Gutkowski.

I say my thanks and goodbyes to Phil and go back into the hospital.

———

A HAND GENTLY SHAKES MY SHOULDER AND I SNAP OUT OF A bizarre dream, which was starting to coalesce in my brain. "Mr. Rogan?" It's one of Tina's nurses.

"How is she?" I ask. Thank God it's not a doctor. It's the doctors who bring the worst news.

"She's stable but she won't regain consciousness for a day or two."

"But she will get better?" I can hear the pleading in my voice.

"Probably, but it's too early to know."

I take a couple of deep breaths to steady myself. The second one turns into a yawn.

"There's nothing you can do here," she says. "Why don't you go back to your hotel and sleep for a few hours. The night nurse said you didn't sleep at all last night. I promise we'll call you if anything happens."

I suppress a second yawn. "OK." I stand up and stretch. "Thank you." She smiles and nods.

I make my way along the corridors and through the doors to the outside.

It's still raining.

There are taxis but I feel a strong need to walk. The rain isn't too heavy and it actually feels good falling on my head and face. A walk back to the hotel will help me sleep. I walk a couple of blocks to Nathan Road, cross the street and turn left in the direction of the harbour. The street is packed with Saturday afternoon shoppers. After a couple of blocks, I come to the street on which the Golden Dragon is situated. A morbid fascination grips me and I cross over and walk half a block down. I arrive at the place where we tried to take the taxi and it's still marked by the stain of Tina's blood, not yet obliterated by the rain.

As if in response to my thought, the rain increases. If I'm going to walk back to the hotel, I should pick up an umbrella. I check my watch. Two PM. The Temple Street night market just opened, I can pick one up there. I retrace the route we took last night, go past the Golden Dragon, which seems to be closed, and come out at the north end of Temple. There is an ornate archway over the entrance to the street, which reminds me of the one in Vancouver's Chinatown. I didn't notice it last night.

As I enter the market, I look down between the stalls, and in the rain it makes me think of a scene from Bladerunner. I pass the stall selling luggage but the stall selling watches is not there. There is just a gap between the luggage stall and the next stall along. I feel a tug of annoyance. In the back of my mind I was hoping he would be here and that I could persuade him to talk to me about the picture of Zelena and the man in the hat. I remember his fear. I wonder if his absence today has anything to do with my conversation with him.

With the stall missing, I can see the sidewalk. Behind where the stall should be, there is a shop selling more luggage and a concrete doorway with writing above it and the number one-oh-five, which I assume is part of the address. There is a bare concrete stairway leading up, with electrical cables hanging down in loops. At the top of the stairs, all I can see is a filthy wall, which was once baby-blue. There's something forbidding about it and I wonder if people actually live up there.

Shaking off the unpleasant feeling it evokes, I turn back to the stall selling luggage.

Immediately the stallholder is at my side. "What type suitcase you like?" she says.

I give her my best smile. "I'm looking for the man who sells watches," I say. I show her the watch on my wrist. "I bought this one from him and I want to buy another one."

"Not here," she says.

I don't comment on the obviousness of her answer but say, "Do you know when he'll be back?"

She waves a hand in the general direction of the other vendors further down the street. "Lots people sell watches," she says dismissively. "You buy suitcase?"

"No thanks."

She hustles off towards another potential buyer and I continue down the market. There are indeed other vendors selling watches, but none of them are the man who was terrified by Zelena's picture.

———

AGAIN I AWAKE WITH A START. I'M SWEATING AND MY HEART IS hammering. I try to muster the dissipating tendrils of the dream. I remember something about finding a box and being terrified. I try to remember why but the details evade my grasp, leaving me with a strong sense of unease. I am in complete darkness. I fumble for my phone on the bedside table. It's almost ten PM. I've slept for six hours. Too long. I need to get to the hospital.

After the quickest shower ever, I'm dressed in clean clothes and sitting in the back seat of a taxi. Having slept on it, I've had a change of heart about the case. If Tina was attacked because of my investigation into Zelena, there are two options: one, I back off and, when she's better, take her home to Vancouver; or two, I find the slime-balls who did this to her. I know it's reckless, but I'm all over option two. Tina's safely in the hospital and I'm going to do what I do best.

Time to check in with Phil Jiang. I pull out my phone. It rings and rings and just as I'm about to hang up, *"Hi Cal."*

"Hey Phil." Something's not right. His voice is little more

than a whisper and there's not much background noise. "I thought you were staking out IF for the guy in the hat."

"I was. He came in, had one drink and then left. I'm following him."

I can feel my heartbeat ramp up.

"Any idea where he's going?"

"No but he's heading into a more residential area."

I can feel the thrill now. "He's leading you to Zelena," I say.

"I hope so. He's..." He stops speaking, I hear traffic noise in the background, then, *"Gotta go. I'll call you back."*

He hangs up. Damn.

I'm on tenterhooks all the way to the hospital then, just as I'm getting out of the cab, he calls.

"Wait a moment," I say to the driver as I tap Accept. "Where did he go Phil?" I ask.

"I lost him."

My hopes evaporate in one big explosion of air from my lungs. I wave the taxi off. "What happened?"

"Because it was a residential area, there weren't a lot of people on the streets, so I was keeping about thirty or so metres behind him. He turned a corner and when I got there he was gone, like he'd just disappeared. Then I noticed there was a white Cadillac SUV disappearing down the street."

"Did you get the plate?"

"No. It was too far away. But I'm pretty sure it was the same one I saw parked outside IF when I left."

I think it over for a second. "He made you. Someone in the club tipped him off that you'd been looking for him."

"Yes. It was my error. Last night, I should have paid the bar staff to keep quiet. I'm sorry Cal."

"No prob." *Big* prob, but I don't have the heart to say it. "OK," I say. "I'll check in with you tomorrow."

I walk into the hospital and make my way to intensive care.

My phone burbles. I snatch it out of my pocket but it's not Phil. It's FaceTime. A big smile spreads over my face. I press Accept and after a hesitation, a grin, matching mine, appears on the screen.

"Hi Dad."

"Hi sweetie. How are you doing?"

"Great! Mom says it's twelve hours time difference but I knew you'd be up." She keeps moving and the background keeps changing. Sam appears over her shoulder. *"Hi Cal."* She smiles and waves then disappears as Ellie dances around.

"Hi Sam," I say through the emotional turmoil stirred up by seeing her. I don't know if she hears me.

"Only five more sleeps until I see you." A wispy cloud crosses El's face. *"You will be back from Hong Kong by then, won't you?"*

"Absolutely," I say with a confidence I don't feel.

She frowns. *"Where are you Dad?"*

"I'm in a hospital."

"OMG are you OK?" It comes out as one word.

"Yes, I'm fine. But Tina's been hurt."

"What happened to her?"

All the memories rush to the fore. People close to me who have been hurt because of what I do: Roy beaten to death, Nick in a wheelchair, Sam and Ellie traumatized by a drug dealer. And now Tina. I can't subject Ellie or Sam to the truth. Or am I just being a moral coward. Either way I say, "She had an accident... on the street."

Fortunately, she doesn't press me for details. *"Is she OK?"*

Sam's concerned face reappears over Ellie's shoulder. She *does* press me for the details. *"What happened?"* she asks.

I chicken out. "I can't go into it right now, I'm about to go into the ICU. I'll call you guys back tomorrow."

"Say 'hi' to Tina for me Dad and give her my love." She makes kissing noises. *"I love you."*

Sam smiles and blows a kiss.

"Love you too sweetie." We do the three... two... one... thing and hang up.

I push open the doors and walk into the reception area of the ICU.

———

I WANT SO MUCH TO TAKE OFF THE SURGICAL GLOVE AND HOLD her hand, skin-to-skin. She is lying silent in the bed, breathing unevenly. Although the nurses keep telling me she's not out of the woods yet, I take it as a positive sign that they are letting me sit here. Or are they just being kind and giving me my final moments with her?

All the emotions I've been bottling up—the frustration of the case, the hatchet job someone's working on us, my conversation with Sam and, worst of all, what I've let happen to Tina—burst through the dam and I find myself sobbing uncontrollably. I just give myself over to it and let the sobs rack my body until I am left drained. I take in a final breath and let it out in an uneven sigh.

I haven't cried like that since I was in another hospital crying over the body of my father.

With the mask and visor they are making me wear, I can't even reach up and wipe away the tears.

"I don't know if you can hear me," I say to her, "but I am so, so sorry I let this happen to you. I just want to say I—"

My words are cut off by the entrance of a doctor with one of the nurses. "Hello Mr. Rogan," he says.

"How is she doctor?"

He smiles gently, "It's difficult to say. If she gets through the night, maybe she'll be OK."

My jaw clamps down and I have difficulty swallowing.

"You'll have to leave now," the nurse says. "Why don't you come back in a couple of hours and we'll let you sit with her again."

I get up and leave her room, divest myself of the mask, gown and visor and walk out through the doors of the ICU.

Like the time I cried over my dead father, the sorrow turns to a rage. But this time it's controlled and silent. I am going to find whoever did this to her and make them pay. I have two hours. I check my watch. Ten-thirty. When Tina was attacked, we had just come from the Golden Dragon. Maybe the bouncer there saw someone follow us out.

The walk to the nightclub takes less than ten minutes. As I walk in, I scan the room. The bouncer is on the same seat as last night. Except that it's not the same bouncer. This one is younger. Last night's guardian of the peace is not in evidence. However last night's barmaid *is* in evidence. She's standing at the left hand end of the bar taking an order from a woman who looks like she's too young to be in here. I walk over to the bar and sit down. The barmaid turns towards me with a big smile but as she sees my face that smile goes slip sliding away. She cuts a glance to the right-hand end of the bar and I follow her gaze. There is a man standing behind the bar. He is dressed in an immaculate suit, which he wears like a model. It must be Leo, Harvey Lim's friend and one of the owners. His black hair is slicked back and his face looks vaguely familiar. As if sensing the combined gazes of his server and myself, he turns toward us. His eyes lock with mine.

Recognition dawns simultaneously on both of us.

The shape of his jaw is the giveaway. It's the man in the

hat. After evading Phil Jiang, he must have come straight here.

I get off my seat and walk along the bar towards him, my mind teeming with questions.

He holds my gaze for a moment, indecision written on his face, but when I'm only a couple of paces away, he turns and vanishes through a door at the back of the bar. I am *not* going to let him get away. I scan the bar looking for the opening the servers use to move between the bar and the customers. There isn't one. The bar is too high for me to vault over but maybe I can climb it. Then I see what I need: beyond the left-hand end of the bar, a server bearing a tray of food and exotic looking cocktails is pushing his way through a swinging door. I can use the door to get into the area behind the bar. I break into a run and just as I get to the door, it starts to swing open again. I grab the handle and come face-to-face with the bouncer who was on duty last night. He looks me straight in the eye. "Staff only," he says quietly.

He's not as big as the bouncer at IF but something tells me he's a lot more dangerous. But right now I don't give a damn. Speed and surprise will win the day. Trying to look as if he has intimidated me, I take a half step back and raise my hands in subjugation. I see him relax his stance. Error. Go for the eyes.

I swivel left, as if about to turn away, and make a fist with my still upraised left hand. I'll only have one shot here. With every ounce of strength, I propel my fist forward.

But it doesn't move.

Newton's third law takes over. I stagger and almost fall over backwards.

My wrist is in the considerable grip of the other bouncer.

A plan B comes to mind. All is not yet lost. "OK, OK," I say. "I know the drill. I'll leave." If I can get out of here quickly enough...

Last night's bouncer reaches forward and takes a more-than-firm grip on my right elbow. "Please come with us," he says. They may not be the Borg, but I know resistance is futile. They lead me through the swinging door into the nightclub's kitchen and take me into a corner where the activity is the least frenetic. The kitchen staff ignore us.

Nothing happens.

We just stand there.

Maybe we're waiting for the man behind the bar—whom I assume to be Leo, the owner and friend of Harvey, Zelena's boyfriend—to come and confront me.

We wait.

Last night's bouncer checks his watch.

I start to feel an unpleasant sensation writhe in my gut.

We wait.

This cannot be good.

I look around the kitchen. One of the staff walks over with a net in his hand; it's holding a fish, twitching vigorously. Deftly, he takes a grip on the fish, pulls it out of the net and slaps it down on a wooden slab right in front of us. With one fluid motion, he pulls a cleaver from an array above his head, decapitates the fish and returns the cleaver to its place. A small knife appears in his hand and within the span of a few seconds, the fish is gutted, filleted and cut into bite sized cubes. He takes a bowl and scoops the pieces into it.

As he turns away, last night's bouncer says something to him. He shrugs, takes down the cleaver and hands it over.

The unpleasant sensation becomes a whirlwind.

I try to pull away from them but it's mission impossible.

I wait for him to make his move.

But he doesn't.

We just wait and I think about the body of the detective, Mr. Wang, with knives through the backs of his hands.

A door in the far-left corner of the kitchen opens.

A man walks in.

It's Leo.

Before the door slams closed behind him, I can see into a small courtyard area with a dumpster. It's a possible escape route. He walks over to us and the bouncer hands over the cleaver.

My captors switch their grips and each of my arms is held by two hands. They pull me over to the food prepara-tion area and against every ounce of resistance I can muster, my right hand is held down on the wooden cutting block.

"Show fingers or I take hand off."

I do as he tells me.

He looks long and hard into my face. Without breaking his gaze, he takes a phone from his pocket. He holds it up to his face, then turns it in my direction.

There is a picture on the screen.

It's a bed in a white room. A hospital bed.

His thumb swipes across the screen. The second picture is a close up. It's Tina.

My gut feels like it's going to explode.

"When you leave here," he says, "go to hospital. Look after friend. When she's better, go home. Vancouver. OK?"

There are a thousand things I want to scream at him but I just say, "Yes."

He puts away the phone and looks down at my hand.

"Please, no." The words make me feel like a complete coward but I can't keep them inside. "Please."

He sneers at me, raises the cleaver... I can see little

smears of fish blood on its razor-sharp edge...he smiles...

From behind me a hand covers my mouth. I try to shout "NOOOOO!" but it comes out as little more than a muffled groan.

The cleaver comes down and I feel an unbearable stab of pain permeating my hand, then my arm, until it takes over the right side of my body. I scream into the hand clamped over my mouth.

In horror, I look down.

There's no blood.

All my fingers are intact.

But the pain is excruciating.

Then I see the cleaver. Leo must have reversed the blade and brought down the back edge across my fingers. My relief at not being dismembered is balanced by the pain of broken bones.

He puts the cleaver back, nods at my captors and pushes through the door into the club.

Within seconds, I am outside, standing beside the dumpster, cradling my injured hand. The door slams behind me.

With my good hand, I hang on to the rim of the dumpster for a moment, trying to steady myself. Although the May air is warm, I feel the chill of evaporating sweat, which is covering every square centimetre of my body.

Although I've paid a price, I have learned something: Leo, the owner of the Golden Dragon, is the man in the hat, Zelena's 'new guy' in her first Instagram post after disappearing.

It answers one question but spawns a hundred others.

Questions someone else will have to answer.

On wobbly legs, I head down the alley and on towards the hospital.

22. ZELENA

There were only two clients tonight. In the third round, no one bid for me. I don't know whether to be relieved or worried. Relieved that I didn't have to live out yet another man's rape fantasy and worried that if they stop bidding for me, I will become of no value to them. Then, what will they do to me?

The soup is hot and delicious. I'm trying to live in the moment and just enjoy the meal. That lasts about two seconds. Leo stamps into the kitchen, slamming the door behind him. It's never good when he does that. He marches over and sits beside me.

He hands me my phone. "Do it," he says.

I open it and look for text messages but there are none. In my old life there would have been so many. I can feel tears pricking my eyes. I mustn't cry. I don't want to show them. I go to Instagram. There are lots of comments and likes on my last post. I comment back to some of them. He is watching me like an evil old crow. I cannot believe I ever thought he was cute. I go to the Matt Standing account. I try to keep my face straight. His first post is an album cover: 'On Our Way'. I feel my heart skip. If there's only even the smallest chance someone's on their way, I'll be able to hang on. The second post says, 'I just played this with my kid brother. He's great at solving puzzles.' The picture is the cover of a game or a book. It's an underwater illustration with what look like long intertwined strands of spaghetti. But it's the title that matters: 'Can You Help Us Find The Way?' My mind is revving hard. I comment, 'Looks cool, I'm going to try that.'

"Post new pictures," he says.

With a newly-spurred confidence, I say, "If I don't interact with my friends, they'll know something's wrong."

He grunts.

I post a couple of the pictures we took the last time we went out, all the time trying to think of something to post that will help them find me, whoever they are. Nothing comes. I've been shuffled out of the building into the van and back again but then we've driven somewhere to take the pictures for my posts. While I try to come up with something, I comment on various posts.

He snatches the phone away from me. "Enough for today," he says.

He stands up and puts the phone in his pocket. "Tomorrow special, we take you to see special client."

This is a complete break with the routine. The clients always come here and bid for the girls. The way he says it gives me a very bad feeling. "I don't want to," I say.

He looks at me and smiles. "You do it or we hurt your brother again."

I can't trust myself to answer.

I just nod.

At least I'll be going out. Then I remember the first day they took me out to take photos. It was near here. And I remember when they brought me back. I just need to find a way to tell them on Instagram.

23. NICK

Adry bursts into the office. "Did you see the email from Cal?" she says. I did but I'm not sure what to make of it. "You don't think we should drop the case do you Nick?" It's the question that's been bugging me for the last fifteen minutes.

"What do *you* think?" I ask her.

I can see from her face that she's not made up her mind. "I understand why Cal wants to drop it: he and Tina are both in danger if he stays on it. But I keep thinking of poor Zelena. She's being held captive somewhere and we're starting to get close to maybe finding out where she's being held."

"I know." I kick it over in my mind. "Zelena's a bright girl. You saw her last post right? She said, 'Looks cool. I'm going to try that.' She's gonna find a way to let us know where she is, but we need Rogan on the ground over there to follow up. She might give us a clue we can't understand because we're not there."

"Exactly." She sits deep in thought. I let her think it over. She's bright. In lots of ways brighter than me and Rogan.

"What about we work with the Hong Kong detective Cal's been working with, Phil Jiang. Cal says he's a good guy."

"Good idea." I check my watch. "It's one in the morning over there, I'm not gonna call him right now but I'll email him for Phil Jiang's contact details."

I fire off the email to Rogan and say, "Good work last night Adry."

She smiles. "Just doing my job," she says.

"And doing it well."

"What did you do with his gun, Nick?"

"On my way home, I handed it in at the Cambie police station. They're gonna run it through ballistics and prints and see if there's anything that could come back and bite Lee on his scrawny ass."

"That would be great," she laughs.

"Do you want to hear the good news?" I ask.

"Do I ever."

"After Jason and I searched Lee's car last night, we got his name and address from the car's registration papers— his name's Lawrence Charles Linsky by the way—so I just did a search for him. We were right, he's got a record. He's got three or four small summary convictions for fraud but he also got done for major fraud. He was running a con-game selling phony securities to rich seniors. That's an indictable offence but he was lucky, he got away with it. I guess he had a good lawyer." I stop speaking.

Adry looks at me and sees the smile on my face. "Who?" she says.

I just grin at her.

Then I see it on her face before she speaks. "Big... Bob... Pridmore."

"Bingo."

"We were right the first time," she says. "The slime ball

who was blackmailing Marly Summers a year ago *is* behind this scam."

I just nod. But something is still not right. "Do you remember how scared Lee was last night? He said he wouldn't tell us anything because 'They'll kill me if I tell you.' It can't only be Bob Pridmore behind this. I think Pridmore is just the front man."

"Who do you think it might be?" she asks.

I think it over. "You know," I say, "it's always bothered me that Bob was prepared to fork over a quarter of a million bucks for drugs to plant on us. What if the people behind him have easy access to drugs?"

"Some drug gang?"

"Not just any drug gang, one that has it in for Rogan and me."

"There must be a few of those," she says with a grin.

"Yeah, but there's one in particular." I tell her about the murder of Rogan's best buddy five years ago and about the drug gang we, or should I say he, uncovered as part of the investigation. "The guy running the gang has been in Millhaven for the last four years. If anyone has a grudge against Rogan it's him."

"Yeah, but does he have a connection with Pridmore?" Adry asks.

"Big Bob has defended a lot of bad guys in his time. Maybe we should do some digging into court records and see what we can find."

"Sounds good but right now, all we've got to go on is Pridmore."

"You're right."

"So how do we stop him?"

"That's what we've gotta work out. Then we have to

follow up on the other thing in Rogan's email. I made the appointment already."

"Right. Looks like another Sunday shot to hell," she sighs.

"No. We'll work out what to do about the Pridmore deal on the way over. Then we can call it quits for the day. We all need a break."

———

"Why did you lie to my colleague, Cal Rogan?" Adry says it gently, no accusation in her voice.

"What about?" She looks confused but I'm betting she's faking it.

Adry turns her phone around. "You said you didn't recognize the man in this picture. The man with Zelena. The man in the hat."

Stephanie White has the good grace to blush. "I'm sorry," she says.

"So why *did* you lie Steph?" Adry repeats it, still gently, still good cop. But I can feel the bad cop in me.

"Leo's a good guy. There's no way he could be involved with Zel."

"But that's no reason to lie to Cal in the first place."

She bites her bottom lip. "Harvey told me not to tell."

Jeez. What is the matter with this girl?

Adry keeps her quiet tone. "Do you know why?"

"When we saw that first Instagram from Zel, Harvey said if she was with Leo, she must be OK. He said she obviously didn't want her parents to find her. So he said not to say anything to Mr. Rogan."

My bad cop bursts out. "Listen, Stephanie. Your friend

Zelena is being held captive somewhere in Hong Kong and your precious Leo has something to do with it."

"How can you say that? She keeps posting on Instagram. She sends me texts. She's fine."

"No she's not!" I bark at her. I get some odd looks. I guess people don't raise their voices in Caffè Artigiano in Kerrisdale. I take a breath. I just broke one of my own rules. Don't let a witness know what you know. Anyway, too late for that. "Stephanie," I say, barely able to hold back the anger. "Rogan is in Hong Kong trying to find Zelena. Already, his girlfriend's been stabbed and he's been attacked and injured by Leo. Zelena is in a lot of danger and if there's anything you know, you have to be honest with us. We have to find Zelena and her brother."

"Is there anything else you can tell us Steph?" Adry asks, still in good cop mode.

"Are you sure about all this?" she asks.

Adry and I both nod.

"I can't believe Leo could be involved in something like that. He seems like such a good guy. Poor Harvey, he'll be devastated to know. Leo was his best friend growing up." She thinks for a while. "I can't think of anything that might help you."

"There is one thing," Adry says. "Can you send me copies of all the texts you've got from Zel."

She nods, hunches over her phone and taps away. While she does it, I start to worry at another bit of the puzzle. Something I'll have to talk over with Rogan.

24. CAL

Monday

The voice comes at me from the end of a long, long tunnel. "Cal?" It sounds like Tina. A dream, I guess. I feel a hand on my head. "Cal, wake up." My head snaps up and a stab of pain shoots through my hand. Her eyes are open, smiling into mine. I grab her hand in my uninjured one and kiss it... several times.

"Thank God you're OK." I blink my eyes, fighting for control.

"What happened?"

I stand and lean over her so I can kiss her forehead. I want to hug her but don't know if I can. I sit back down. "You were stabbed."

She frowns and looks around the room. "Stabbed?" Her eyes come back to mine. "Why would anyone want to stab *me*?"

What will my next words do to us? "No one wanted to stab you," I say. "They were trying to stab me but got you by mistake."

She takes this all in and looks down at our hands, still clasped together on the bed. She doesn't speak. I look away. Through the window, I can see the grey light of dawn. A new day. What will come and what will pass away in the next twenty-four hours?

We sit in silence.

Finally, "Cal?" There is a sadness in her voice and in her eyes. "I don't—"

The door opens. "Oh my God!" I recognize her mother's voice. It sounds just like when Tina imitates her, rich with the wonderful tones of India. "How did this happen?"

I stand and move away from the bed, letting go of Tina's hand so her mother can bustle her considerable bulk closer. She pauses only to throw me a glare. It brings me face-to-face with her father. His face stoic, he just nods, "Cal."

"I'm sorry," I tell him. "This is probably my fault."

He nods again and moves to his daughter's side, leaving me standing apart feeling like an intruder into their family grief.

A nurse and a doctor have followed the Johal's into the room and take up their positions on the other side of the bed. I look back towards the bed. All I can see of Tina is the outline of her legs and feet under the blankets. I turn and leave.

———

STAMMO'S EMAIL IS KIND OF A ' GOOD NEWS/BAD NEWS' deal: we know Big Bob Pridmore, and maybe even George Walsh, is behind the scam being pulled on us, but how are we going to prove it to the satisfaction of the VPD when all our evidence is circumstantial? Steph White has confirmed that the man in the hat is, in fact, Leo but she concealed this when I spoke to her. So what other lies or omissions might she have dealt us?

With Leo complicit in Zelena's kidnapping, does Harvey —his childhood friend and her boyfriend—have something to do with it too? Does he procure young girls for Leo to enslave? A part of me wants to call him at the Kerry and go have breakfast with him but it's all moot. I can't put Tina in any more danger. The unrelenting throbbing in my hand reminds me I've been warned off. I'll just pass the info on to Phil Jiang.

I check my watch: six-thirty; probably too early to call him.

I look around me. I've wandered away from the hospital and onto Nathan Road, near the road leading to the Golden Dragon. Like a homing beacon, the throbbing in my hand intensifies. I step up my pace and pass the intersection. The further I move away from the Golden Dragon, the better I feel. I pull out my phone and email Nick, telling him to contact Janusz Gutkowski on Monday morning Vancouver time and resign us from the case. Zelena's father can pay Phil Jiang to pursue it for him.

I'll just take a walk for an hour or so then go back to the hospital to be with Tina and her parents—if they'll have anything to do with me. I brush away this disturbing thought, straighten my back and quicken my pace.

Getting Tina better is my priority.

———

I WALK INTO THE ICU RECEPTION AREA AND NOD TO THE NICE woman at the nursing station as I head towards Tina's room. "Mr. Rogan," she calls me back. "Did Ms. Johal forget something?"

"Sorry?"

"Did Ms. Johal forget something?" she repeats.

I shrug. "I don't know. I'll ask her."

She reads the confusion on my face and matches it with a confusion of her own. "Didn't you know?" she asks.

"Know what?"

"Her parents moved her. Against her doctor's advice they discharged her and took her away in a private ambulance."

"When?" I ask, my voice in a higher register.

"About an hour ago. That's why I thought you'd come back to—"

"Which hospital did they take her to?" I interrupt.

"They didn't take her to another hospital, they took her to the airport. They're flying her back to Canada."

I pull my phone out of my pocket and call Tina's number. No reply. I scroll through my contacts. About a month ago, we swapped emergency-contact phone numbers with each other. It was romantic at the time, another little step forward in our relationship. I call her father, then her mother. No replies. By accident or design?

I run down the hallway knowing there'll be a red taxi waiting just outside the hospital doors.

———

I KNOCK ON THE DOOR WITH THE LIST OF COMPANY NAMES meticulously printed on the pebbled glass. The door opens. "Cal?" he says.

"Hi Phil."

He ushers me into the office and settles me on the sofa. His partner, the taciturn Mr. Lee, is not there. "How's Tina?" he asks.

"Her parents have taken her back to Canada. I went to

the airport to try and find out which airline they were taking her on but no one would tell me anything. I wasted a good part of the morning there."

He walks over to a small fridge. "Maybe that's better, she'll be safer in Vancouver." He takes out two bottles of water and hands me one. His eyes widen. "What happened to your hand?" he asks.

I tell him about my visit to the Golden Dragon.

"So the man in the hat, who's holding Zelena as a prisoner somewhere in Stanley, is an owner of the Golden Dragon and is the best friend of Zelena's boyfriend?"

I just nod.

"Do you think the boyfriend is implicated in her kidnapping?"

"I don't know. I've met him a couple of times and he seems like a straight-up guy. I don't want to believe I read him so wrongly but maybe I have. On the way back from the airport, I called him and arranged to meet him at the Kerry this evening. I need to get another read on him."

"So you're planning to stay on the case?" he asks.

"To tell the truth Phil, I don't know. A big part of me wants to go back to Vancouver and be with Tina, but I've never let a client down before. I emailed my partner to tell Mr. Gutkowski we're resigning from the case but it just doesn't sit well with me."

"What about your hand?" he asks. "Next time it may be worse."

He's right but he's just triggered my contrarian gene. I've had bad guys gunning for me before and it never stopped me. And I think of Zelena, hanging on to the hope that someone's coming to rescue her. Tina's on a plane on her way back to the safety of Vancouver. Phil is a great guy and I'm pretty sure he's a good detective but...

I take in a big breath.

"I'm not going to let Leo or his gang tell me what to do. I'm seeing this thing through."

Phil eyes me for a long moment then a big smile breaks over his face. "Good." He extends his hand. "*We're* seeing this thing through." I reach out my hand to shake and then think better of it. I grab his hand with my left one.

"Done," I grin.

"What's the next step?" he asks.

"While I was sitting in the hospital with Tina, I wondered about bringing Inspector Ho up to date. But I don't have any evidence of where Zelena's being held. All I have is the photo with her and Leo and the story of what happened at the Golden Dragon. What's he going to do with that?"

"You're right. We need something more solid. What about the boyfriend? When are you meeting him?"

"I said I'd meet him at five in the bar at the hotel."

Phil mulls it over for a while. "Why don't you get him to meet you in your room. I'll come with you and, if we have to, we can apply some real pressure on him. Break him if we need to. If he's involved in this, maybe we can get him to tell us where she's being held." I nod. "Meanwhile, I'll do some research on the Golden Dragon and on Leo. See what I can come up with."

"Sounds like a plan."

He checks his watch. It looks like a Rolex but then again we're in Hong Kong, the home of knock-off designer watches. "I have a lunch appointment with another client." He looks a bit grim. "And I don't have any good news for them. While I'm gone, you're welcome to stay here if you want."

"Thanks for the offer but I haven't had much sleep over

the last few days. I think I'll head back to the Kerry and take a nap."

As I leave Phil's office, I take Harvey Lim's business card out of my wallet. As I look at his cell number, I get the feeling I'm missing something important. Maybe it will become evident when we speak to him this evening.

————

HE TAKES IN THE ROOM AS HE ENTERS. IT'S PROBABLY A LOT smaller than his room and I'll bet his room has a view of the harbour too. He doesn't seem fazed that Phil Jiang is here. I make the introductions. They sit on the guest chairs and I perch on the corner of the bed, feeling the height disadvantage.

"Harvey," I start, "how well do you know Leo?"

Not the question he was expecting.

"Leo? Really well. He and I were friends growing up. Since my family moved to Vancouver, we've seen less of each other but I always see him when I come over for a visit. Why?"

"We believe he's somehow involved in Zelena's kidnapping."

"Kidnapping?! What are you talking about?" he almost shouts.

"We think she's being held against her will."

"Why would you think *that*?"

I don't want to tell him about how we are able to communicate with Zelena in case he's in on the kidnapping. Which reminds me I haven't even told Phil. I must remember to let him know the details.

"I can't go into that right now. I just need you to tell us what you know about Leo."

"You really think he's involved?" he asks.

Phil speaks for the first time. "When you saw the picture of Zelena with Leo why didn't you tell Cal who he was?"

He looks from Phil to me and back again. "I was embarrassed. Leo's a good friend but he can't keep his hands off beautiful women. I was embarrassed he'd taken Zelena away from me." He turns to me. "I didn't want you to think I was…"

He seems sincere but then again he seemed sincere the last time I talked to him and he lied about not knowing who the man in the hat was. "When we sat in the bar downstairs on Friday evening, you told me you thought someone might have been following you and Zelena on the ferry over to Hong Kong Island. You said it might be the man in the hat. Was that all bullshit too?"

"Not a hundred percent. I think there was someone following us but it wasn't Leo."

"And you've no idea who it was?"

He just shakes his head.

"Was Leo ever involved in anything criminal?" Phil asks.

"No, not directly."

"What does that mean?" I ask.

"When Leo started the Golden Dragon, he needed investors. He tried everything to get people he knew to invest in it. I asked my parents but they refused. No one was interested. Anyway, Leo knew some people who ran other nightclubs, people who were not entirely legit. They agreed to invest. Leo won't talk to me about them, but I have the feeling they're involved in triads."

"Would the IF nightclub be one of the clubs these people run?" Phil asks.

"Yes. How did you know?"

Phil and I exchange looks. This explains why Leo was at the IF last night.

"So you think Leo might just be doing what his investors tell him to do?" I ask.

"It would make sense. Leo's not a criminal. He would never hurt Zelena himself."

I look at Phil again. He gives the slightest of nods.

I look Harvey in the eye. "You are going to have to take us at our word that Zelena is being held against her will. That said, will you help us find her?"

"Of course, I'll do anything I can."

"We need you to set up a meeting with Leo," I say and he agrees without hesitation.

25. ZELENA

Today was the worst yet. They hustled me out into the van and took me somewhere for more photos. Then they took me to the client's house. It was a lovely house but he was horrible. He slapped me and punched me and spat in my face. When he raped me I got a shooting pain, which hasn't completely gone away. But when they brought me back here, I remembered to look up and I saw the number. When we got back, the old woman in the kitchen said, in her broken English, that the girls always get a day off after a visit to that client. They put me in a better room too. It's not cold like the other one and it has decent sheets on the bed.

For once I want Leo to show up. I worked out how to communicate where I am. I remember the first time they took me out for the photographs. They took one with Leo. That was the only time they took the pictures near here. Right afterwards, they hustled me inside. I think I can tell them without *him* knowing what I'm doing. If I can pull this off, Zander and I could be out of this place before I have to see another client.

The door bursts open. Is he reading my thoughts?

He hands me my phone. I open Instagram and comment on a couple of posts. I search for Matt Standing and go to his post with the picture of the album cover 'On Our Way'. I comment, 'Great group. Loved their first hit Behind the Watchman.' I'm betting my captors don't follow Swedish Rock Groups that closely. Now to clinch it. I go to Steph's texts.

"Enough," he says. "Post pictures now."

My mind revs. Can I put my second message into an Instagram post without it looking obvious? I choose the first picture. It's of me in front of a restaurant. I put it in a post and start typing. 'Reminds me of the restaurant we went to for my fifteenth birthday. We were 7 15 year-olds.' I hesitate. How do I add the last word without it being obvious to him?

Too late. He snatches the phone away from me and taps 'Share.'

"Enough for tonight," he grunts. "You sleep now."

I have to work out a way to tell them I'm on Temple Street, then they'll have everything.

26. NICK

I'm not too sure we're doing the right thing here, baiting the bear in his cage. But the cop in me wants to look him in the eye. As I wheel out of the elevator and into the reception area, I see that everything has changed since the last time I was here a year ago. Everything except the receptionist. She is what my mother would have called brassy. Dyed blonde hair with half an inch of black roots showing, over-made-up and dressed more 'Hastings and Main' than downtown lawyer's office. The name plate on the reception desk says her name is Doris Blake. It only takes a second for her to recognize me. The wheelchair gives it away. She looks from me to Adry and back.

She greets us with, "What do *you* want?"

"I want to speak to your boss."

A sly smile creeps across her bright red lips. "And which boss would that be?"

"Pridmore," I say.

"Look around you." I just stare at her. "Go on," she says. "Just take a look around."

I rotate my chair through three hundred and sixty

degrees and it clicks. Last year the walls were plastered with pictures of Big Bob posing with all sorts of semi-famous people. Now there are just cheap prints, which look like they were picked up at a thrift store.

"Where is he?" I ask.

"At home probably." Her smile is nasty.

"And where would that be?"

Her smile broadens. "Why should I tell you?"

Damned if I can think of a reason.

"To avoid being arrested," Adry says.

That gets her attention. Way to go, Adry. "What do you mean by that?" Doris says.

"Mr. Pridmore has been involved in some illegal activities. We are about to inform the RCMP fraud squad about them. If we can't find Pridmore first, we're just going to have to send the police here to look for his files."

"He moved out a few months back. Got disbarred. Lost everything. There's none of his stuff here."

"You'll have to explain that to the RCMP when they come to turn this office over."

Adry turns to leave and I start to follow her.

"He lives on Union Street," Doris says. She grabs a piece of paper and starts writing. "Here's the address." She holds out the paper and Adry takes it with a smile.

She hands it to me. The address is about three blocks from Roland McCoy, the little shit who started all this. I'm guessing that's not a coincidence.

———

I WAS EXPECTING A GENTRIFIED FAMILY HOME, NOT THIS. IT'S old, small and ugly. There's no front yard and the front door, without a bell or knocker, opens straight onto the sidewalk.

Maybe, in years past, it was a shop of some sort. Adry's knuckles rap on the peeling maroon paint. After a second rap, the door opens.

He's still Big and he's still Bob but I hardly recognize him. No tie, no suit, no shirt. He's wearing a grubby tee, track pants and a good three days growth of beard and not in a fashionable way either. He's lost a lot of muscle tone and replaced it with fat. He's been on a downhill slope for a while. He looks at Adry with glazed eyes, then his gaze stumbles its way down to me.

"What do you want?" he grunts. I can smell the stale alcohol on his breath.

It makes no sense. This sack of shit can't be the one who conned Marly Summers out of five million bucks and planted a quarter of a million bucks of heroin on us. He's certainly got the motivation but he's more washed up than a beached whale. But now we're here I might as well ask the question.

"Did you set your boy Lawrence Charles Linsky and his sidekick Roland McCoy on us?"

"What the fuck are you talkin' about," he slurs. "And who the fuck *are* you?" He blinks his eyes and looks at me for a moment.

If he doesn't recognize me, he is so far gone as to be useless to us. Have we got this all wrong? Could it be someone else is behind the scams?

"Come on Pridmore," I say. "You know who I am." He still has a blank look on his face. "Nick Stammo," I prompt him. Still nothing. He just stares at me, scratching the scar on his temple. "The guy who helped Marly Summers get away from you a year ago."

"Marly Summers?" he says. Then some sort of under-standing seems to break through his alcoholic haze. "Oh, yeah." A sly look takes over his face. He chuckles, taps the side of his nose with his finger and slams the door in our faces.

"What the heck was that all about?" Adry asks.

"I have absolutely no idea. Something's wrong here but I don't know what."

———

ADRY'S SHOUT PULLS ME OUT OF MY BAD MOOD. "ZELENA'S posted new stuff," she yells.

She gets up and puts her laptop on my desk and kneels down beside me. Luce comes in and looks over her shoulder. "Look at this," Adry says. "She commented on the Matt Standing post. 'Great band. Loved their first hit Behind the Watchman.' What does that mean?"

"I can tell you this,' Lucy says, "The Royal Concept doesn't have a tune called Behind the Watchman. It's definitely a message."

"She also posted this." Adry scrolls to a post. "She says, 'Reminds me of the restaurant we went to for my fifteenth birthday. We were 7 15 year olds.' I wonder if that's a message too."

"We could ask," Lucy says.

"How?" Adry and I say together.

"Call her friend Steph and find out if she remembers Zelena's fifteenth birthday party. Ask her if seven girls went to a restaurant."

Adry jumps up, hugs Lucy and grabs her phone. Right now I'd give anything to jump up and hug Lucy too. I make do with, "Great work, Luce," and get a big smile back. It's almost as good.

Adry makes the call, asks the question, thanks Steph and

hangs up. "Zelena didn't have a fifteenth birthday party. She had mono that year."

So it is a message. Zelena sent us two messages.

"I wonder if '7 15' means a time," Adry says.

"Maybe it's a street address," Lucy adds.

"No," I say. "It would be too obvious. If someone's watching what she types they would spot that."

"If you put the clues together maybe it says she'll be behind the watchman at seven-fifteen."

We sit in silence trying to make sense of it. "Maybe Rogan can figure it out." I check my computer. "It's two in the morning over there," I say. "He can't take any action on it in the middle of the night. Let's wait for a few hours before we wake him up."

"OK." Adry sounds disappointed.

"Good work, you guys," I say with more confidence than I feel. "We're going to save this girl for sure."

I take a deep breath, which turns into a sigh as I turn back to my computer.

"What's the matter Dad?" Lucy asks.

"It's the Pridmore thing. Everything points to him being the one who scammed Marly Summers and us. But the pathetic drunk, who Adry and I visited this morning, couldn't find his ass with both hands *and* he definitely wasn't someone who had five million bucks of Marly's money in his bank account."

She gives me a big smile. "Don't worry Dad, you'll sort it all out; you always do. Why don't you work on some other cases and maybe a solution will pop into your head."

"I suppose."

"Plus, you're going to be able to talk to Cal in a few hours. Maybe he'll have an idea."

"Lucy's right Nick," Adry says. "Let's focus on the clients we've still got."

No man's a match for a smart woman, so when two smart women agree on something, who am I to disagree?

———

I CLICK 'SEND' AND THE REPORT I SPENT THE LAST FEW HOURS on is on its way to the client. Adry and Lucy were right. Focussing on other clients was a good idea. It's kind of cleared my mind.

I check the time. It's six-thirty in the morning in Hong Kong. "Let's wake Rogan up," I say.

I fire up Skype and start the call. Adry and Lucy come and sit either side of me and Lucy opens a new packet of chocolate digestives. She must have read my mind.

Rogan's face pops onto the screen. He's dripping wet. I grin. "Did I get you out of the shower? Sorry about that," I say.

"Yes you did and no you're not," he says, wiping his face and hair with a towel.

"Yeah, well just make sure you don't drop the phone."

"What's up?" he says.

I tell him about the encounter with Big Bob.

"It doesn't make sense," he says.

"You better believe it," I grunt. "The only person who connects us to Marly is Bob Pridmore. If someone is trying to ruin both of us, it's gotta be him."

"Could he have been putting on an act for you guys?"

"No way. Living in a hovel, smelling of booze at ten in the morning waiting for us to find him and question him: who would do that?"

A faraway look comes into his eyes. The cogs in his brain

are turning over. *"He went downhill fast,"* he says. *"A year ago he was a practicing lawyer, presumably making good money. Then he gets disbarred and in the space of a year he... Wait a minute. Do we know when he was disbarred?"*

"No," I say, "but I could look it up."

"The receptionist at his old office said he moved out a few months ago," Adry adds.

"It makes even less sense. A few months ago he's functioning well enough to have a law office and now he's an incoherent drunk. Something doesn't add up here," he says.

"Well duh! I've been kicking it around in my mind most of the day."

We slip into a silence. Adry breaks it with, "Did you check Instagram yet Cal?"

"No. What did she post?"

When she says the words 'Behind the Watchman', he looks like he's been hit by a bolt of electricity. "There's a building behind where the watch vendor used to be on Temple Street. It was number one-oh-five."

"One-oh-five?" A frown comes to Adry's face but only for a moment. "OMG! Zelena's other post talked about, '7 15 year old girls.' Seven times fifteen is one hundred and five. That's the place."

He gives a whoop. *"At last a real lead!"*

With a bit of luck, Rogan will be talking to Zelena before the day's over.

He outlines his plan. "Sounds good," I tell him. "Make sure you keep us up to date."

After he hangs up, Lucy laughs. "This is so exciting. I so hope Cal finds Zelena and her brother too."

"I'm looking forward to making the call to the parents telling them their son and daughter are safe," I say.

"Go team!" Adry high fives us.

A new voice intrudes. "Has the great Nick Stammo solved yet another case?"

I swivel my chair around and feel my smile getting bigger.

"Hi Stewart," I grin.

"Hi Lover," he says and I feel myself blushing. I suppose I'll get used to being gay at some point, but after rejecting the way I was born for so many long years, it still feels a bit strange.

"What are you doing here Stewie?" Lucy asks. She always calls him that; apparently it's a reference to some character in a TV show. He seems to like it. They get on so well.

"Didn't he tell you? No, of course he didn't. I'm here to pick him up. We're catching an early movie and then I'm taking him out for dinner. Friday's our five-month anniversary but I'll be on nights, so we're celebrating this evening."

"You guys are so cute," she laughs.

"Huh" I grunt, pretending to be annoyed.

I haven't been called cute since I was five.

———

WE ARE IN THE CACTUS CLUB AT ENGLISH BAY BEACH. IT HAS an amazing view of the sunset and has the added advantage of being a couple of blocks from Stewart's apartment. We are sharing the white chocolate cheesecake and drinking cognac. As the last sliver of the sun disappears, my phone pings. I look across the table at him. He smiles and nods. I pull out my phone. It's a text from Cal and it's not one-hundred percent what I wanted to hear. I show the text to Stewart.

"It must be tough on the parents," he says.

I nod. "I'll have to call them and pass the news on."

Something tells me not to do it right now.

After a moment Stewart speaks. "I lost my older brother a few years back."

"You didn't tell me about it. I'm sorry."

He shrugs but I can tell he's close to tears. "Still too painful," he says. "He OD'd. He lived in the States. Got addicted to Oxycontin after an operation and went from there to fentanyl and then…"

I reach out and put my hand on his.

With his other hand, he takes out his wallet and slides out a photograph. "This was us a few weeks before. I begged him to come back to Canada for the operation but he was stubborn."

I take the photo. Stewart and his brother are standing on a pier with the ocean behind them. "Newport Beach," he says. They are very much alike. Not like Roland and Connor McCoy who don't look like brothers at all. Stewart's older brother looks less fit and doesn't look like he has the same unlimited energy Stewart always has. It's probably the illness. They are so similar yet so different. It's like—

Then it hits me. "Oh," I say.

"What?"

"You may just have solved a mystery," I tell him. I squeeze his hand. I want to tell him I love him. But I'm not ready.

Not yet anyway.

27. CAL

Tuesday

He gives me a dead stare across the table. "Mr. Rogan," he says in his perfect British accent, "how many times do I have to say this? You say you were a policeman, so you must know I can't just raid a building without any evidence. No judge in the territory is going to give me a warrant to search a privately owned building, based on the social media posts of a young woman who appears, in those self-same posts, to be free to come and go as she pleases."

Trying hard to curb my irritation at his pedantry and general prissiness, I say, "But Inspector Ho, the posts where she's asking for help—"

"Not evidence, Mr. Rogan, not evidence. It's just your interpretation of her turn of phrase."

"Could you just come with me to the building? We could go in and you could ask whoever's there to let us look around."

He sighs and looks up at the ceiling. "I would be happy to do that, *if and when* you have any evidence."

I look into his eyes and get an implacable stare in return.

If it's evidence he wants, I know how to get it.

————

I CALL PHIL JIANG FOR THE THIRD TIME THIS MORNING. There's still no reply so I leave him a voice message outlining my plan. I'm going to have to go it alone.

Temple Street looks completely different in the morning. There is no sign of the stalls, which will line both sides of the road this afternoon and evening, but, from across the street, the entrance to number one-oh-five looks as forbidding in the daylight as it does at night.

It looks like a cheap apartment building, shabbier than the buildings on either side. There are windows at each level, some with air-conditioning units. But there's something missing. Almost every apartment in Hong Kong has laundry hanging out to dry on racks or clothes horses. This one doesn't have a single item. And something else is wrong: all of the windows have either roller blinds or paper covering them. Whatever happens behind those windows is kept from the neighbours' eyes.

I cross the road and stand on the threshold.

I have only the vaguest idea of how to proceed. I'm going to have to wing it.

The stairway up has an almost-abandoned feel to it. The concrete walls are covered to about elbow height in what used to be white paint. Loops of white and grey electrical wire hang from the ceiling and the stairs look like they haven't been swept since the Lunar New Year. I get the sense that this air of both dilapidation and menace is a purposeful device to keep strangers from entering.

Taking a deep breath, I start up the stairs, ducking under the wires so they don't even brush against my hair. At the top of the first flight is a scuff-marked wall, which used to be powder blue. There is a black, window-sized piece of metal set into the wall and I have absolutely no idea what it might be used for. I turn around and with a last glance back to the safety of the sidewalk below, I take the second flight up. It ends in a bare concrete hallway.

At the end of the hallway is a panelled door, unusual in two respects: one, it looks new, painted in black, with expensive-looking brass fittings, one of which is a five-pointed star, set exactly between the upper panels; two, there is a brass-and-leather barstool beside the door.

The occupant of the barstool looks up from his book. He is a young man in an expensive suit, with a mild expression which changes when he sees me. He smiles, stands and places his book on the stool. Although his smile is welcoming, I recognize his stance. It screams 'martial arts.'

"How can I help you sir?" he says in passable English. He has a lisp and the last world comes out as 'thir'.

I step very close to him. "I've come to see Zelena," I say.

He shows no sign of surprise or puzzlement at the mention of her name.

"Come back. Thicth tonight." His smile is a model of polite, friendly service.

I look at my watch. "But I have a special appointment to see her now," I say. Then, as an afterthought, I add, "I arranged it with Leo."

That causes a smile and a nod. "OK," he says.

He turns and reaches for the door handle.

I wait just long enough to ensure the door is not locked.

With just a touch of regret at how I'm repaying his politeness, I step forward and with as much force as I can muster, I drive my left fist into his kidney. Before his "Ooof" is fully exhaled, I grab his hair and smash his head into the concrete wall beside the door. He goes limp and slides down the wall to the floor.

I step over him and push through the door.

I am in a small, elegant bar, empty of people. There is seating arranged on an expensive carpet but the chairs are enveloped in dust covers. Behind the bar there's a small array of liquor featuring several brands I can't afford. But it is only a quarter full. There are boxes on the bar full of bottles. I say a silent thank you that whoever is stocking the bar is not there right now. There are two doors off the bar. One is a replica of the door through which I just entered, complete with brass star. The other, off to the right, is similar with a small plate bearing Chinese characters and the word 'Staff.'

I take the staff entrance.

Elegance is replaced with utility and I smell food.

Again I'm in an anteroom with doors leading off. I can hear the sounds of people and a huge clatter of kitchen implements. If I take any of the doors I am going to encounter people, something I don't want to do just yet.

To the right is a wooden staircase. If Zelena is being held here, it will likely be upstairs. Prisoners are always held in high places. I take the rickety stairs two at a time, as quietly as I can, using what Ellie calls marshmallow feet. At the top of the stairs is yet another door, held closed by a heavy-duty bolt. I feel the thrill of getting close.

I need to be fast.

The guard won't stay unconscious for ever.

As I slide back the bolt, I hear one of the doors below

open. I made the right choice. I am in a hallway with eight doors leading off. I open the closest one. It's a tiny bedroom and it's freezing cold. It has a bed and nothing else. Two of the walls are bare concrete. In one there is a barred window high up close to the roof. In the other there is a vent and I can hear the sound of some sort of motor or pump.

The next door reveals a similar room except that all four walls are covered in particle board and it's much warmer. I keep going. They are all the same until I get to the last door on the left.

It's locked.

This is it.

The door is cheap. The frame is cheap.

I'll risk the noise I'm going to make.

With a firm hold on the door handle, I take a half step back and propel my shoulder into the door. A sharp crack and it gives way. I manage to stop myself from falling into the room.

It's a mirror image of the first room.

Except that it has an occupant sitting up in the bed, eyes wide.

It's not Zelena.

But through the bruises and incrustations of dried blood, I know who it is.

"Aleksander," I whisper. "My name's Cal. Your father sent me to get you."

"Thank God," he grunts pushing himself up off the bed.

He stands swaying.

"I have to get you out of here fast. Can you walk?"

He nods.

"Let's go then," I say, taking him by the elbow.

"We have to get Zel. She's here too."

I process it for a second. "I need to get you out of here

first. With your evidence, we can have the police raid this place and rescue her."

"No." He says it more loudly than I would like. "I'm not leaving without her."

"Keep your voice down! Zelena's not on this floor. She's in a part of the building that's full of people. I can't get you both out at the same time."

"Then leave me here. I'm not going without her. Go tell the police and have them come for both of us and the other girls too."

I think of the intransigent Inspector Ho. Will he take my word for it or will he go on about hearsay evidence? I'll need Aleksander in the flesh to force Ho's hand.

"I respect your loyalty to your sister but I can't leave you here. I can only persuade the police to raid this place if I have you as a witness."

He thinks this over.

I pull gently on his elbow. "We don't have time."

Footsteps.

Trudging slowly up the stairs.

Only one person... I think.

I weigh the dwindling options.

He's probably been sent to investigate the noise I made pushing in the door.

I have to take him out.

"For Zelena's sake, follow me!" I hiss at Aleksander.

As quietly as I can, I sprint down the corridor towards the open door at the top of the stairs. As I get within about two metres, I hear a grunt of surprise. He's seen the door's unbolted. I have to take him out before he calls for rein-forcements.

I step into the doorway and come face to face with an

old woman. She's carrying a tray bearing a meagre supply of food.

Her surprise gives me a fraction of a second.

My left hand reaches down and grabs a big handful of her clothing below her throat as my right hand takes hold of the tray. I yank her and the tray up the last two stairs. It only partially worked. A bowl of rice and a plastic cup of water drop to the floor making way too much noise.

She opens her mouth and takes in a breath.

I drop the tray and, fighting against all feelings of chivalry, I jab my right fist forward into her jaw and a horrendous pain shoots up my arm from my broken fingers. I can't suppress the grunt of pain.

She goes limp.

The clatter of the tray hitting the wooden floor is eclipsed by a shout. The woman's not alone. Of course! Her guardian lunges for me. His enthusiasm is greater than his fighting technique. I let go of the woman's clothing and smash my elbow into his throat.

He staggers back. I reach out to grab him but he pitches backward down the stairs, making enough noise to be heard throughout the building.

Our window of time is slamming closed.

At least Aleksander obeyed my command to follow me. He is standing wide eyed beside me.

"Let's go." I lead the way down the stairs and hear him follow.

At the bottom, I'm amazed to see the doors to the ante-room are closed.

I pull open the door that leads to the bar.

It brings me face to face with the young man who was at the front door.

Before he can react, I use my forward momentum to snap my right foot up into his crotch.

He drops gasping to the floor.

Today is definitely not his day.

I look over my shoulder. Behind Aleksander, I see one of the doors to the anteroom crash open. A man in chef's uniform comes through. "Come on!" I shout and dash across the barroom. I can hear Aleksander behind me.

I wrench open the outer door and rush down the hallway. As I get to the top of the stairway down, I hear a crash.

The chef has pushed Aleksander to the ground. He yells something over his shoulder, a call for reinforcements, I guess.

As Aleksander scrambles backwards, the chef reaches down and takes hold of an ankle.

Behind them, a tough-looking thug bursts through the doorway. He shouts something to someone back inside. It's in Cantonese but I recognize one word in the stream of sounds: 'Rogan'. He turns back and starts to race toward us.

There is no way we are both going to get away now.

Do I run and try to persuade Inspector Ho to raid this place or do I stay and try and fight these two with one good hand and one broken hand?

The decision is made for me.

Aleksander arches his back, putting his weight on his shoulders and pulling his entrapped foot down hard. The movement forces the chef to bend down further or lose his grip. As the chef's head pitches down, Aleksander's other foot smashes up into his face. In an instant he's free and on his feet. That move was a thing of beauty.

"Go, go, go!" he shouts.

We dash down the two flights and burst out onto the street.

I turn north and run into the intersection, almost smashing into a red cab.

We scramble inside.

As the cab pulls away, I see the tough-looking thug standing in the middle of Temple glaring at us.

I smile and wave.

———

FOUR HOURS LATER, I AM STANDING ON THE STREET OUTSIDE one-oh-five Temple. This time I'm under strict orders from Inspector Ho: I am to wait here while he and his squad of armed officers go through the building. They went in about five minutes ago. This time Phil Jiang is standing beside me. As I get to the end of telling him my story of breaking Aleksander out of there, I remember something odd.

"As we were leaving, one of the guards shouted something and I'm sure he used my name."

"How would he know your name?" Phil asks.

"I don't know but I'm sure he said 'Rogan'"

He thinks for a moment. "The Cantonese word ruògān sounds like Rogan. It just means several."

Further speculation is interrupted by Inspector Ho. He exits the building and crosses the street to where we are standing.

"Come with me." He does an about face and heads back across the street. We follow. He leads us up the stairs and along the corridor. As we go through the first door with the star on it, I see the smear of blood on the wall from where I rammed the guard's head into it. Except for an armed police officer, the bar is empty. Not one of the expensive bottles of liquor is in evidence. The chairs are moved over to the side of the room and are still under white dust covers.

"Did you arrest anyone?" I ask.

"There was no one here to arrest." Ho replies.

Phil and I exchange glances. I wonder if he is thinking the same thing as me.

"Where did you find Mr. Gutkowski?" Ho asks.

"Through here," I say. I lead them through the staff-only door and up the stairs. Ho looks in all the rooms and makes a cursory examination of the room in which Aleksander was held but gives no indication of his thoughts.

We go back downstairs and I take the door through which the chef appeared on my last visit a few hours ago. It leads into a big kitchen. The kitchen is as bare as the bar. There is no sign of any pots and pans or other implements. It is, to all intents and purposes, abandoned, but the earlier smell of food lingers on.

"Come and see this," Ho says.

He leads us back through the bar and into the room behind the second door with the star on it. The room is large, about ten metres on each side. It has a luxurious feel and it is lit by hundreds of tiny LED lights in the ceiling, twinkling above like stars. There is an expensive carpet on the floor but no other sign of furniture. Facing us is a stage. Along the back of the stage, at about shoulder height, are five loops of golden-coloured rope connected to the back-drop and above each rope is a large brightly-coloured star: red, yellow, green, blue and purple.

I turn to Phil and Ho. "What do you think this room is used for?"

"An auction," Ho says. With a nod of his head he moves towards a door to the side of the room. We follow. This door has five small stars on it: red, yellow, green, blue and purple. It leads into another corridor, with five doors leading off it. On each door is a small golden hook. On each hook, hanging from a thin, golden chain, is a star: red, yellow, green, blue and purple. Ho throws open one of the doors, inviting us to step inside.

It's a bedroom with a subtle and delicate smell. It is immaculate, to a hotel-like standard. There's an expensive-looking chair, some sort of wooden stool, partway in height between a chair and a barstool. On one wall there are four chain restraints strategically placed for hands and feet. The bed's a four-poster with creamy-white, silk sheets. Each of the posts has a light-tan, leather restraint attached. On a low cabinet at the foot on the bed, is a large pair of tailor's scissors and small array of leather instruments. I recognize a whip, a riding crop, a blindfold and what might be a gag but have no idea what the others are used for.

I am seized by an overwhelming desire to throw up.

———

"IT WAS DESERTED WHEN WE GOT HERE," HO SAYS. AS HIS MEN file out of the building, the vendors are starting to put up their stalls for the market's start of business at two.

"Who owns the building?" Phil Jiang asks him.

He shrugs. "It's owned by a company on the mainland."

"Who's behind the company?" I ask.

He gives a crooked smile. "The Hong Kong police don't have access to the records of companies in mainland China, Mr. Rogan."

"Can't you phone a colleague over there?" I ask but he just shrugs, a resigned look on his face. I can feel my anger stirring. Is he telling me the truth or is he just too lazy to do anything? I try another tack. "Four hours ago, the place was full of people. Someone must have seen them leave. They must have used vehicles to transport the girls and the things they took with them. Someone must have seen something."

"Mr. Rogan, this was obviously operated by a triad from the mainland. Trust me, no one who saw anything is going to talk to the police. They know there are dire consequences for themselves and their families if they do."

"But what about Zelena Gutkowska? She was in there. People were bidding to take her into one of those torture chambers disguised as bedrooms. You have to do something."

He looks long and hard at me. "If you hadn't acted like a cowboy and gone in there to rescue her brother, they would all still be in there. My men could have arrested them all and saved the girl."

It all explodes out of me. "You refused to raid this place when I came to see you this morning. It wasn't until I came back with Aleksander that you bothered to get off your fat ass and put together a team to take this place." I'm shouting now. "*And* it took you almost four hours to do that. Four hours in which the gang were able to clear out of the place and take Zelena with them and probably a bunch of other girls too."

When I stop for breath, I feel Phil Jiang's hand on my arm. "Steady Cal," he says. He turns to Ho. "Mr. Rogan is understandably upset Inspector. I'm sure you understand his outburst," he says quietly.

Without a word, Ho looks at Phil then at me, turns, and walks to his police car. He gets in and drives off.

My anger deflates with a long sigh. "No wonder he's still an Inspector, he's too incompetent to go any further."

"Maybe not," Phil says. "Didn't you say you thought someone shouted your name as you were leaving?"

"Yeah, but..."

Then it hits me.

"You think Ho warned them I knew about this place and that I might come here?" I ask.

"He wouldn't be the first. Two years ago, five Hong Kong officers were arrested for taking bribes in exchange for protecting gangsters from one of the local triads."

I answer with a single expletive.

He nods.

"So how do we go about finding Zelena?" I ask.

"Ho's right when he says people won't talk to the police about the triads. But I have a couple of people who work for me from time to time. They're tuned in to what's happening on the streets. I can get them to make a few inquiries."

I think of Ghost and Tommy. "I've got a couple of guys like that back home," I say with a smile. I check my new watch—the one I bought from the still-missing vendor— "It's almost eleven o'clock at night in Vancouver. I'd better email my team and give them an update. Then I'd like to go check out Aleksander in the hospital. Maybe he has something that might help us track down his sister."

"Good idea," he says. "I'll talk to my guys and get them working on it. Then I've got to deal with a couple of other clients' cases. Why don't we get together at my office first thing in the morning?"

"Sounds like a plan."

He turns to go.

"Phil," I say. He stops and turns back. "Thanks for stopping me. I might have lost it and hit him." He just nods and smiles. "And watch your back. Remember what happened to Henry Wang."

"You too," he says as he heads off.

Despite the setback in finding Zelena, I'm feeling confident that with Phil's local knowledge and contacts, and my ability to communicate with Zelena via Instagram, we are going to find her. And maybe, just maybe, I'm going to find a way to expose a corrupt cop in the process.

––––––

"DID YOU FIND HER?" ARE THE FIRST WORDS OUT OF HIS mouth. I know he means Zelena, but being back here in the Kwong Wah Hospital reminds me of Tina. Is she as lost to me as Zelena is to him? I shake off the thought and look at Aleksander. He is sitting up in bed, looking a lot better than he did when I dragged him into the Mongkok police station earlier.

I shake my head. "No, when I got back there with the police, the place was empty."

He bites his lip.

"Don't worry," I tell him with a confidence I only partly feel. "We'll find her. Through the credit-card payment you made to Jiang and Lee, I was able to track down Phil Jiang and he's working with me. He has some people making inquiries."

"There was another detective," he interrupts. "Henry Wang. You need to talk to him."

"I know. I found Mr. Wang."

"That's great! What did he tell you?"

There is a real hope in his voice. I hate to have to be the one to shatter it. "I found him in his office. He was dead. Murdered."

The shock on his face is palpable. "But he..." He shakes his head. "How did you...?" A tear starts to form in his eye.

"Why don't you tell me everything that happened after you got to Hong Kong," I say as gently as I can.

After a moment he nods.

"When I got into Hong Kong on the Wednesday after-noon, I checked into the Hilton—my father's company has a corporate rate there—but I immediately took a taxi to the Kerry. I talked to the staff and discovered that Zelena and Steph had been staying there with two men. I was really shocked, I knew I couldn't tell my parents. They thought Zelena was... well, you know."

"A virgin?" I supply the word he seems scared to use.

He nods. "I went back to the Hilton and the next morn-ing, I went to the police and met with Inspector Ho. He didn't seem in the least interested in trying to find Zelena. So I went back to the Hilton and talked to their head of security. He gave me the name of a private detective Mr. Wang. At first, I was a bit unsure of him. He wanted to be paid in cash and his office was a bit old-fashioned but I went ahead and paid his retainer because of the recommendation I'd got. I preferred Mr. Jiang, he seemed more professional and, although his partner Mr. Lee was a bit odd, I thought he had a better chance of finding my sister." I nod, thinking about my drive with Mr. Lee to the IF nightclub. 'A bit odd' is putting it mildly.

He continues, "I gave all the details to both detectives and waited for them to conduct their initial inquiries. To my surprise, Mr. Wang got back to me first, on the Friday evening. He told me Zelena had last been seen at a night-club that was owned by one of the local triads. He said they were known for kidnapping girls and forcing them into prostitution. He said he would have good evidence of where she was being held and would I meet him the following morning so we could go to the police station together. I agreed of course, but the next morning early there was a knock on my room door. It was a uniformed policeman. He said they'd found my sister and he was there to take me to the hospital to see her but when I got into the police car, he and another officer put a cloth over my face and the next thing I knew, I woke up in the room you found me in."

"Did you see Zelena at all?" I ask.

"No. They just kept me there and fed me twice a day. Twice, a couple of men came in and both times they beat me up and took video of it. The second time they held a knife to my throat in front of the camera. When you broke in and rescued me, I'd been there about eight or nine days."

"The nightclub, which Mr. Wang said Zelena was seen in, was it called either IF or the Golden Dragon?"

He thinks for a bit then says, "I don't think he mentioned the name."

"The place you were held was one-oh-five Temple Street. Did Mr. Wang say if Zelena was being held there too?"

"No."

"When the police officer showed up at your hotel door, did you mention Mr. Wang to him?"

"Yes, I did. I asked him if Mr. Wang had sent him. He said 'Who?' and I said, 'Henry Wang, the private detective.' He shook his head and asked if I'd hurry up and get dressed. Why do you ask?"

"Just wondered," I lie.

But he's too smart for me. His face goes white. "Do you think those phony cops killed Mr. Wang because I told them his name?"

"No," I lie again to save his feelings of guilt. "And I don't think those cops were phony either."

"What?!" His eyes are like saucers.

I think over his story. "You said that men came twice to beat you up and that they took videos both times." He nods. "Did they say why they were taking the videos?"

"No. But I thought about it. I think they probably

showed them to Zel and maybe told her they were going to kill me if she didn't do as they asked her."

Smart kid. I suspect he's right.

"Did the doctors here say when you can leave?" I ask.

"Yes. When those guys beat me up, one of them punched me in the kidneys. The doctors are just waiting for some tests to come back and if they are OK, they'll discharge me right away."

"Good," I say. "As soon as you get out of here, take a taxi to the Hilton, grab your things and get the next plane back to Vancouver."

"No. I want to help you find my sister."

"Just leave that to Phil Jiang and me. We'll get her back, I promise. Your parents need you back safely in Vancouver."

"That's what they said when I called them and told them I was safe."

"Then that's what you need to do. We'll have Zelena back to you in no time at all."

The thought flits through my mind that Janusz Gutkowski told me he was only prepared to pay for the return of his son, not his daughter.

But if he thinks I'm going to stop now, he's crazy.

———

HARVEY LIM HASN'T GOT BACK TO US ABOUT SETTING UP A meeting with Leo. So I'm doing the next best thing. Stake-outs can be a real pain but I'm enjoying this one. I'm sitting at a table, on the sidewalk outside a restaurant, with a good view of the entrance to the Golden Dragon. It's right on the corner of the first intersection east of the club. If I turn my head forty-five degrees, I have a perfect view of the entrance to the alley that runs behind the Dragon. With the building on Temple Street abandoned, Zelena will be held captive somewhere else and my one shot at finding her is to follow Leo. So I've been sitting here for over an hour nibbling dim sum and people watching.

The other good thing about this stakeout is that it has given me some thinking time. If the gang were using Aleksander as a lever to get Zelena to do what they want, she now knows that lever is gone. I only hope the Instagram post I just did is not obvious to whomever is supervising her posts.

Knowing Inspector Ho is working for the triad answers a lot of questions. It's why Aleksander was kidnapped. When Ho found out about his other private detective, Mr. Wang got killed for his trouble. It also explains how the gang knew my name; Ho must have warned them about me.

I glance to my right. Two men are walking out of the alley. One of them is almost certainly Leo. He is the right height and build but the fedora is the giveaway. It's the same one he wore in the very first picture Zelena posted on Instagram. The man walking with him looks vaguely familiar but I can't see him clearly in the street lighting. He has a severe limp, which makes him walk with a strange, rolling gait. They are alone. There is no sign of either of the bouncers from the club. They head down the opposite side of the street in the direction of Nathan Road. With a twinge of regret at leaving the dim sum, I get up from the table and follow them. At Nathan, they separate. The man with the limp crosses the street and Leo does a left turn. I hurry to the corner and peek around. Leo is walking quickly now and is about a hundred meters ahead of me. I follow him for a couple of blocks until he turns into what looks like another alley. I hurry ahead. Above the point where he turned in, there's a sign with a picture of a smiling Buddha.

It's a temple. What a brilliant place to hide a captive. I turn left and am in a courtyard. Two meters ahead, facing me, with a smile on his face, is Leo.

Except it's not.

It's one of the bouncers from the club wearing Leo's hat. "Hello, Mr. Rogan," he says. I take a step towards him and as I do, he glances over my shoulder.

I've been played.

I start to turn and my world explodes in bright white light.

28. ZELENA

Everything was different today. This morning, while we were in the kitchen eating, the cook and the old woman were packing things into boxes and then there was a huge commotion and the chef ran out. There was all sorts of shouting and the next thing we know, we were all pushed into one of the vans and driven here. There was no auction and no men living out their foul fantasies on us. We are all in different rooms but they are nice rooms, with soft beds and good, clean linen. The rooms are not even locked but they told us there was a guard outside and we would be punished if we opened our doors.

Best of all, my room has a small bathroom with a shower. I hated using the communal washroom in the other place. This is my third shower of the day. I can't get over the luxury of having a shower in private without there being four other girls and a guard leering at us. I will never take a simple shower for granted ever again.

This has been the best day since they first took me.

The last of the suds ran down the drain five minutes ago.

Regretfully, I turn off the water and slide back the shower curtain.

He's standing there.

Looking at me with that dead look in his eyes.

I grab a towel which is barely big enough to cover me.

I want to scream at him. Tell him he's a filthy pervert. But I can't. The last time I lost it with him, he beat Zander badly and showed me the video.

"Leo." I force a smile onto my face. "You startled me."

He says nothing. Just waggles the phone at me.

He stands there looking as I try to dry myself. When I wrap the skimpy towel around me, he walks into the bedroom and sits on the bed. I follow. He hands me the phone.

I don't want to sit beside him, so I clamp my arms down to stop the towel from slipping down and tap on the phone. I go into Instagram and check my feed. Yes! There's a post from Matt Standing. Huh? There's a picture of the old guy from Jeopardy. My parents love that show. The post says, 'He's safe at home now.' He's had cancer. Does that mean he's dead? Why would whoever is...? Wait a minute! His name's Alex. Alex Trebek. Does this mean Aleksander is safe at home now? I can feel my heart racing. Are they telling me Zander is safe? Maybe that's what all the noise was about.

"Post pictures. Answer texts," Leo grunts.

I do as he says, trying to keep the excitement off my face. I need to tell them I'm not at the same place. I reply to Matt's post, 'I'm really moved.' They'll get it, whoever they are.

I do a few more posts and reply to some others and then hand him back the phone. Maybe with Zander safe, I can take some chances. They're not going to damage me permanently, I'm too valuable to them.

"I've used all the pictures," I say. "We'll have to go out to take some more." I try to sound bored with the whole idea.

He puts the phone in his pocket and stands up.

Thank God that's over. I won't have to look at his face again until tomorrow.

But he doesn't go.

He just stands there looking.

He smiles.

In a blur, one hand darts out and grabs my hair. I feel his other hand snatch the towel from my body.

He throws me backwards onto the bed and, as I try to cover myself with my hands, the look on his face tells me this is going to be bad.

29. ADRY

There's a big smile on Nick's face as I walk into the office. I grin. "Your romantic dinner with Stewart must have gone well," I say. He grunts and looks embarrassed. I love it.

Lucy is making coffee in the kitchen area. She sings, "Dad and Stewie, sitting in a tree. K I S S I—"

"Alright you guys. If you must know, Stewart solved the Pridmore mystery." He reacts to our shocked faces by looking smug.

"What?"

"How?"

"Listen and learn," he says. He just sits there with a smile on his face. It's his turn to tease us. Finally he says, "It's just good old-fashioned logic. We're being scammed and Marly's being scammed. Both at the same time. Right?"

He's making us work at it. "Right," we say in unison.

"The only person who holds a grudge against both of us is Bob Pridmore. Right?"

"Cut to the chase Dad," Lucy complains.

He laughs. "Pridmore's old receptionist gives us an

address where we can find him. We go there and we find a
pathetic drunk who couldn't plan a piss-up in a brewery."
He looks from one of us to the other. "Therefore..."

"It's not Bob Pridmore who's scamming us?" Lucy asks.

"Oh, it's Pridmore who's scamming us," he says.

Then I get it.

"That wasn't Big Bob we talked to yesterday morning," I
yell.

"Bingo! Last night Stewart showed me a picture of him
and his brother. They were like two peas in a pod. That's
when it clicked. The old drunk was Bob's *brother*. He sure as
hell fooled me until I did some research. His name's Jeff
Pridmore; him and Bob are twins. The mistake we made was
when we first suspected Big Bob was behind it all, we didn't
look into what Bob is up to these days. If we had, we would
have been ahead of the game."

"But the receptionist said—" I cut myself off in mid-
sentence. "Bob knew we'd suspect him, and that we'd go to
his old office to confront him. He must have got her to give
us the brother's address to throw us off the scent."

Nick nods. "He probably gave his brother a crate of
Scotch to get him to go along with it."

"Sneaky son of a..." I exhale.

Lucy puts coffee in front of us, together with the oblig-
atory plate of chocolate digestives. I swear I'm putting on
weight working here. "Was the receptionist lying about him
being disbarred too?" I ask around a chocolaty mouthful.

"No," he says and turns his computer monitor around so
we can see it.

It's a website, all very modern and professional-looking.
The company name is Erom Investments Inc. Nick clicks his
mouse and there, on the page headed 'Our Team', is a
picture of Bob. I lean forward to squint at the bio. There are

a lot of very impressive words in it but lawyer is not among them.

"So we know what he's doing with the money he scammed from Marly," I say.

"I guess," Nick says. "I looked at the website in detail. Part of it is a pitch to companies who are looking for investors and part of it is a pitch to high-net-worth individuals to get them to invest in Erom. I think he has his sights set on bigger money than just the five mil he took from Marly Summers."

"Is there a company address on the website?" I ask.

"Yep. He's in Park Place."

I whistle softly. Park Place is a big step up from his old office.

"Are you guys going to go see him?" Lucy asks.

"Maybe," Nick says, then adds, "I did some other digging." He waits with a smile on his face. We both look at him expectantly and he waits until I open my mouth to ask him. He laughs, "Big Bob defended a gang-banger name of Guy Chang. Guess who his boss was?"

Lucy gets it first. "The guy in Millhaven prison who hates Cal and you?"

He nods. "George Walsh. Guy Chang was a big man in his gang. I bet Walsh got his guys to supply Big Bob with the drugs to plant on us. That amount of drugs is penny-ante change to him. He'd be happy to drop a quarter of a million bucks of bad shit on us if it got Rogan into prison. And if they sent Rogan to Millhaven, Walsh would see him dead on his first day there."

There's a moment of silence while we absorb it all.

"The point is," I say, voicing what they must be thinking, "how are we going to prove to the VPD that Big Bob was the one who planted the stuff on us?"

We all lapse into silence again and I take another cookie. My own words have reminded me that if we can't prove it, this company could be over and Nick and Cal could even end up in jail. The next crime they solve might be who killed who in the prison yard. It must be burning Nick up. Life in prison in a wheelchair doesn't bear thinking about but I still think about it and I can feel a tear starting to form.

My phone pings.

I quickly brush at my eye and focus on the screen. "There's an Instagram post from Zelena." I click through her posts until I get to the reply to Matt Standing. "She says, 'I'm really moved.' She must be telling us she's been moved to a new location."

"We already knew from Cal's email last night."

"Has anyone heard from Cal this morning?" I ask.

"No, I've been trying to get him every half hour since six o'clock this morning." Nick pulls out his phone, taps away and I hear the FaceTime ring. It continues for thirty seconds with no response. "Not a good time to flake out on us Rogan," he grunts, but he's looking really worried.

I think about Cal's email. "At least the Gutkowskis got their son back," I say.

"Yes," Nick says. "It means I can bill them a progress payment."

Lucy chuckles and says, "Sometimes I think all you care about is billi—" The look on Nick's face stops her in her tracks.

"Progress payment," he repeats, half to himself.

"What?" I ask.

He doesn't look worried any more, in fact he's smiling. It's that smile he gives when he's got a bad-ass idea. It's a bit scary but it's good.

"What?" I say again.

"I know how to solve Marly's problem with Big Bob and, more to the point, ours too."

"How?" I ask.

He doesn't speak but his smile just gets broader.

———

THIS TIME I DIDN'T HAVE TO SPAR WITH THE RECEPTIONIST TO get to see the real Connor McCoy. Nick and I are sitting in his office enjoying a cup of the best coffee I've ever tasted. Nick has explained to him how his brother Roland helped to swindle five million dollars of Marly Summers' money and how he transported a quarter of a million bucks worth of heroin to our office.

Connor's face has gone from shocked to appalled to mortified in the space of five minutes.

"I am so sorry, Mr. Stammo," he says. "Roland has always been one to take the easy way through life and he's had a couple of minor brushes with the law but this..." He looks really down. "I suppose you'll have to take it to the police. What's going to happen to him?"

Nick shrugs. "Well, there'll be fraud charges of course, transportation of a controlled substance, blackmail maybe. He will definitely face some serious jail time if convicted."

Connor puts his hands up and massages his face. "It'll kill our parents," he sighs. "Why would he do something like this?"

"He got involved with a couple of bad guys."

Nick stops and waits. I feel a strong desire to fill the silence but Nick warned me in advance not to say anything. Connor looks from Nick to me and back again and I feel really sorry for the guy but I still keep quiet. I don't even show him any sympathy in my expression.

"I suppose I'd better get a lawyer for him. I don't know any criminal lawyers. Is there someone you could recommend?"

Nick waits a beat. He looks off into the distance and grunts "Huh" like he just thought of something. He looks Connor in the face. "You know what," he says, "maybe, with your help, there's a way to keep Roland's name out of all this."

"I'll do anything. Anything Mr. Stammo," Connor almost pleads.

If Nick hadn't been a cop, he'd have made one hell of a con man.

"Let me run this idea by you," he says.

Connor McCoy may be CEO of Dark Energy Systems and a powerful man in the world of high tech but Nick has him in the palm of his hand.

———

NICK THINKS ARNOLD YOUNG MAY BE A HARDER NUT TO crack. I'd never heard of him before today. He's a big-time investor who manages the estate of a rich Vancouver businessman named Wallace and he has referred quite a few rich clients to Stammo Rogan Investigations. Apparently, he also manages a trust fund for Cal. Mr. Wallace set it up for Cal before he died. I'll bet there's an interesting story how that all came about. Nick has given me strict instructions not to mention anything about Cal's drug relapse a year ago after Em's death. He explained it's a condition of the trust fund that Cal doesn't use.

As he strides into the reception area to greet us, the first word that comes into my mind is soldier. He moves like an officer on a parade ground. I was a military brat growing up and would recognize that walk anywhere.

"Mr. Stammo," he says. "A pleasure to see you again." He has what sounds to me like an upper-class British accent. He shakes Nick's hand and they hold on quite a while with eyes locked like there's some form of contest going on. Finally they let go.

"Thanks for seeing us at such short notice," Nick says. Arnold just nods, so Nick introduces me.

"Good afternoon Ms. Locke, I'm pleased to meet you." He extends his hand and I prepare for a vice-grip, but his shake is firm without being painful.

"Pleased to meet you too sir," I say.

"Please, call me Arnold, everyone does." Nick also told me he would say that but that I shouldn't do as suggested.

He leads us down a short corridor to his office. Unlike at Connor McCoy's office, there is no offer of coffee.

"So what can I do for you Mr. Stammo?" He gets straight down to business.

"About a year ago you referred Marly Summers to us," Nick says.

"Yes, yes, I remember. Shocking business," Young says, shaking his head. The first two words come out as 'ers, ers'. Definitely upper-class Brit.

"Ms. Summers has engaged our services again. Her former lawyer has swindled her out of five million dollars."

His bushy eyebrows go up. "Who's the lawyer?" he asks.

"A slime bucket named Bob Pridmore."

"Aaaah. Robert Pridmore Esq. Yes, we've met." From his tone, it was clearly not a good meeting. Good news for us.

"We have come up with a plan to get her money back but in order to do it we are going to need your help."

"Really?" He thinks it over for a bit. "The late Mr.

Wallace had a very satisfactory business relationship with the Summers family, although I do understand that Ms. Summers doesn't have any contact with Luke Summers, her former brother-in-law." He intones it to sound like a question but Nick doesn't rise to the bait.

Young looks off and absently taps his finger on the desk. Tap tap-tap, tap tap-tap, tap tap-tap. There's some sort of calculation going on in his head. Finally he speaks. "Well... Damsel in distress and all that. What can I do to help Mr. Stammo?"

"Pridmore has started a company called Erom Investments Inc."

"Never heard of it," Young grunts.

"I suspect he used the money he conned from Ms. Summers to start it."

"Huh," he grunts again.

Nick takes a big breath. "I want you to invest ten million dollars in Erom."

The eyebrows go through the roof this time.

Talk about getting someone's undivided attention.

———

"Do you think it will work Nick?" I ask when the elevator doors are closed behind us.

"If Bob Pridmore's as greedy as I think he is, he'll go for it like a seagull at a landfill."

"I hope you're right."

"I'm always right," he says with a chuckle. "Just ask Rogan."

The elevator doors open into the parkade. "I'm worried we haven't heard from Cal," I say.

"Yeah, I'm a bit pissed off at him. What's the time?"

I check my watch. It's a simple thing but I realize it's something he can't do while he's wheeling his chair. "Three-thirty."

"That's six-thirty tomorrow morning in Hong Kong. Why don't you call him."

I pull out my phone while he operates the lift on his truck. Yesterday, we caught Cal in the shower but today it just rings. It's not like Cal. I google the Kerry Hotel and get the number. They put me through to his room but it also just rings. I leave a message.

As I climb into Nick's truck, I get a sinking feeling in my gut.

Something's not right.

30. CAL

One question pushes its way through the throbbing in my head: how come I'm still alive? It spawns a second one: for how much longer? I force my eyes open. I'm in a room. It's small. A bit like a hotel room. It's not fully light, maybe six or seven in the morning. Unless it's evening and I've been unconscious for what... twenty hours? I'm on a bed. It's clean. It smells nice. A woman's smell. It reminds me of Tina. I should have gone back to Vancouver when her parents took her back. I feel an overwhelming desire to see her and talk to her and tell her I love her.

"You had a chance to leave Hong Kong." It feels like he's reading my thoughts. I try to roll over and face the speaker but my wrist is handcuffed to the bed post. He walks round the bed and into my line of sight. It's Leo. He smiles, but not in a nice way. "You are dead man now," he says in his accented English. "Understand?" I do, so I nod. "Good. You can die easy or die hard." His dead eyes bore into mine but I won't give him the satisfaction of responding. I stare back. "Only one reason you still alive. One question. Answer question, you die easy. No answer, you die hard." He sounds like he's watched too many bad movies. I suppress an insane desire to laugh.

"What's your question Leo?" I ask.

"How you know we at one-oh-five Temple Street?"

Any desire to laugh drains out of me. If I tell him we've been communicating with Zelena via Instagram and that she told us, God knows what he'll do to her. I rack my brain for an answer, any answer. Nothing comes and he sees my hesitation. He smiles again, reaches down and takes my hand in his. It's the hand he smashed with the blunt edge of a meat cleaver two nights ago.

"Last chance," he says.

What can I tell him? The truth will probably be a death sentence for Zelena and for me. There must be some credible lie I can concoct.

I scream in pain as he crushes my hand in his. Bolts of electricity course up and down my arm between hand and brain. I scream again as he bears down and grinds the broken bones together. It feels like my hand has been pierced by knives. It reminds me of... "Henry Wang!" I shriek.

He lets go of my hand. Through my whimpering, I think about the other private detective hired by Aleksander: garrotted and with knives through the backs of his hands, maggots feasting on him. It's probably the fate that awaits me.

"What you mean Henry Wang?" Leo asks.

For a lie to be convincing it has to be embedded in truth. "I went to Aleksander Gutkowski's hotel and went through his suitcases. I found a notebook. It mentioned a private detective, a Mr. Henry Wang." Now for the lie. "Underneath Mr. Wang's name and address it said 'Temple Market. 105,'" and back to the truth. "I went to Mr. Wang's office to find out more but he was dead."

He takes out his phone. "Which hotel?" he asks.

"The Hilton." He nods and makes a call. Through the stream of Cantonese I recognize two words: Rogan and Hilton. He's getting one of his thugs to check with the Hilton, to check I'm telling the truth. Good. He makes a second call. This time the words I recognize are Rogan and Wang. This call is probably to his tame cop Inspector Ho to verify I was at the crime scene. He's showing no sign of spotting the big weakness in my story: the timing. If he asks me why I waited four days between— Oh crap. I told Ho about our communications with Zelena. If he tells them, we're sunk.

He puts his phone away and takes a seat near the door.

We wait.

And in the silence the Bard's word provide no comfort.

> That you yourself may privilege your time
> To what you will; to you it doth belong
> Yourself to pardon of self-doing crime.
> I am to wait, though waiting so be hell.

And I worry.

But the wait is not long. The door opens and two very large men walk in. One is large from long hours of dedicated labour in the gym with a stiff cocktail of steroids to top it off. The other is large from long hours of dedicated labour at the dinner table with probably several stiff cocktails to top it off. They confer quietly with Leo and he gives them their orders.

He stands and shows me that dead smile of his. "Goodbye Mr. Rogan. Die hard." I'm pretty sure that's not a reference to the Bruce Willis movie. Ho must have given the truth to my lie and told them about the Instagram communications.

"Don't hurt the girl," I blurt out.

His smile broadens but still doesn't reach his eyes.

Without a word, he turns and leaves.

His men uncuff me from the bedpost.

Steroid man stands behind me and holds my arms in vice-like grips.

Fat man opens a drawer in the bedside table and takes out a leather mask. He slips it over my head. There are holes around my mouth and nose for me to breathe through but no holes for me to see through.

Steroid man marches me out of the room.

Waiting may be hell but what comes after may be worse.

31. NICK

Rogan's starting to piss me off. It's over twenty-four hours since his last email. It's ten in the morning over there. He can't still be sleeping, so why the hell isn't he answering my calls? When you're partners with an addict, you always worry they've gone off to get high. Since he's been seeing Tina, he's been doing real good but I wonder if her getting stabbed has pushed him over the edge, like Em's death did.

"You OK Nick?" Adry's voice cuts into my thoughts.

"Yeah, I guess. Just worried about Rogan."

"I know, I have this creepy sensation something's wrong."

I nod. "It's six-thirty. Why don't we call it a day. I left a ton of emails and messages for him. If I don't hear back from him by the morning, I'll call Phil Jiang. Maybe he'll know what Rogan's up to."

"Why don't we—" Her phone pings. She checks it. "Zelena's made another post. That's odd. It's morning over there. She usually posts late in the evening." She makes a couple of taps, looks and frowns. "It says, 'Would someone please tell my stupid parents to stop trying to find me. Call off the private detective. I want to be left alone. Hey, everyone likes privacy.'" She hands me her phone. "What's that all about?"

"Assuming the people who have her are still making her post, it must mean they're worried about Rogan. He must be getting close." I read the post again and hand her back the phone. "Look at the last sentence again."

"'Hey, everyone likes privacy.' It's a bit— wait a minute, H E L P. Way to go Zelena! And way to go Nick. I think I would have missed that."

"Nah. You'd have got there in the end," I tell her.

"Thanks Nick," she smiles for a moment and then gets more thoughtful. "Do you think we should reply to it?" she asks.

"Normally Rogan does that but with him going AWOL maybe we should."

Before she can answer, my phone starts pinging. Please God it's Rogan.

It's not.

"Stammo," I say.

"Hi Mr. Stammo, it's Connor McCoy. I just came out of the meeting. We're on."

"Great!" The grin on my face almost hurts. "How much?"

"Five."

"The full five million?" I ask.

"Yes."

"When?"

"Day after tomorrow."

"That was quick."

I hear him chuckle. *"You don't get to build a company like Dark Energy without being a fairly decent salesman."*

We say our goodbyes and I update Adry.

She smiles and crosses her fingers for good luck. We're

probably going to need it, it's all going a bit too easy for my liking.

"You look worried Nick," she says.

"Something doesn't add up," I say. "He scammed five million from Marly but he had to have paid Roland McCoy and Lee Linsky at least fifty grand each, probably more. So how come he still has the full five million to invest in Dark Energy Systems?"

"Maybe he put some of his own money into his investment company."

That brings a smile to my face. I like the idea of him losing his own money as well as Marly's. It has a good ring to it.

Now if Rogan would just call back, we'd be firing on all cylinders.

32. CAL

I've lost all track of time. I've been handcuffed in this van all day. The leather mask has me in inky blackness but I'm guessing it's after sundown because the stifling heat is slowly waning. I can smell the stink of my own sweat and urine. After a drive of about an hour, they stopped the van and left me here, wherever here is.

In the distance I can hear what I think is the hum of traffic but I can't be sure.

Earlier, I spent some time shouting for help. It's left me with a sore throat and I am getting to the point where I would give just about anything for a drink of cold water. Maybe they've just abandoned the van and are leaving me here to die of thirst. There are worse ways to die. But that's not compatible with Leo's parting shot. 'Die hard.' They aren't going to just let me die.

To keep myself from dwelling on it, I've been working the case in my mind. Something doesn't add up but I can't work out what it is. There's something missing. I wish I could talk it over with Nick and Adry. I'm sure that between us we could figure it out.

For the hundredth time I think of Ellie. She's coming back to Vancouver and I won't be there for her. With Sam's MS, what will become of her? If Sam doesn't make it, Ellie will probably grow up with her grandparents.

And I won't need to think about how to answer the email from SFU.

And Tina. Will she be able to forgive me.

With a screech of metal on metal, the van door opens. I hear a stream of Cantonese. There is disgust in their voices. It's their own fault, if they don't like the smell they shouldn't have left me here all day. Rough hands drag me out of the truck. One of them unlocks the handcuffs from behind my back. They push me to the ground and, amid the clanking of chain, I can feel metal on my wrists, then on my ankles. They pull me to my feet. The mask is pulled off and I get to take in my surroundings.

I look down. I am manacled like a prison inmate. My feet are connected by a one-foot length of chain. My hands have a bit more freedom of movement but a length of chain runs between the hand and foot manacles. I feel like I'm in *The Green Mile*. On the ground by my feet is a spade.

It's night. We are on what looks like an area of scrubland. It's fenced in. I look around. In the distance I can see the lights of high-rise apartments. Steroids and Fats are standing in front of me; the latter holds a gun with a silencer trained at my chest. He nods toward the spade. "Dig," he says.

Now I really feel like I'm in a movie. A bad movie. Do they really expect me to dig my own grave? "You've got to be joking," I say.

Fats smiles without any semblance of humour. "You dig, I shoot," he says. "We dig, he..." He gestures towards his partner. Steroids has a knife in his hand. He mimes removing body parts: eyes, ears, lips, tongue. A smile creases his face as he points the knife below my waist.

Fats nods. Sounding like a good friend offering advice, he repeats, "You dig."

I crouch down and pick up the spade. As I straighten up, I see he's taken a couple of steps back and is keeping his gun trained on my chest. He's a pro.

I look around. Just in front of me is a patch of land that looks softer than what's underfoot. I shuffle forward as fast as the manacles allow and plunge the spade in. The ground gives a little but it's not going to be easy.

My guards go and squat on the edge of the van's back bumper. They are about five metres behind me and to my right.

I dig.

It's slow and back-breaking work. I do the math in my head. I'll need to make a shoulder-width hole just short of two metres long and a metre deep. At the rate I'm working it will take an hour. At the end of it I'll be exhausted. I'll appreciate the chance to lie down and have a nice long sleep. Gallows humour. *And in that sleep of death, what dreams may come, when we have shuffled off this mortal coil.* Dreams... huh... I remember the dream.

It gives me an idea.

The idea becomes a plan.

And I dig.

33. NICK

I snap out of the dream and check my phone. Five AM. I'm not going to sleep any more tonight. I push off the covers and sit up. Stewart's on nights, so I don't have to worry about waking him up. My chair's right beside the bed so I slide my rear onto it and pull up the armrest behind me. I dial Rogan again but it goes to voicemail. Something's seriously wrong.

I scroll through the numbers he gave me and dial.

A Chinese voice answers.

"Hi, is this Phil Jiang?"

"Yes."

"Hi, it's Nick Stammo calling from Vancouver. I'm Cal Rogan's partner."

"I am so glad you called Mr. Stammo," he says. *"I was going to call you. Do you have any idea where Cal is?"*

My heart sinks. "No," I say. "I was calling you to see if you knew."

There's a moment of silence and then he asks, *"Does Cal often... what's the phrase? Go off the radar?"*

Swallowing the worry about him using again, I just say, "No."

"The last time you spoke to him, did he give you any idea of what his next step might be?" he asks.

"The last thing we got from Cal was an email telling us he'd found Aleksander. He said he was going to try and track down Zelena by following Leo, the owner of that nightclub The Golden Dragon."

He's silent for a while. Then says, *"OK, I'll see what I can do to track him down. It's eight PM here, I'm going to see what I can find out at the Golden Dragon."*

"I'd really appreciate that."

"And there's nothing else you can tell me about where he might be Mr. Stammo?"

"Please call me Nick," I say. I agree with Rogan. I get a good feeling about this guy but my worry about the drugs issue sets my heartburn going. Rogan started using after Em's death about a year ago. Maybe Tina getting stabbed has pushed him over the edge again. I don't know what to think here. Maybe I should—

"Nick, you still there?"

"Yeah, sorry Phil. I was turning something over in my mind."

"Anything I can help with?"

I think it through and make my decision.

"Maybe," I say.

———

"There's a Mr. Young on line one," Lucy calls out. I look over at Adry. She's giving the thumbs-up sign.

I pick up the phone. "Good morning Mr. Young," I say.

The Brit accent comes through strong. *"Just wanted to tell*

*you that Mr. Pridmore is very keen on having us invest in his
new company. He and I are meeting later today."*

"That's great," I say, returning Adry's thumbs up.
"Thanks for calling and letting us know."

"My pleasure," he says and hangs up.

"Pridmore's all over it," I say.

She grins. "You were right. You said he'd go for it like a
seagull at a landfill."

I nod. "So there's just one duck we need to set up."

She laughs now. "What is it with the bird metaphors?"

I roll backwards from my desk.

"Let's go get high as a kite," I say.

Still chuckling she follows me out of the office.

———

I HATE THE SMELL OF POT. BACK IN THE DAY, IT WAS THE
worst part of making a drug bust. He looks up as we enter
the store. "What the fuck do you losers want?" he says.

I look up at Adry. "Do you want to explain the situation
to Mr. Linsky?" I ask her. She nods.

"Pretty nice store you've got here Lee," she says.

His eyes go to slits. "So?" he says.

"You'll miss it when you lose your licence to operate it."

"What are you talking about?" he says with an uncertain
laugh.

"When the police arrest Bob Pridmore for fraud, your
name's going to come up. You were the guy who got Roland
McCoy to cheat Marly Summers out of five million dollars,"
she says.

His eyes go wide. "*Five* million?" he says.

Oh, it just keeps getting better. Big Bob must have lied to
him about the size of the scam.

Adry ignores his interruption. "*And* you got young Roland to transport a briefcase containing a quarter of a million bucks of heroin to our office."

"Heroin!" he literally gasps. "I had no idea what was in that briefcase. Pridmore said it was documents, he said—"

"I'm not interested," I interrupt. "You can tell it to the police when they come here to revoke your licence to operate this place."

His face takes on a lighter shade of pale. I can almost hear the calculations going on in that brain of his. He's no fool, he'll get there. His eyes go all slitty again. "So why are you here telling me all this?"

He got it.

"Good question," Adry says.

She can't keep the grin off her face as she gives him the answer.

34. CAL

A phone rings behind me. Probably someone calling to check if I'm dead yet. I'm not. The grave is not yet deep enough to bury me but it is just about deep enough for me to execute my plan. I keep digging while I wait for the phone call to end. I don't want the caller to hear what happens when I turn the tables on my captors. I listen to the short bursts of Cantonese from Fats as he responds to the caller. I hazard a look when he stops talking and see him put the phone back in his pocket.

Game on.

Now to test the acting skills I learned as part of my Masters in English Lit.

I push the spade into the soil. "What the...?" I shout.

I push the spade in twice more.

"Oh my God," I shout and scramble out of the grave. I throw a quick glance at the thugs and then stare back into the hole. "How the *hell* did that get there?" It's not good enough for an Academy Award, but it should get them running.

As I hear movement behind me, I firm up my grip on the

spade. I'm hoping Steroids will be quicker to act than Fats. I want to take him out first.

My muscles tense as someone moves fast into my peripheral vision. "What?" It sounds like Steroids.

I take a small backswing.

A hard, round piece of metal presses into the back of my head.

"Drop spade," Fats says.

Crap. He moved fast for a man of his epic proportions.

"Drop," he repeats.

I drop the spade at my feet.

I will not be offering effusive thanks to the Academy tonight.

I grit my teeth waiting for Fat's gun to fire.

I tense up and close my eyes.

Will I hear it?

Silence. A grim form of torture.

Finally, "Change of plan. Get in truck," Fats says.

My breath comes out in a whoosh.

I open my eyes as Steroids grabs my bicep and hustles me towards the van. The manacles limit the length of my pace and I shuffle forward as fast as I can.

He bundles me into the back and slams the doors behind me.

Within seconds, we are moving again, leaving me to wonder what earned me the reprieve.

Unbidden, Shakespeare comes to me.

> No, you are deceived;
> therefore, back to Rome, and prepare for your
> execution: you are condemned, our general
>   has sworn
> you out of reprieve and pardon.

I fear that, as usual, the Bard is right.

———

THE VAN COMES TO A HALT AND THE ENGINE IS SWITCHED OFF. They open the doors and drag me out into an alleyway. Steroids pushes me towards a door, which Fats opens for me. I shuffle inside and they follow. I am in a dingy hallway with a naked bulb hanging from the ceiling. Fats levels his gun at me while Steroids unlocks my shackles.

They hustle me along the hallway, up a flight of stairs and into an apartment. It shows no sign of habitation. The furniture is faded and shabby, the carpets look like they haven't been cleaned in an eon, and it smells. A frightened old woman is standing beside a rickety table. The black bruise on her chin washes a feeling of guilt through me.

Fats waggles his gun at me. "Take clothes off."

"What?"

He repeats his order.

I look from him to Steroids to the woman. She averts her eyes.

"Now!" he commands.

I strip down to my underpants, aware of the stink of sweat and urine on my garments as I drop them to the floor.

"Everything," he says.

I take off my underwear. Now all I'm wearing is my watch.

Fats fires off an order and the old woman shuffles forward, takes my things and hurries into another room, slamming the door behind her.

"Sit." He gestures towards a decrepit sofa, the pattern of the fabric being formed by a variety of dark stains.

"You're kidding," I say.

His eyes tell me otherwise.

Squirming inside, I lower my naked rear onto the seat and sink deep into the filth.

Fats and Steroids take seats on wooden dining chairs.

And we wait.

I don't know what we are waiting for but I'm guessing it's nothing good. However, it does give me time to think. Through the apartment's one grimy window, I can see neon lights and hear the noise of traffic. We are in the city. If I can find a way to escape, maybe I can get help somehow. Although the sight of a naked, fleeing man would only get me into the hands of the police and, if we are in Mongkok, that will inevitably put me under the control of the corrupt Inspector Ho.

I sneak a look at my captors. Steroids is cleaning his nails with something metal and Fats is sitting, cradling his gun in his lap. His eyes are fixed on me. He has obviously been given orders not to kill me, not just yet anyway. If I made a charge at him, would he obey orders and hold off using his weapon? He's a professional. Getting me to sit on this sofa was brilliant. The springs are wrecked and I have sunk so deep into it that my knees are at chest level. It would take an extra second to get up. Also the broken bones in my hand, courtesy of Leo, will be a huge impediment in any fight.

Now is not the time. *I am to wait, though waiting so be hell.* And so we wait.

Again.

———

AFTER WHAT FEELS LIKE ABOUT AN HOUR, THE OLD WOMAN appears in the doorway through which she exited. She says a couple of words and turns back into her room. Steroids and Fats get to their feet and the latter gestures to me to do the same. I struggle out of the deep seat. What now?

Fats waggles the gun at another door I hadn't noticed before.

"Clean," he says, gesturing again.

As I step towards the door, Steroids stops me. He takes my injured hand and removes the bandage. It's not a pretty sight: purple and yellow bruises and fingers like sausages about to burst through their skins. I go through the door and find myself in a tiny bathroom with a tiny shower. The walls are decorated with black patches of mold. I'm not sure why they want me cleaned up but it works for me, I guess. I turn on the water, which gushes out of the shower head. No low-flow shower here. To my surprise it is warm and I step inside. On the floor of the shower is a bar of soap. I pick it up and lather my head and body. A second surprise: the soap smells good; it's a lot like the soap in the Kerry Hotel. It feels good to wash off the stale sweat and urine from today's imprisonment in the truck.

When I step out of shower, there is a towel hanging on the back of the bathroom door. It's small but it does the job. Clean and dry, I step back into the apartment's living room, feeling a lot better.

The scene has changed. Steroids has gone but Fats is still here and he trains his silenced weapon on me again. There is a short, bespectacled man standing in the centre of the room, holding a paper bag, which I don't think holds take-out food. And the old woman is back. My clothes, clean, pressed and folded are in her arms. She hands them to me in silence and scuttles out by the door through which we entered.

Gratefully, I put my clothes back on. They feel slightly damp.

As I dress, the new character in the scene walks across the room and pours the contents of his paper bag onto the rickety table.

I recognize the items that clatter down.

Now I understand why the shower and why the clean clothes.

What I don't understand is why they decided on this way to kill me.

35. ZELENA

They did the auction again today. This time it was online, which I guess is better than being in that star room, but it was the only thing that was better. They drove me to the guy's house and he was a pig. He made me do things I don't even want to think about.

And now Leo is standing over me watching while I post on Instagram. But the worst thing of all is that there is no reply to my last message to 'Matt Standing.' This morning Leo made me post about calling off a private detective so I'm guessing Matt Standing is the private detective. So why hasn't he messaged me? He can't have given up on trying to find me so soon, can he? I can't keep this up much longer. If I don't hear from him tomorrow, I'm going back to Plan A. Being dead is definitely preferable to living another day like this.

36. NICK

I feel as twitchy as a crack addict right now. With any luck by the end of the day tomorrow, Bob Pridmore will be off our backs. But what's making me twitchy is all the things that could go wrong. Everything depends on Big Bob's greed being greater than his caution. He may be disbarred now but when he was practicing law he was pretty good at it. He's no fool. Connor McCoy is a smart cookie for sure but has he really fooled Big Bob? Adry's sure it's all going to go down OK but I've got my doubts.

But what's really making me twitchy is Rogan. He's been out of touch too long. My gut tells me he's back on the drugs but nevertheless, I shouldn't have told Phil Jiang about Rogan's history. Phil was really sympathetic and encouraging and I just felt I needed to share the information with him. But now I feel like I've betrayed Rogan's trust. Hopefully the subject will never come up and he'll never know I told Phil.

Adry breaks into my thoughts. "Zelena just made an Instagram post."

"What did she say?"

"Just the usual stuff, how much fun she's having blah-blah-blah. But she did message Matt Standing. She said, 'Are you OK? Haven't heard from you?' Cal hasn't done any posts as Matt. I think we need to do one and let her know we're still trying to find her."

"Yeah, you're right. Though with Rogan out of the loop, we're going to have to rely on Phil Jiang to find her." I check my watch; it's after midnight in Hong Kong. "When I spoke to him early this morning, I didn't think to tell him we are communicating with Zelena via Instagram. I'll call him in eight hours and let him know, it'll be morning his time. Maybe he can think about some questions we could ask her that might pinpoint where she's being held."

"How about I message her something to give her some hope. Something like 'we're getting closer' but not so obvious. What do you think?"

"Yeah, I guess we should. But I wonder if she has any idea where she is."

"If she did, I'm sure she'd have given us some sort of clue." She thinks for a second. "She said she was worried she hadn't heard from Matt. How about I say 'Sorry, I was out of cell range but I'm closer now.'"

"That should work. Do it."

She taps away at her phone. "Done."

"I hope we're not giving her false hope," I sigh.

"If it's enough to get her through another day, it's worth it," she says.

My cell rings.

I don't recognize the calling number. Probably one of those friggin' telemarketers or scam artists. Some asshole's going to say, 'This is the Canada Revenue Agency, we have a warrant for your arrest, blah-blah-blah.'

I let it ring.

Screw 'em.

37. CAL

I stare at the items lying on the rickety table. The baggie looks like it has enough heroin in it to kill a bull. If they inject just half of it into me I'm going to go out in one last burst of ecstasy. The thought rouses the Beast inside of me. He's lain dormant for half a year and as my love for Tina has grown, I dared to think he was gone for good. But he's back. He wants that hit even if it will kill both of us. I wonder if a hit that big will match the bliss of the very first time I used.

But the big questions are: why would they change the method of execution at the last moment? And how did they know? Maybe Leo asked his buddy Inspector Ho to look into my background? If Leo and his thugs know I was a user, it would be a smarter way to kill me. They shoot me up to the moon and leave my body on the street somewhere with the syringe beside me. It means everyone will think I just backslid. No one will think I was murdered by the people holding Zelena. What will Tina think? Will she grieve for me or will she have contempt? And Ellie, how will she handle it?

Thinking of Ellie and Tina gives me an inner boost of strength.

I take stock of the room.

People: Steroids and the old lady are gone. Fats is still sitting cradling his silenced gun in his lap. The man in the glasses is sorting through the paraphernalia on the table, diligently preparing the execution cocktail. He knows what he's doing. Maybe he's a user too.

Potential weapons: Fats' gun is the obvious one but he has a firm grip on it and he's shown he can move quickly when he needs to. He's two metres from me and with my broken fingers I don't rate my chances too highly. I can't see any obvious weapons in the shabby apartment. I look at the man with the glasses. He's standing on the other side of the table, bent over, shaking the white powder onto the table-spoon. It won't be long before he's ready. Then I see it.

Calculate: Step one will take maybe two seconds, two-and-a-half tops. Fats knows I'm not supposed to die by bullet; a half second of indecision on his part may give me the advantage I need. Step two, another couple of seconds.

I run the sequence in my head and check for any imped-iments that could slow me down.

Looks good.

A quick glance towards Fats and...

Go!

I take a quick step forward and take the only wooden chair still pushed up to the table. I grab it with both hands, pull it towards me and spin towards Fats.

Everything goes slo-mo.

Realization comes into his piggy eyes. I make the first step with my right foot and bunch up my shoulder muscles. Is that indecision in his eyes? I flow forward and start my swing. No indecision now. The gun comes up off his lap.

The extra weight of the silencer may slow its trajectory. With all I have, I complete the swing. The chair hits him full force before he can level his weapon.

Unlike in the movies, the chair doesn't shatter into a number of pieces but there is a sharp crack, which may be wood or bone. I'm hoping the latter. Either way, Fats and his chair topple over onto the floor and lie still.

I spin towards drug man.

Behind his glasses, his eyes are like saucers. He drops the spoonful of heroin as I drop the chair. I take two fast steps forward and push the table with every ounce of strength I have left. It hits him in the upper thighs, toppling him backwards and I follow through, tipping the table onto his chest and slamming my body down on top of it. *That* crack was definitely bone.

I straighten up and the world returns to normal speed.

Man, that was a loooong five seconds.

I stand in the centre of the room, drained, the broken bones in my hand throbbing. Now to sneak—

The apartment door flies open and Steroids fills the doorway.

We both take stock. He smiles. I don't.

I glance at Fats. He is lying on top of the gun with just the tip of the silencer protruding beneath his belly. Steroids eyes follow mine and his grin disappears. I dive toward Fats and land on the floor beside him. I get as good a grip as I can on the silencer and pull. It only moves about a centimetre. His hand must be underneath him too, still gripped around the stock. I slide my hand further up the silencer and get a better grip. I pull and this time it starts to move more freely. Another pull and—

Oooof!

Steroids' boot connects with my chest. I roll away and

look up at him. His foot is raised and he stamps down on my hand holding the gun. Just in time, I let go and whip it away. He moves his size twelve off the gun and makes a rookie mistake: instead of kicking the living snot out of me first, he reaches down for the gun.

Just before his hand grabs the prize, my hand snakes out and grabs his wrist. My foot comes up and with everything I've got I kick him under the chin, snapping his head back.

Any normal man would be out cold after a kick like that but Steroids just shakes his head a couple of times. However, it gives me enough time to take hold of the gun. I manage to yank it out from under Fats' gut but before I can take the stock with my other hand, he roars and throws his body down on top of mine. Every millilitre of air whooshes out of me and I start to see stars. His face ends up an inch from mine. I remember my Scottish instructor at the Justice Institute. *Always be on the offensive, laddie.* I make the only attack I can. I push my mouth into his face and bite down hard on his nose. It tastes foul. He bellows, filling the air with the smell of garlic and the ravages of poor dental hygiene. I bite down extra hard and then let go. Still howling, he rolls off me, hands over his injured part.

It gives me just enough time to manoeuvre the gun into my good hand, stick it into his belly and pull the trigger.

Nothing happens.

The safety must still be on.

I roll onto my hands and knees and jump to my feet.

As I fumble for the safety, something pushes me forward and I stumble over Fats' body. The floor comes up to meet me. I roll onto my back. Spectacles is there blinking down at me. I wait a split second for him to make his next move but he's not a fighter. He just stands there. He looks to Steroids who is lumbering to his feet but now I have the time I need.

My fingers find the safety, slide it to fire and point the gun at Steroids.

"Freeze!" I say, smiling grimly at the cliché.

He freezes.

Wow. I never knew a nose could bleed like that.

Holding the gun steady, I get gingerly to my feet.

I look at my prisoners. There is fear in their eyes.

I want to say, *Think'st thou I am an executioner?* But I think the quote might be wasted on them. However, it does beg the question of what to do with these mooks. The last fifteen seconds have been loud and may have attracted attention from the surrounding dwellings. I need to get out of here fast.

"Turn around," I say.

Glasses understands and turns his back on me. Steroids looks at me blankly. He may be one of the few people in Hong Kong who doesn't speak English but he looks at his companion and follows suit.

When they are facing away from me. I look around and see what I need. The crack that resulted when I hit Fats with the chair, was one of its legs breaking. I pick up the broken leg and, with two swift blows, put my other two prisoners into the land of nod.

I don't want to take the gun with me. I'm not sure what Hong Kong law says about carrying guns but I'm pretty sure it won't err on the liberal side of the equation. I take it into the bathroom, remove the silencer, wipe off my fingerprints and put both items into the toilet cistern.

I return to the main room and wipe my prints off the chair leg. I don't know why I'm bothering to clean off my prints, I doubt anyone is going to call the police. I chuckle at the thought. I scan the room and my eyes come to rest on the toppled table and what's on the floor beside it.

Pause.

Why not?

I take two paces and crouch down. In seconds, the heroin and paraphernalia are back in the paper bag and as I stand I stuff it into my pocket.

Why did I do that?

The Beast inside just chuckles as I head out of the apartment.

Outside, I walk past the parked van and out of the alley. There are not a lot of people on the street. It must be well after midnight. That's morning in Vancouver. I need to talk to Nick a.s.a.p. He must be worried sick. I look each way and to my right I can see bright lights. I make my way towards the lights and soon find myself on Nathan Road, Hong Kong's big shopping street. I'm in Mongkok. Not too far from the Golden Dragon and Inspector Ho's police station. With no phone and no money I feel naked. I see a nice-looking young couple approaching me.

"Excuse me," I say. "Do you speak English?"

"Yes," they say simultaneously.

"I've lost my phone, could I borrow yours to make an emergency call?"

They look at each other and a silent communication goes between them. "Certainly," the man says. He unlocks his phone and hands it to me.

I dredge up Nick's cell number from my memory and dial. It rings... and rings... Maybe I've got his number wrong. I normally just tap his name or get Siri to call him. *"This is Nick Stammo..."*

"Nick, it's Cal—"

"...I'm not available right now..."

Voicemail! I hang up. I'll call the office. I smile apologetically at the couple and they seem OK with me using it a second time. I raise my finger to dial and then stand there like a complete idiot. I don't know our office number. The only numbers I know are old ones from before the days of smart phones. I hand back the phone. "Which way is south?" I ask. I thank them and walk off in the direction they indicate. A brisk thirty minute walk should get me back to the Kerry where I can look up the office number and talk to Nick.

I increase my pace and enjoy the fresh air.

38. CAL

Thursday

Fortunately, the front desk check-in clerk recognized me and was happy to give me a replacement card despite it being after one in the morning. She even remembered my name—ah, the joys of five-star hotels. When Leo's thugs kidnapped me, they took all my stuff including my room's keycard. They know where I'm staying. The Kerry is no longer a safe haven for me. It is not outside the bounds of possibility that one of them is in my room right now, but unless Steroids and Co. have regained consciousness, I will have the element of surprise on my side.

Taking a deep breath, I swipe the card over the lock and burst into my room.

It's empty. My open suitcase is on the little stand provided by the hotel and the rest of the room is immaculate. Everything looks undisturbed. In an excess of paranoia, I check the bathroom. It too is empty but hey, even paranoids have people out to get them.

I open the safe and take out my passport, Vancouver keys, spare credit card and the remainder of the cash I withdrew in case I need to bribe someone. I must remember to cancel the card that was in my wallet. I pack my suitcase and carry-on bag as quickly as I can and head back to the lobby, dropping the keycard on the front desk and asking the clerk to check me out.

As I head to the main door, I walk past the concierge desk. There is just one person there at this time of night, an older man with a kindly smile. I remember the first time I spoke to the concierges—all five of them—about Zelena and Steph. This must be Mr. Zhao, the night concierge; he was on duty the night Zelena went missing.

I approach the desk and his smile broadens. He gives a slight bow, which I reciprocate. I fumble in my carry-on bag and pull out the photographs of Zelena and Steph. "Do you remember these guests?" I ask.

"Yes sir, I do. Very nice ladies."

I indicate Zelena. "She went missing on..." I check the date on my new watch—the gang obviously didn't think it was worth taking—and do the math. "...Friday night three weeks ago."

His forehead furrows. "Yes. I remember. There was a big dinner in the hotel that night. We were very busy. I called a taxi for her."

"How did she seem?" I ask. "Was she worried, or happy, or excited?"

"Oh very happy. Looked like she was in love." He gives a big smile.

"Why do you say that?" I ask.

"She was with her boyfriend. They looked very in love."

Now it's my turn to furrow my forehead. Zelena's boyfriend, Harvey Lim and the spiky-haired Chad left Hong

Kong on the Thursday, the day before Zelena vanished. Harvey, Chad and Steph already confirmed that. Could Leo have come over to pick her up? "Would you recognize the boyfriend if you saw him again?" I ask.

"Of course," he laughs. "He's a regular guest here. He's staying here now."

"Do you mean Harvey Lim?" I ask.

"Yes, Mr. Lim."

"It couldn't be. Mr. Lim flew off to California the day before."

He taps the computer mouse and after a couple of clicks, he nods to himself and types and clicks some more.

"Sorry sir. You are mistaken. Friday was definitely the night of the big party. That was when I saw them. Mr. Lim didn't check out until the Saturday."

Could Harvey be involved in Zelena's kidnapping? If he didn't leave on the Thursday, could Chad and Steph both have lied to me? But why would they? I think over my conversations with each of them. Steph and Zelena didn't go to the airport with the boys so Steph wouldn't know for sure whether Harvey actually left. But Chad *did* see Harvey leave... I think over my conversation with him. He and Harvey checked in together... except that's not what he said. They were on different flights, Chad to Vancouver and Harvey to somewhere in California. When Chad went through airport security, Harvey was still lining up at the check-in desk and after he went through security, he didn't see Harvey again. It could all have been a ruse.

Why didn't I see this before? It's so obvious. He and Leo are working together. Harvey procures girls and Leo puts them to work as sex slaves. I can see it all. On the Friday night Harvey calls Zelena and gives her some line, something like he couldn't be without her so when he got to California, he missed her so much he took the next plane back to be with her. He asks her would she come down and meet him in the lobby right now. She rushes down and falls into his arms and he takes her off to the Golden Dragon and Leo. He and Leo are big buddies from way back. It makes complete sense.

Except that it doesn't.

There's one thing that doesn't fit.

Phil had the security manager at the hotel check videos from the front door cameras. Zelena got into a cab alone and Phil tracked down the cab driver from his licence plate. He took her to IF, not to the Golden Dragon.

I turn back to Mr. Zhao, who is standing patiently ready to help. "She took a taxi by herself that night. Do you know where Mr. Lim went?"

"I don't know sir. They walked past me towards the front door and I had to help another guest. Maybe ask one of the doormen."

I thank him effusively and head for the front door.

I pull out my photo of Zelena but neither of the doormen have any memory of seeing Zelena on that Friday night.

I get in a cab and head for the Hilton.

———

THIS TIME HE PICKS UP. "NICK, IT'S CAL."

"What the hell are you doing at the Hilton? We were worried sick about you."

"I called you a couple of hours ago but you didn't pick up."

"Oh crap. Was that you? I thought—"

"Never mind. I got taken by Leo and his thugs. They tried to kill me but I managed to escape."

"What happened?"

"I'll give you the details later. I found out it's the boyfriend who set her up." I tell him about my conversation with Mr. Zhao.

"Jeez. What a slime. What are you going to do next?"

"It's two in the morning here. I'm going to go see Phil Jiang first thing and see if we can put together a plan. I'm thinking we could turn the tables on them and kidnap Harvey Lim. He's still here staying at the Kerry."

"Committing a crime in a foreign country may not be the smartest plan you ever had Rogan. You should definitely talk it over with Phil first. He seems like a good guy."

"You talked to him?" I ask.

"Yeah." He hesitates for a second. *"Yeah"* he repeats, with another pause. *"When you went missing I phoned him to see if he knew where you were."*

"Good idea. You're right. He is a good guy. I'm sure we can work this out together."

"Maybe you should go to the police. With the evidence of the concierge guy and the hotel cameras plus Phil talking to the taxi driver who took her to that nightclub, it's probably enough for them to pick up Harvey and ask him some hard questions."

"Normally, I'd agree, but Phil and I worked out Inspector Ho is dirty. He tipped off the guys at the place where I found Aleksander. By the time he got his act together to raid the place, they'd cleared out." As I say it, something picks at my mind. I stifle a yawn. Maybe I'm too tired to think straight.

"Inspector Ho's not the only cop in Hong Kong. Phil must know at least one clean cop."

"You're right. I'll talk to him tomorrow."

"You sound like you need a good night's sleep."

"You're right again. Before I go, how's it going there?"

He tells me about his plan for Big Bob Pridmore and I feel a wave of relief hit me. I can feel my old optimism return. With Stammo Rogan Investigation restored and a good result with Zelena we'll be back on top.

I KNOCK ON THE DOOR. FIVE HOURS OF SLEEP AND A HILTON English breakfast have restored me. No response. I stare at the door. There are five company names in both English and Chinese. Jiang and Lee is at the bottom. I wonder if Phil and his partner, the taciturn Mr. Lee, own all these companies. I raise my hand to knock again just as he opens the door. Phil's face is priceless: surprise, followed by an instant of puzzlement and then a broad smile. "Cal, I am so glad to see you. Where have you been?" He opens the door wide and I step inside.

Everything is the same as on my previous visits except Mr. Lee is sitting at one of the desks with the computer monitors on them. He gives me a glance so I smile and nod, but he turns back to his screens and studiously ignores me.

Phil gestures towards the sofa and chairs in the corner of the office. "Sit down. Make yourself comfortable," he says.

As I do, he asks again, "Where were you?"

"Leo's thugs kidnapped me. They tried to kill me."

"What happened?" he asks.

I tell him in detail about my abortive attempt to follow who I thought was Leo and how they turned the tables on me outside the Buddhist temple.

"When I woke up, I was in a room, like a hotel room, and Leo came to interrogate me."

"What about?"

"It was odd, he only had one question. He asked me how I knew Zelena and Aleksander were being held at one-oh-five Temple Street."

"How *did* you know?" Phil asks.

"Didn't I tell you, we've been—" I stop in mid-sentence. I just saw the implication in Leo's question. "Wait a minute..." I think it through again. Why the hell didn't I see this before? "I've made a big mistake," I tell him. "When Inspector Ho raided one-oh-five, no one was there. We assumed Ho had tipped off Leo so he could get the girls and most of their stuff out of there. But earlier that morning, I told Ho how I knew about one-oh-five. If Ho's working for Leo, Leo would have known too. He wouldn't have needed to ask me. I've done Ho a disservice. He can't be working for Leo. I need to go and see him."

Phil digests this for a moment.

"Maybe Ho is playing a clever game," he says. "He takes money from Leo for warning him about possible actions against him but keeps the source of his knowledge a secret. When you're taking bribes you don't want to reveal too much to the people who are bribing you."

"Wheels within wheels," I murmur. Maybe I won't go to see Ho after all.

"So how did you know?" he asks.

I chuckle. "I gave Leo a cockamamie story about seeing it in Aleksander's papers. The truth is, Leo, or someone, makes Zelena post stuff on social media. They're obviously trying to keep up the pretence she's a free agent and everything is fine. However, she is a smart cookie and we have found out a way to communicate with her over Instagram."

"Are you serious!"

I tell him about Zelena's H E L P messages and how we have been communicating via the fictitious Matt Standing.

"That's amazing."

He's cut off by the loud scraping of a chair across the floor. I turn and see Mr. Lee getting awkwardly to his feet. The normally quiet Phil snaps rapid-fire Cantonese at his partner who looks embarrassed for a moment before flopping back down into his chair. He replies with three syllables. Phil gets up and walks over to the filing cabinet. He opens the top drawer, riffles through until he finds a file folder, which he pulls out. Without a word he drops it on Lee's desk, turns and comes back to sit across from me.

Making no reference to the odd scene that he and his partner just played out, he asks, "How did you escape from Leo's people?"

I tell him about last night's grave digging episode, followed by the change of plan and the attempt to fill me full of drugs.

"Why didn't they just kill you and dump your body in the grave?" he asks.

Now it's my turn to look embarrassed. I take a deep breath. "I used to have a drug problem. I guess they figured it would be best for me to be found in an alley, dead from a massive overdose, than to go missing. Everyone would think I just relapsed and had one final high."

"But how would they know about your problem?" he asks.

"*That* is the mystery," I sigh. "Maybe Ho made some inquiries with the Vancouver Police Department."

He thinks for a while. "Did you tell your partner about this?"

"No. I talked to him at two o'clock this morning. I told him they'd kidnapped me but I didn't talk to him about the details." It reminds me of what we did talk about. I tell him about my conversation with Mr. Zhao, the night concierge.

"That makes complete sense," he says. "When I looked at the video of Zelena getting into the taxi, just before she got in she looked back and smiled. At the time, I thought she was smiling at one of the doormen but she must have been smiling at Harvey. Son of a—" he looks crestfallen. "I should have thought of that."

"You couldn't have known," I tell him.

"So what were you planning to do?" he asks.

"I think I need to take it to the police. Inspector Ho is out of the question but I was wondering if you knew any cops who could be trusted."

"Yes, sure. I know a couple, do you want me to call one of them?"

"I think we should."

He pulls out his phone and is soon having a conversation with his contact. In the stream of Cantonese, I recognize my name and Zelena's but nothing else. He hangs up with a big smile. "It's all good," he says. "My contact wants to meet with us. I mentioned Inspector Ho, and he told me Ho is under investigation at the moment. Anyway, he's at the court house right now, he has to give evidence at a trial this morning but he said he'd meet us here at two this afternoon."

"You don't know how relieved I am," I sigh. "Leo's pretty tough but I think Harvey Lim may very well break under interrogation. Maybe by this evening, we'll know where Zelena is." I check my watch. "It's just after six in the evening in Vancouver, I should call Nick and give him an update."

Phil chuckles. "You know what, Cal? You should relax a bit. From when we sit down with my guy, it's going to be all action for a while. Take a break. You're a block and a half from Nathan Road. Why don't you go and buy some stuff for your girlfriend and your daughter?"

I feel a pang of guilt that I haven't even thought about Tina or Ellie, or Sam for that matter. "You're right."

I stand up and shake his hand. "We'll soon have this all tied up."

"We sure will," he says with a big smile.

I like working with this guy.

He's one of the good ones.

———

"Hello, this is Tina Johal." My heart skips at the sound of her voice and I find myself tongue-tied for a second. *"Hello,"* she repeats.

"Tina, it's me," I say.

She's silent for a moment... a long moment. "Hello?" I say.

"Why didn't you call me? I've called you so many times over the last two days."

"I got kidnapped by the people who stabbed you. They held me captive for a day and a half. I only just bought a cellphone." Even I can hear the guilt in my voice caused by the fact I didn't call her sooner.

"Oh," she says, *"That's why I didn't recognize the number."*

"How are you?" I ask.

"Much better now," she says, *"They kept me in VGH for a day and a half then my parents brought me home. They have been driving me batty. I only managed to convince them to go home this evening."*

Another bout of uncomfortable silence.

I break it with, "I am *so* sorry about what happened."

The words tumble out of me. "It was my fault. I should never have taken you with me. I should have known it would be dangerous. I am so, so sorry. I shouldn't have put you at risk."

She gives a little laugh. *"It wasn't your fault. And if you remember, you didn't take me, I took myself."*

"I love you," I say.

I hold my breath for two long seconds before she says, *"I love you too."* A beat and then, *"When will you be home?"*

"With a bit of luck this will all be over tonight or tomorrow and believe me, I will be on the first plane out of here."

She laughs, then yelps. *"It hurts when I laugh. No need to rush. I'll be here when you get home. Besides, my stomach is still stitched together—inside and out—so I won't be very active for a couple of days. Nudge, nudge, wink, wink."*

I laugh, not because I understand what the last four words mean—I don't have a clue—but because I'm happy.

———

I'm sitting in a restaurant across the road from Phil's office. It's twelve-thirty. The meeting with his colleague in the Hong Kong police is not for another ninety minutes. I didn't eat anything yesterday and I am compensating with a large array of deliciously smelling dishes and a glass of Heineken. It's nice, but I do miss my craft beers.

My phone rings. The first call on my cheap-o cellphone. "Hello. Cal Rogan."

"Hi Daddy, why do you have a new phone number?"

"Hi Sweetie, thanks for calling me back. What time is it there?"

She giggles. *"Past my bedtime. And you didn't answer my question."*

Sheesh! You can't get anything past this girl. "Some bad guys stole my old one."

"Have you found the missing girl?"

Did I tell her about this case? "Not yet, but I'm hoping we are going to know where she is tomorrow."

"Is Uncle Nick over there with you?"

"No he's in Vancouver dealing with another bad guy. I'm working with a local private detective over here. His name's Phil. He has a partner too but his partner's a bit weird."

"Not like Uncle Nick."

"No Sweetie, not at all like Uncle Nick." I can't suppress a chuckle. There was a time, not so many years ago, when I thought Nick was a bit weird... and a lot worse than just weird. When I think back to the time of Kevin's death, Nick and I pretty much hated each other. We've come a long way. Maybe I should cut Mr. Lee some slack.

Ellie switches gears. *"You know it's only two more sleeps until Mommy and I arrive in Vancouver."*

"I *do* know that," I say, the big smile on my face getting wider. "I can't wait."

"I've been messaging my friends at St. Cecelia's. I've really missed them. Did you know what Ariana said the other day..."

As she prattles on about a bunch of girls I don't really remember, I dip a shrimp dumpling into some soy sauce and pop it into my mouth. As I chew appreciatively, my gaze drifts across the street. One man stands out from the lunchtime crowd thronging the sidewalk. He has a pronounced limp, which gives him an unusual rolling gait. I recognize that gait. I have seen this man before. Then I get it. Two nights ago, he left the Golden Dragon with the thug I thought was Leo. At the time I thought he looked familiar but now I know why. He steps off the sidewalk to avoid a gaggle of students and I can see his face clearly.

A bolt of electricity gallops up my spine.

It's Phil's partner, Mr. Lee.

I watch as he pushes through the doors into Phil's building.

I interrupt Ellie's ramble. "Sorry, sweetie, I have to go."

"You sound excited, have you seen the bad man who stole your phone?"

"Kind of. I'll talk to you tomorrow, OK?"

We make kissy sounds at each other and hang up.

I take three deep breaths to calm the maelstrom that is my consciousness. I need to think this through calmly. OK. Another deep breath. I saw Phil's partner walking and chatting with one of Leo's gang members two nights ago. The most charitable take on it is that Lee was staking out the Golden Dragon, just as I was, and he approached Leo's guy to try and pump him for information. Even as I think it, I reject it as unlikely. I have to assume Mr. Lee is part of the same triad as Leo.

But I've gone wrong before by assuming stuff.

What if—

And then it gets worse. On the sidewalk, I spot two old friends, one with his nose encased in bandages. It's Steroids and Fats. They too push through the doors into Phil's building.

So where does Phil Jiang stand? All my instincts tell me he's a heads-up guy. Maybe he doesn't know about Lee's connection with the gang. Maybe Lee is using him. I think through all my interactions with Phil. Nothing seems wrong. Except for one thing.

This morning in his office, Lee stood up and Phil made him sit down. Phil got the file Lee wanted. Why would he do that? The answer comes instantly. I told Phil how the gang kidnapped me on Tuesday night, I told him about the man with the limp walking beside Leo. Phil would know I'd recognize Lee's limp, so he stopped Lee from walking the three paces from his desk to the filing cabinet.

The disappointment sinks like cement into the pit of my stomach.

The problems I've been blaming on Inspector Ho have been caused by Phil Jiang. Then again, maybe Ho and Jiang are both dirty.

Phil misdirected me to investigating IF. It must have been Phil who tipped them off at one-oh-five Temple Street

Phil knew I was going to stake out the Golden Dragon on Tuesday night. He orchestrated for the gang to take me. I think about the fear I had digging my own grave. And then the change of plan to pump me full of heroin. The idea that Ho contacted the VPD and found out about my addiction was a bit tenuous even when Phil suggested it. It was Phil who told Steroids and Fats about my addiction.

And when I realize how Phil knew, the cold wind of betrayal hardens the cement in my gut to concrete.

Then a worse thought coalesces: I told Phil how we have been communicating with Zelena.

When Leo learns that, what will he do to her?

I have to find her fast.

But how?

I have no clue where she is.

I have no way of finding out.

And I have no friend to help me.

———

SOMETIMES STUFF JUST POPS INTO YOUR MIND. SO OFTEN FOR me, it's Shakespeare. As I leave the restaurant via the back door, silently bemoaning my bad luck, Claudius' words from Hamlet pop into my mind: *That sweepstake you will draw both friend and foe.* And the words trigger something. I've drawn several foes in this case but just maybe I can turn a foe into a friend, albeit an unwilling one. As a plan starts to form in my mind, I think perhaps I can turn two foes into friends.

In the taxi back to the Hilton, I think through the plan.

By the time I get into my room, I have the details worked out. It's shaky as hell but it's all I've got. I make a list on a piece of hotel stationery of the things I need to do. It's a long list but doable. Now for step one.

I still have his business card in my pocket unless the old woman took it out before she cleaned my clothes. I feel a crumpled mass in my pocket. I pull it out. I straighten it out carefully and for the first time I really look at it. I am such an idiot. The name of Harvey Lim's company leaps out at me. I knew I'd seen this name before. It's one of the company names painted on the door of Phil Jiang's office. If I had *really* looked at it before, I would have made the connection and it would have saved me a lot of trouble. But it's water under the bridge now. His number is just legible. I dial it.

"Lim Jian Xun."

"Good afternoon Harvey, it's Cal Rogan."

Silence. The silence of the guilty methinks.

"Yes?"

He doesn't know what to think. If he has been kept up to date with the rest of the gang, he will be expecting that in five minutes I will walk into Phil's office and into the trap, which has almost certainly been prepared for me.

"Did you know Phil Jiang is screwing you over?"

Silence again.

"What exactly do you mean?"

"You mean you can't guess?"

I can almost hear the gears turning in his mind.

"No, why don't you tell me."

"At seven-thirty this evening, I want you to leave your hotel and get the Hung Hom ferry. When you are on the ferry, call me on this number for further instructions on what to do when you get to North Point. Do you understand?"

"Why should I bel—"

"Do you understand?"

"Yes, bu—"

I hang up. I don't know a lot about the gang but they may very well be able to track me through my phone, so I power it off.

I wonder if he bought my assertion that Phil Jiang is cheating him in some way.

I don't care one way or the other.

Slinging my carry-on bag over my shoulder, I wheel my suitcase out into the hallway. I have a hell of a lot to do after I've checked out of the Hilton.

———

THERE IS A BUS TERMINAL UNDER THE KERRY HOTEL. I park the rental car right by the pedestrian exit that gives onto the seawall. At weekends this area is taken over by young immigrants who sit in the sun, play music, chat and picnic. At this latitude the sun has set and, fortunately, there are not a lot of people around. I take the sawn-off baseball bat off the back seat and slide it up the sleeve of the oversized jacket I purchased in the market. I pull the peak of my new baseball cap down over my eyes and get out of the car. I didn't have time to reconnoitre the area so I have no idea where the cameras may be.

I walk onto the seawall and move to where I have a decent view of the concrete stairway that leads down from the hotel to the seawall and the ferry terminal. I squat on the edge of a planter and try to look like I belong.

The wait is short. I can see Harvey Lim is coming down the steps. I see he didn't buy my story about Phil Jiang cheating him because he's not alone and his companion is Steroids; won't he be pleased to see me. I have to execute the riskier Plan B. I slowly get to my feet and, affecting a slight limp, I cross the seawall and move into the shadow of the concrete stairway, out of their line of sight.

I let my weapon slide down my sleeve into my hand, then conceal it behind my back. Soon enough they step off the bottom stair and I see their backs as they walk toward the ferry terminal.

"Hey, Harvey!" I call out.

He turns and I wave. He barks an order to Steroids who also turns. He sees my face and grins.

They come towards me.

So far so good. They are walking side by side. Harvey is not a warrior in this scenario. He has taken out his phone and is tapping at the screen.

He stops about three metres from me but Steroids keeps on advancing.

Timing will win the day.

At two metres, I wait a split second, genuflect, and with every bit of strength I can muster, swing the foreshortened bat in a wide arc and smash it into the side of Steroids' knee.

I snap back up to my feet and cut off his bellow of pain by cracking the bat across his skull. It's a glancing blow, which won't kill him but will raise a goose egg to make a nice match with the one I gave him yesterday.

Before his body hits the ground, I make a beeline for Harvey. Definitely not a warrior, he does exactly the wrong thing: he turns and runs. But I have the momentum. I jab the bat hard into his back, making him stumble and fall. His cellphone shatters into several pieces.

I kneel on his back and cuff his wrists behind him with the toy handcuffs I also bought in the market. I open my jacket, peel off one of the strips of duct tape I secured there earlier, and slip it over his head and across his mouth.

I get up and drag him to his feet and within ten seconds, I am bundling him into the back of the rental car. Taking a moment to secure his wrists with more duct tape—just in case the toy cuffs are as shoddy as I suspect—I put my last strip of duct tape over his eyes, throw the cheap blanket over him, get in the car and drive off.

We are heading for the one place they will not think to look for us.

39. ZELENA

There was no auction this evening. At least, there wasn't for me. I hope there wasn't one for the other girls either. I don't know whether that's good or bad. It's good that I don't have to be abused by some pig of a man, but changes in routine are never good. Maybe they are going to move us back to that awful place where I was so cold at night. At least the rooms here are decent. It must be late. Leo will be here soon to make me do another post. I wonder if 'Matt Standish' will have commented on my post. I can't think of any way to give him a clue as to where I might be. From the post Leo made me send, he must be some sort of private investigator. If he reads the post, he will have seen the help message I added. 'Hey everyone likes privacy.' That was pretty good. Hey, I'm smiling. It's the first time I've had a genuine smile on my face in a while. Maybe it's a good omen. Maybe the detective is going to find me tonight. I get a surge of hope, which I thought had abandoned me. He is going to be here soon. He's going to free me and all the girls here. The weight of the last however-many days lifts from my shoulders and the smile is back.

When I'm free of this place I'm going to start thinking more seriously about stuff. I'm kind of over the whole party-til-you-drop thing. Maybe I'll switch to law. I could use it to help kids caught up in the slave trade. I don't quite kno—

The door opens.

Leo.

I force a smile to my face. This smile is definitely not genuine. "Hi," I say.

He just stands there glaring at me. And he doesn't have the cellphone in his hand. This cannot be good.

He quietly closes the door behind him and walks slowly over to me. I stand up and face him. I'm almost as tall as he is.

He stops in front of me and looks hard into my eyes. I return his stare. There's no way I'm going to let him see how scared I am. I see him tense up then feel a stab of pain as he slaps me. The whole side of my face feels like it's on fire. He shouts something at me in Cantonese. I turn my head back to face him and although I feel the tears running down my face, I don't make a sound.

"You tried fool me," he says in his broken English. "Bitch."

I just stand there looking at him but this seems to make him even more angry.

Before I can look away, his hands reach out and he starts tearing off my clothes. No! Not this time. I reach up and scratch his face with both hands. He flinches as one nail rakes over his eye. I bring up my knee as hard as I can but it just hits him in the thigh. He pushes me hard and I fall over backwards onto the wood floor. Before I can react he pounces on me and kneels on my legs.

Now he has a knife in his hands. I can't suppress the

scream that rises to my lips. He uses the knife to cut away the remnants of my clothes then holds it to my throat.

"Don't move bitch," he says.

I can feel the tip of the knife penetrate my skin.

I don't move.

But he does.

40. CAL

He winces as I rip the duct tape off his eyes. "Recognize this place, Harvey?" I ask. He looks around and shakes his head. He's lying. "Sure you do," I say but he still shakes his head. He tries to sit up but he is bound tightly to the bed. I take the newly-purchased knife from the newly-purchased holdall and slide it out of the sheath. His eyes go wide. "I'm going to remove the tape from over your mouth so we can have a conversation. If you yell or scream, I will ruin your face so that no girl will ever look at you again, let alone allow you to sell her into slavery. Do you understand?"

He nods.

I rip away the tape. He grunts at the pain of his facial hairs being torn from their follicles but makes no other noise.

"Where is Zelena being held?"

"I don't know. Why would I know? She's my girlfriend, I love her. I want to find her as much as you do."

"Oh, that is so heart-warming," I say. "But you lied to me

about leaving here and going to California. A lie of omission perhaps but a lie nonetheless."

"But you don't understand—"

"Can it Harvey," I interrupt. "Your cousin Leo is holding Zelena captive somewhere. You need to tell me where she is."

"I told you I don't know," he says.

"When we sat in the bar at the Kerry, and I told you I was working with a private detective named Phil Jiang, you omitted to tell me you know Mr. Jiang and know him well."

"I've never heard of him," he protests. He sounds so genuine, I could almost believe him.

"When I called you, I had to check your business card for your phone number. I recognized the name of your company." His face tightens. "I knew I'd seen it before somewhere. Then I remembered: it is one of the companies whose names are painted on the door to Phil Jiang's office."

"It must be a different company with a similar name," he says, but the tone of his voice belies his assertion.

"Really Harvey?"

He pauses a beat.

"Ok, so I know Phil Jiang, so what?"

"Come on Harvey, I know everything. Phil Jiang is in the same gang as you and Leo. You find the beautiful girls, they take them captive and put them into slavery, auctioning them off to perverts, and you all make big bucks doing it." As I speak all the assurance slides from his face.

"How did you find out?" he asks.

"Because I'm good at what I do. So believe me when I tell you, unless you tell me where Zelena is right now, you are going to regret it very much."

He drops the façade. "Go take a flying fuck, Rogan. If I

read you right, you're not going to slice me up with that knife of yours. It's not your style."

I remember my earlier thought that I can turn two foes into friends. I can use one against the other. I rummage in my holdall and pull out the paper bag containing my other foe.

"Phil Jiang made a big error," I tell him as I start to remove items from the bag and put them on the bedside table. "He talked to my partner in Vancouver who, out of a misguided worry for me, must have told Phil I used to have a problem with this." I wave the baggie at him then put it down. "Phil realized if I was found dead of an overdose, it would be treated as a tragic error in judgement. If I went missing, the police might get off their fat asses and start investigating the things I had talked to them about. So he called the guys who were about to shoot me and bury me, and told them to pump me full of smack instead. Unfortunately for them, I had other plans."

I pour all the powder into the little metal container and add some water, all the while watching Harvey with a smile on my face. There's no reciprocating smile on his but there *is* a sheen of sweat on his brow. I fire up the butane lighter and heat up the solution.

"There's enough here to kill a stable full of horses. When I inject it into your vein you are going to get the most unbelievable high, which you will really, really enjoy for the few seconds before your heart explodes."

"You wouldn't," he almost gasps.

I say nothing and take out the syringe. His eyes go wide. "Oh, do you have Trypanophobia by any chance?" I say conversationally.

"What the fuck?"

"Trypanophobia," I repeat. "It's fear of needles."

I get a stream of expletives back.

"I'll take that as a yes." I fill the hypodermic from the metal container. No need for any sanitary precautions here. He tries to thrash about but the duct tape has both arms firmly attached to the frame of the bed. "That's good," I say. "The more you strain against the duct tape, the more your veins will swell and the easier it is for me." He goes limp and with the ease of long practice, I slide the needle into a vein in the crook of his arm.

"No, please, take it out, take it out."

As much as I want to get the information, I long to ram the plunger home and watch his reaction.

"Please don't. I'll tell you, I promise. Just take it out of my vein." There is a rising panic in his tone.

"*Meum opium, meae leges,*" I say with a grin.

"What the fuck is—"

"It's Latin. It means my heroin, my rules," my grin gets wider. "And here are my rules. You tell me where Zelena is being held and I remove the needle. If you lie to me, I will come back, reinsert the needle and send you to heaven or wherever it is you're bound. Then I'll track down Leo and make him the same offer. I'm sure he'll be happy to cooperate."

"All right, I'll tell you." His words come tumbling out. "There's a small hotel that Leo owns. Just before this place was raided, he took all the girls there. It's called the Bright Sun in English, it's in Wan Chai. Now, take the needle out please."

"What's the exact address?"

He gives it to me and I write it down.

"Now, *please* take out the needle."

I take out the duct tape and tear off a new strip, which I stick over his mouth and wrap twice round his head.

"Thanks for your help Harvey," I say. "You know, in my career, I have met some of the real dregs of humanity: murderers, drug dealers, child kidnappers, a serial killer, gang bosses and perverts. But you guys take the cake. It has *got* to be a better world without you in it." I can smell the fear on him. "So have a nice trip," I conclude.

His eyes go like saucers as I push home the plunger on the syringe, pick up my holdall and leave. I am followed by the sound of his bowels voiding.

41. ZELENA

At last it's over. He rolls off me and lies on his back beside me, smelling of sweat. I managed to get through it without fighting or crying or screaming, though God knows I wanted to do all of those things. I can take a little satisfaction in knowing I spoiled it for him.

"You are useless bitch," he says as he gets up.

I get off the floor, pull the quilt from the bed and hug it around me.

"Thought you talk to detective." His words fire through me like electricity. He sees it and smiles. "Oh, yes. Thought you give him message. Detective told us everything. Silly *gwáilóu* girl. No one never gonna find you now."

All my hopes of twenty minutes ago shatter and I feel a volcano of heat rise up in me. I hate him for telling me. How stupid was I to believe I would be rescued? Leo will never let me go. I will be here until I die. Living the same nightmare every day.

He took away my one dream.

I have never hated like this before.

For the first time I actually believed I would get out of

here. They must have scared the detective off or maybe bought him off. Either way doesn't matter. But my contempt for him is totally eclipsed by my hatred for Leo. He buckles his belt and bends down to pick his tee shirt up off the floor.

And I see it.

His knife. It's on the bedside table, three paces from where I stand.

As he pulls the tee over his head, I drop the quilt, take the three steps and grab it. It feels good in my hand. For the first time I feel I have some control. I hear some yelling as I turn towards him. His head pops out through the neck of the tee and he must hear the yelling too because he turns away from me towards the door.

He's a metre away.

Perfect!

I whisper a silent prayer and, with a feeling of victory, I plunge the knife in, right up to the hilt.

42. CAL

I don't know what prompted Inspector Ho's change of heart but I am grateful for it. When I showed up at the Mongkok police station, demanding to speak with him, they had him on the phone within minutes—despite the late hour—and he immediately sprang into action.

This time he equipped me with a bulletproof vest and let me follow his SWAT team into the Bright Sun Hotel. I hear yelling and the sounds of struggle as Ho's team take down the staff. After a couple of minutes all goes quiet on the main floor and there are several people face down on the floor and in handcuffs. I recognize Fats among them.

There is more yelling going on upstairs but it soon quiets down. As ordered, I wait on the main floor. It is a small but elegant hotel with furnishings that must have cost a fortune. I know less than nothing about Chinese art but there are some beautiful vases, which must be worth thousands, and even I can tell the artwork on the walls is original.

I don't have to wait long.

Ho appears at the top of the stairs and waves me up.

As I get to the top, I see several men in handcuffs and a group of scantily dressed girls standing together hugging each other silently. Zelena is not among them.

"Come," says Ho.

I follow him down the hallway and into the last-but-one room on the right.

There are two SWAT guys in the room.

One is holding the arm of a handcuffed Leo.

The other is kneeling beside the naked body of a girl. A knife is protruding from under her chin. It has been pushed up through her throat and the roof of her mouth and into her brain.

The kneeling cop looks up at Ho and shakes his head.

And I feel the tears stream down my face.

43. ADRY

I watch Jason as he makes breakfast. Before I met him and started staying over at his place, breakfast for me was a cookie and a cup of coffee. I worry about the additional calories but Jason is a breakfast-is-the-most-important-meal-of-the-day kinda guy. Even when I told him Kellogg started that idea in TV ads before either of us was born, he still insists on making me start the day with a meal and I love him for it.

Last night, we had the discussion about moving in together. The plan is to get a new place rather than one of us moving into the other's apartment. I'm just waiting to see if Nick can pull off the plan and restore Stammo Rogan Investigations to its former glory, so that I know I have a job moving forward.

Just as Jason puts poached eggs and toast in front of me, I hear my cell ringing. I think about letting it ring... but only for a second. "I'd better take it, it might be Nick," I say. Bless him, he just smiles and nods. He knows how important the next eight hours are going to be.

I get into the bedroom by the fifth ring. I grab the phone. It's Cal's new number.

"Hi Cal, what time is it there?"

"It's over," is all he says.

"You found Zelena?" I can hear the excitement in my own voice.

"Yeah."

Silence.

"Is she OK?" I ask but I know the answer.

"She committed suicide minutes before we got to her." I can hear the break in his voice.

Through the tears, I manage to speak. "I'm so sorry Cal. You mustn't blame yourself."

"I... do blame... myself," he manages to say.

"Don't Cal. It wasn't your fault." Silence again. "What did Nick say?" I ask.

"I don't want to speak to him just yet. Do you think I could ask you to do it for me?"

I can feel a frown wrinkle my brow. What's going on? "Sure, of course. Is there anything else you want me to do?"

He thinks for a moment. Then, *"There is one thing. The Hong Kong police will talk to the VPD who'll send someone over to tell her parents. I think they need to hear it from one of us first. Could you ask Nick to do that? He's had experience telling parents. You might not think so but he's good at it."*

"Sure, no problem. We'll go together."

"Thanks."

More silence.

"Cal, there is some good news. Connor McCoy called, everything seems to be going according to plan."

"Oh, right. OK. That is good news I guess." His words give me an uneasy feeling. It's more than just the guilt and

distress of losing a client. I need to ask him. I take a deep breath but before I can say anything he hangs up.

I hope it's just the shock but I don't think so.

44. CAL

Friday

The Jaguar is new and the smell of the leather is good as I slide into the back seat. But the good stops right there. I can't shake the feeling that Inspector Ho is going to take me to his police station rather than to the airport. He gives an order in Cantonese to the driver and we pull away from the curb.

"Mr. Rogan," he says in his posh English voice, "I appreciate your desire to leave Hong Kong so soon but I did want to speak with you before you left the Territories."

"Sure. But let me ask you something first."

"Of course," he says it more graciously than I can manage right now.

"When I came to you and told you I thought Zelena was being held at one-oh-five Temple Street, you basically blew me off. It wasn't until I came back, after getting her brother out of there, that you agreed to make the raid and even then it was too late. Why?"

"Yes, you will never know how much I regret that. But I

had a good reason. I have spent most of my career fighting organized crime. When you first came to see me, I was suspicious of you, so I had one of my men follow you. When you left the police station, you went straight to the office of Jiang and Lee. We have long been suspicious of those two but never had any solid evidence to tie them to the triads. Needless to say, when you went there, you fell under suspicion too. So when you came to me with your story, I thought it might be a trick to lure me into a trap. It wouldn't be the first time they have tried to kill me.

"When you came back with Aleksander in tow, I didn't know what to think. I knew I needed to raid the place, but it took me some time to put together a task force big enough to take the place if it were heavily guarded.

"Then of course you threw me into another round of confusion immediately after the raid when I found you waiting outside with Jiang."

His words have the ring of truth. "Have you arrested them?" I ask.

He chuckles. It's the only time I've seen him exhibit any genuine humour. "Oh, yes," he says. "Your sworn statement was enough to get me arrest and search warrants. Messrs Jiang and Lee are in the cells right now, as is the man you know as Leo and several members of their gang. Providing you keep your word and come back to give evidence at the trial, I feel confident we can put them all behind bars for a very long time."

"That reminds me," I say. "If you go back to Temple Street, in one of the upstairs rooms you'll find a young man named Harvey Lim duct taped to a bed. He'll be hungry and thirsty and will smell pretty bad but, apart from about ten millilitres of sugar water in his veins, he'll be OK. He lives in Canada and has the job of procuring girls for the gang to enslave. We don't want him back, so if you could put him in jail here, the Canadian people would thank you."

He smiles again. "Well done. We were wondering about Mr. Lim. When we raided the Bright Sun Hotel, we rescued several young ladies from different parts of North America who have been victims of the gang. They all mentioned coming to Hong Kong with a Mr. Lim. We wondered who he was."

"It must have cost them a lot of money to kidnap these girls," I say.

"It's all relative Mr. Rogan. They were probably charging their clients somewhere between fifty- and a hundred-thousand Hong Kong dollars for a night with each girl."

"You can tell them they were rescued thanks to the smarts and the bravery of Zelena Gutkowska."

"I will do that."

He spends the rest of the trip to the airport, telling me about the evidence they have found so far at Jiang's office and at the Bright Sun Hotel. It's an impressive list but I'm only listening with half an ear. I'm thinking about seeing Ellie and Sam at the airport; our planes arrive at about the same time. And I'm thinking about Tina. And I'm thinking about two emails: one I just sent and one I received eleven days ago. But most of all I am thinking about one element of the case that I don't understand and the answer to that is back in Vancouver.

45. NICK

The reception area is weirdly familiar. It's a lot more luxurious than his old office, with modern décor and expensive-looking leather chairs, but the same photos are on the walls. They all feature Big Bob in various settings with the glitterati and the wealthy of Vancouver. Vanity pics Rogan calls them... Hmm, Rogan... He'll be getting on the plane soon. He's avoided my phone calls. There can only be one reason for that.

"We'd like to speak with Mr. Pridmore," Adry says to the receptionist.

"Do you have an appointment?" she responds. She's very pretty but with a bit too much makeup.

"Tell him Nick Stammo and Adry Locke are here to see him."

"Mr. Pridmore doesn't see anyone without an appointment," she says with a smug look on her face.

"Just tell him we're here," I growl at her. "He'll see us." I say it with more confidence than I feel. Then again, maybe Pridmore would like to gloat over us.

She makes an elegant gesture and looks at her watch. "He has another appointment in ten minutes, so I am afraid he won't be able to see you."

"That appointment's cancelled. He's meeting us instead." She looks confused for a moment then picks up the phone. I think of something that'll get his attention and make him want to speak with us. "Tell him Connor McCoy sent us."

She relays the message, pauses, repeats it, pauses again and hangs up. "He'll be right out." The surprise in her voice makes me chuckle, less at her but more in anticipation of Pridmore's surprise.

He steps out of a corridor into the reception area. That was quick. "What do *you* want?" he says, drilling his eyes into me.

"Good afternoon, Bob." I give him a big grin. "I'm fine. Thank you for asking. How are *you* doing?"

"Cut the crap Stammo, what's this about Connor McCoy?"

I glance at the receptionist. "Are you sure you want to have this conversation out here?" I ask.

"Yeah, I am. It's going to be a short conversation anyway."

"Yes." I can't keep the grin from my face. "I suppose it is. I have a message from Connor. He said to say thank you so much for the five million dollars investment in his company. He was surprised when the cheque cleared by the way. He said he decided to change the use-of-funds clause in your agreement. He's going to pay the money to Marly Summers so she can pay it to the Royal Bank."

Confusion, surprise, anger: they're all fighting for position on his face. "He can't do that," he splutters.

"Oh, I think you'll find he can. As a matter of fact, he already has," I say. God, I am loving this. "By the way, Marly asked us to say a big thank you as well."

The anger comes to the front of the line. "Well you can tell Mr. Connor McCoy I'll sue the ass off him. He's going to be spending most of the next few years in court."

"Hmm. That sounds like an expensive proposition. You're a corporate lawyer, not a litigator. How are you going to come up with the five-hundred-an-hour fee for a good litigator?"

"That's for me to know." He checks his watch. "Now get out of here before I call security."

"Expecting someone are you?" I ask. His eyes narrow in uncertainty. I wish Rogan was here to share this. "You see Bob, I don't know a lot about corporate finance but it seems like you don't either. Normally investment deals, like the one you made with Connor McCoy, take months. Yet you pulled it off in two days. Didn't that seem odd to you?"

"It was a great deal. McCoy was desperate for money so he agreed to all sorts of shit clauses. In six months, I'll have control of his precious Dark Energy Systems."

"Oh, Bobby, Bobby, Bobby. You didn't do your due diligence did you?"

"My contract with him is airtight. Like I said, he's gonna be spending a lot of time in court."

"Do you think Arnold Young will want you to spend his money in litigator fees?" Arnold's name is like a slap in the face. Bob's eyes go wide and his mouth is moving, but nothing's coming out. "Oh, yeah, I forgot to tell you. Arnold says he won't be here for your meeting in what..." I make a big deal of checking my watch, "...ten minutes. Or, for that matter, ever. He said to tell you the deal's off."

"You sons-a-bitches."

He collapses onto one of the leather chairs. I just sit in my wheelchair watching the gears turn in his mind but he finds no way out. "Fuck!" he says, but it's more to himself than to us. Then a sly look comes onto his face. "At least I'll be able to enjoy watching you and Rogan fighting off the drug charges in court. With a bit of luck, you could get convicted. How'd you feel about being in jail in that chair Stammo?"

"Drug charges? What *do* you mean?" I ask.

"Come on Stammo. You know what I mean. The police busted you for having possession of the drugs I got Lee Linsky to plant on you."

"Drugs? Busted?" I fake confusion.

"I saw you on the news being led away by the police. By the way, did you ever wonder how the CBC and the Vancouver Sun got those pictures and videos?"

"One of your many problems Bob is you don't know how to delegate. You see, Lee Linsky didn't plant those drugs on us. Mr. Linsky didn't want to get his hands too dirty. When you decided to scam Marly you asked your boy Lee to seduce her and get some financial details. Without telling you, he sub-contracted the job to an actor he knows. Then when you decided to scam us too, Lee got the same actor to pretend to be a blackmail victim. You know about actors, don't you Bob. You hired one in Toronto to pretend to be Marly Summers and take out that loan."

He now looks bewildered. He wonders how I know all this stuff.

"But do you know about facial recognition software Bob? The Vancouver Police Department used it to analyze that tape. They were able to track down the actress you used. When they got their colleagues in Toronto to pick her up, she told them everything."

The bewilderment has vanished. Now he looks like a caged animal trying to find a way out.

"Anyhoo... the actor Lee Linsky used was named Roland McCoy and, being a lazy s.o.b., Roland used his successful older brother's name with Marly and with us."

"It's all circumstantial," he growls.

I pull out the digital recorder covered by the blanket across my lap. "Except that you just admitted to getting Lee Linsky to plant drugs on us. On top of that Lee and Roland have both agreed to turn Queen's evidence and testify against you."

Everything else disappears from his face and gets replaced with rage. He stands and starts towards us, then stops in his tracks looking past us. I hear the door being opened and soon-to-be-Inspector Steve Waters walks in. He strides over to Big Bob.

"Robert Charles Pridmore, I have here a warrant for your arrest..."

I don't need to hear the rest of it. I've heard it so many times before.

Besides, we've got a party to go to.

————

IT'S A SMALL PARTY, JUST FOUR OF US HERE SO FAR. ARNOLD Young politely turned down our invitation. Just as well, I don't think he's a party kind of guy. Marly Summers looks her usual stunning self and Connor McCoy is pouring champagne for all of us. To my surprise, he's not all over Marly. His smiles seem directed at Lucy more than anybody and she is glowing in his attention.

"Where's Cal?" Marly asks.

"On a plane coming back from Hong Kong," I tell her.

"I love Hong Kong," she says. "Was he there on vacation?"

"No, not exactly."

"It's a shame he's not here, I wanted to thank you all for what you did, rescuing me from Pridmore's clutches... again." She hands me an envelope. "The balance, with a little bonus. It's an extra thank you for getting your friend at VPD to call the Royal Bank and confirm they had been the victims of a crime. They were effusive in their thanks when I transferred the five million dollars to them."

"Thank you." I feel a bit embarrassed for some reason but I'm saved from having to say more by the arrival of Adry, Jason and Stewart with a tray of fancy snacks from the caterer downstairs in our building.

As everyone is being introduced to everyone else, I feel so grateful I have this group of people in my life.

Lucy puts on some music and it starts to feel like a party. Stewart brings me a glass of champagne and a plate of nibbles. "Better than coffee and cookies," he says as he sits beside me. He raises his glass. "Cheers, Nick."

My phone buzzes. I take a sip before I check it. The champagne is courtesy of Marly and it's better than any I've ever had on my budget. I look up at Stewart. "Cheers," I say and I hope he can read the other words in my eyes.

I check the phone. It's an email from Rogan.

I read it and my good spirits disappear.

46. CAL

Friday

She sprints past the baggage carousel and flings herself into my arms. All the dark thoughts, which have inundated me on my thirteen-hour flight, are washed away: thoughts of Zelena and Stammo's betrayal of me and what to do about it and the last question I still have to get answered. They all dissipate in the glow of her hug. "I am so glad to see you Daddy," she says. I hug her tightly. I love that she called me Daddy, rather than Dad. Silly but I love it.

"I have missed you so much," I say. We just hold onto each other.

After what seems too short a time, she tries to wriggle free but I keep holding on. I don't want to ever let go. I want to protect her from the world. As long as she's in my arms she's safe. She stops wriggling and hugs me tighter and I'm safe in her arms too. A wave of tenderness washes over me. "Did you find the missing girl?" she whispers.

"Yes, sweetie." It's all I dare say.

But before she can ask more, I hear Sam's voice. "Hello Cal."

I open my eyes and the shock of seeing Sam in a wheelchair brings me back into the world. It's five years since I first learned of her MS, not even five years ago. The disease has progressed fast.

"Hi Sam," is all I say.

She reaches out a hand and I take it in mine. Time stops for a moment as our history replays on the screen of my mind. The tenderness I feel for Ellie seems to transfer to Sam. Maybe tenderness is the wrong word. Maybe it's compassion or maybe it's love. I don't know any more. Then I become aware of Ellie watching us and the expectation in her eyes cuts into me.

I give Sam's hand a squeeze. "I'll get your suitcases," I say. "Come on Els Bells, you can point them out to me." I grab my daughter's hand and we walk towards the carousel.

She looks up at me. "Well?" she says.

"Well what?"

"Are we going to be a family again?"

"We already are one," I say.

"You know what I mean," she insists.

"I do know what you mean."

Despite her demands for an answer, I'll refuse to give one until the turmoil in my mind resolves itself.

———

I'm glad he agreed to see me here. I couldn't face intruding upon his parents' grief. That's what I tell myself anyway. He walks over to my table, coffee in hand, and sits down opposite me. "Thanks for seeing me on such short notice Aleksander, I appreciate it."

"No problem Mr. Rogan," he says. "I don't know if I ever thanked you for rescuing me from that place. You almost certainly saved my life."

I don't know what to say. I just smile and nod and try to hold it in, but it all burst forth. "I am so, so sorry I couldn't get to your sister before she..." The words stick in my throat.

He just reaches over and gives my forearm one quick squeeze. He withdraws his hand with an embarrassed look. "What was it you wanted to ask me?"

Glad of the chance to just deal with facts, I say, "Did you know Phil Jiang was part of the triad who kidnapped your sister?" His eyes go wide, giving me the answer. "It's been bothering me ever since I learned Jiang was in on it. It just seems too much of a coincidence that the security manager at the Hilton referred you to the one private detective in Hong Kong who was part of the problem."

"He didn't."

"Didn't you tell me in the hospital that it was the security manager at the Hilton who referred you?"

"No. He referred me to Mr. Wang."

"So who referred you to Phil Jiang?"

"Inspector Ho."

It's the turn of my eyes to go wide as I try and make sense of this.

Aleksander sees my confusion. "Why are you surprised?" he asks. "You told me Ho was in on it. It was him who sent the police to kidnap me wasn't it?"

"Except that I was wrong then. Ho turned out to be one of the good guys." And then I get it, at least I think I do. "Ho knew Phil Jiang was crooked, I think he sent you to Phil to stir things up, hoping Phil would make a mistake. Did Ho tell you to report back to him on what actions Phil took?"

"No."

"But I'll bet he asked you not to tell Phil who had referred you."

"No. The opposite. Inspector Ho said to make sure I told Mr. Jiang that the referral had come from him."

Wheels, within wheels, within wheels.

I give up. I'll never know whether Ho was one of the good guys or one of the bad guys.

I have to try and purge my mind of this case.

And there's only one way to do that.

———

THE LOOK IN TINA'S EYES SAYS IT ALL. SHE THROWS OPEN THE door and runs into my arms. "I've missed you so much," she says. We stand there in the hallway, arms clasped around each other. "Why didn't you use your key?" she whispers.

"I didn't know if you'd still want me to—"

"Don't be silly."

She looks up into my face. "I love you." Her kiss is long and sweet.

She draws me inside and I look around her apartment.

I suddenly feel a great clarity of thought. I know what I should be doing from here on out. I want to tell her everything I know and feel but I can only think of one thing to say.

"I'm home."

AFTERWORD

Thank you for reading *Captive*. Reviews are the life blood of an independent author. If you have a minute to do a review on Amazon, it would be *really* appreciated. Also, a review at Goodreads or Bookbub is always appreciated.

The next book in the series is *Jailed* it is available in paperback and large-print paperback from Amazon. The other books in the series are

Junkie (Cal Rogan Mysteries Book 1)
Oboe (Cal Rogan Mysteries Book 2)
Lockstep (Cal Rogan Mysteries Book 3)
Three (Cal Rogan Mysteries Book 4)
Cabal (Cal Rogan Mysteries Book 5)
Jailed (Cal Rogan Mysteries Book 7)

All are available in paperback and large-print paperback from Amazon.

ABOUT THE AUTHOR

Hi. I am a former software developer, turned actor, turned author. The Cal Rogan mysteries are set in Vancouver Canada and, I hope, reflect the best and worst of the city. If you would like to know more about my views on the drug scene, publishing and writing, or would like to contact me:

My website: robertpfrench.com.

Facebook: facebook.com/robertpfrenchauthor